# CRASHING HEAT
# RICHARD CASTLE

**TITAN** BOOKS

CRASHING HEAT
Paperback edition ISBN: 9781789095548
E-book edition ISBN: 9781789092905

Published by Titan Books
A division of Titan Publishing Group Ltd.
144 Southwark Street, London, SE1 0UP
www.titanbooks.com

First Titan paperback edition: September 2020
10 9 8 7 6 5 4 3 2 1

This edition published by arrangement with Kingswell,
an imprint of Buena Vista Books, Inc.

A CIP catalogue record for this title is available from the British Library.

Printed and bound by CPI Group Ltd, Croydon CR0 4YY.

*To games played in the dark.*
*You know who you are.*

# ONE

Marriage. It was a double-edged sword, or at least it was for Nikki Heat. Her husband, Jameson Rook, infuriated her in a way no one else in her entire life had ever done. He also took her to heights of pleasure she'd never experienced. But most of all, she loved the man with all her heart and she'd do anything to protect him. Which is just what she had done not so long ago. It had almost cost them everything. She'd beaten herself up over pushing Rook away during her last big case. In the end, she'd done what she had to so he'd be safe. But at what cost? Working with Derrick Storm had taken her away from the things she loved. The man she loved. But it had also brought her to her mother. She'd gained, but she'd lost. Why was life so complicated?

Her mind swirled back to a single word—*Reykjavík*. It invoked titillating memories of the earliest days of her marriage to Rook. Their honeymoon had taken them from the green hills of western Switzerland, to terraced vineyards and remote fishing villages in Italy, to Buddhist temples in Tibet. *Reykjavík*. It sent her mind on a vivid reenactment of every blissful moment she and Rook had spent together exploring wondrous parts of the world. And of each other.

Warmth spiraled through every part of her body. In short, their code word, *Reykjavík*, set her on fire.

For a short time, they'd been in a good place again. Back where they belonged—together. But now there was another word just as powerful as *Reykjavík*, and far less metaphoric. Actually, it wasn't one word, but three hyphenated words. Three very literal hyphenated words that, instead of igniting passion for her husband, turned her body stone cold.

*Writer-in-residence.*

She only had to think *writer-in-residence* to have a layer of Arctic ice form inside her. And not even a Hudson River barge full of his cavalier charm could melt it. In fact, for once, she almost felt immune to that charisma, focused as she was on the fact that Rook would be leaving. It wouldn't be for very long, but still . . .

She chastised herself. She was a captain, for Christ's sake, and a damn good one. She'd paid her dues to get to where she was, starting where everyone did, as a rookie, and climbing the proverbial ladder. Patrol. Sergeant. Squad leader. Lieutenant. Detective. And now she led New York City's Twentieth Precinct detective squad.

It was a damn good squad. And she was damn proud of it.

The fact that her husband taking a stint as a writer-in-residence at his alma mater could rub her so wrong was her failing. He was her Achilles' heel. Depending on someone was something she was not comfortable with. And falling in love with Jameson Rook hadn't changed her fundamental wiring. But it did make that wiring zip and zing and go haywire sometimes. They hadn't even gotten to the down and dirty details of the thing. She'd shut him down each time he'd started to tell her. If she didn't know the specifics, it wasn't real.

"The coatroom," Rook whispered in Nikki's ear. "We've never, mmm, explored our passion, to put it delicately, in a coatroom."

She came back to the moment. Her skin tingled from the heat of his breath on her neck, but she kept her body still. Her voice steady. It was a game she liked to play: pretend that her husband didn't move her as much as he did. It thrilled them both. "Does this place even *have* a coatroom?"

"If it doesn't, it should." He took her hand, tugging gently to rouse her from her seat. "Inquiring minds want to know. Shall we investigate, Detective?"

"*Captain* to you, Mr. Rook."

"Does that mean you'll wear your captain's hat for me? Just that, and nothing else." He stroked his chin. "On second thought, maybe your tie."

She pulled her hand free, shaking her head at him. "Rook," she said, making her tone take on a trace of warning to hide the saucy response she wanted to give. *My hat, my tie, and my handcuffs.* "Tonight you need to be a grown-up. It's an awards ceremony—"

He sat back in his chair, arms folded across his chest. "My idea was so much more fun," he said, pouting.

"And you're nominated."

There was a gleam in his eyes, a light that never ceased to amaze her. Jameson Rook was a kid at heart. Tragedy and death had been left on her doorstep, obliterating the lighthearted side of her, but Rook had grown up in a loving household with a mother who indulged him far too much. He had saved Heat from the tragedy of her own story, and the glint she saw in him now reminded her how much she loved him. How much she needed him.

"If we leave now, you'll miss the chance to hear your name called," she said. His mouth quirked just the tiniest bit and she knew she had him. "You might even win."

This rattled him. He spun his head to face her. "*Might* win? If I don't win, it'll be the crime of the century. No other journalist has done as much for this city as I have." He started ticking off the list of his journalistic credits on his fingers. "I mean, this year alone, I put the spotlight on corruption at the hands of the New York and New Jersey crime families, I uncovered a scam of the highest level at only the most elite Upper West Side preschool, I stopped—"

"Exactly. You deserve this award," Nikki said, and she meant it. Jamie worked hard, digging deep for a story. He was not afraid of getting his hands dirty, and he always sought the truth. "All the more reason not to go in search of the—probably nonexistent"—she whispered that last part to herself—"coatroom. You need to be here when they announce your name."

He rubbed his hands together before placing them palms down on the tops of his thighs, leaning forward in anticipation. All thoughts of a coatroom encounter had been wiped from his mind, at least for the time being. She nodded with satisfaction. Her job was done. Rook would wait with bated breath until his category was announced. It really was an honor, and she was proud to be on his arm. To be his wife.

They'd both dressed for the occasion. He was dapper in

a pin-striped bespoke suit from Nolita's exclusive Duncan Quinn store. Its classic cut made him look like a secret agent, à la James Bond. Which brought no complaints from her.

She had opted for a just-above-the-knee sleeveless sweetheart dress with a dark pink background and intricate black flowers embossed in velvet. In her experience, it was always cold in venues like this, so she'd brought along a lightweight black shawl to keep her bare shoulders covered, if necessary.

So far, she hadn't needed to use it, and Rook suddenly seemed to notice. "Did I tell you how stunning you look?" he said, his eyes scanning her appreciatively.

"Once or twice," she said, the heat she suddenly felt making her think maybe she'd been too hasty in dismissing his coatroom idea.

Like happened so many times when they were together, he seemed to know just what she was thinking. "Rethinking the coatroom rendezvous, aren't you?"

She shrugged noncommittally. "Am I?"

"Oh, you definitely are. You forget how well I know you, Heat."

She met his gaze, upping her level of nonchalance. She wanted to turn the tables. To drive him to distraction instead of the other way around. "Just how well do you know me?"

"I know your mind," he said.

"You do, huh?" she said, schooling her face to keep him from seeing that she wanted to find that coatroom, and pronto.

He flicked his eyebrow up. "I do."

"Okay," she said, challenging him. "What am I thinking right now?"

He lightly pressed his fingers against his temples as if he were a clairvoyant, and raised his eyebrows in surprise. "Why, Nikki Heat, you are a naughty, naughty woman. I can't wait for you to get me alone."

She scoffed to hide the fact that he'd been dead-on. "That was a lucky guess," she said.

The angle of his head told her he didn't buy that. "I don't do lucky guesses."

"So what am I thinking now?" she challenged.

He rubbed his hands together. "I'm liking this game, Heat."

"Quit stalling, Rook. Give me your second sight."

"I know your body," he continued, speaking slowly. Suggestively. "Every square inch, and every firing neuron." He gave her a playfully salacious grin and let his gaze travel up and down her body. "I know your toes. Your calves. Your shoulders." He paused, his eyes lingering on the rise of her breasts.

She fanned herself with her hand. "Where's that coatroom?"

"Oh, but Heat, there's more."

She closed her eyes for a beat. Her body and her mind— God, she was dying inside. What more could he do to her from across the table?

He leaned toward her, dropping his voice to a whisper. "I know your heart, Nikki Heat. I know your heart like no other, and you melt mine."

She was melting, too. She'd had plenty of men in her life, but none that made her feel the way Rook did. "How'd I get so lucky, Jamie?" she asked as she leaned in and kissed him.

She felt his smile against her lips. "How did I?"

They parted and he raised his hand to summon an imaginary waiter. "Garçon, if you please. The coatroom! The coatroom! My kingdom for a coatroom!"

"Ah, but sadly, there is no coatroom. Now is the season of our discontent." Although she'd graduated from college with a degree in criminal justice, she'd had enough time as an English and then theater major to learn the classics.

They sat at a ten-person round table in the center front of a historic nineteenth-century Brooklyn rope factory. The exposed brick and original woodwork carried the history of two hundred years. They'd had a drink on the roof-deck before the ceremony began, and those thirty minutes, with a picture-perfect view of the New York City skyline, had made the evening more remarkable than it already was.

Now, as the low buzz of the room died down, they directed their attention to the stage at the front of the room. Suspended from exposed beams and perfectly centered behind the stage was the event's signage: THE NELLIE BLY ANNUAL EXCELLENCE IN JOURNALISM AWARD. The emcee, an old college chum of Rook's, spoke into the microphone clipped to his lapel. Instead of standing behind the protection of the podium, he worked the stage, as if he were about to give a TED Talk.

"Freedom of the press," he began. "That concept, first adopted in 1791, at a time when 'press' meant only books and newspapers and pamphlets. It was more than a century later that the first radio was invented . . ."

Rook leaned back in his chair, drawing in a deep breath, the smile still gracing his lips. "Settle in, my love.

Raymond Lamont is nothing if not long-winded."

Nikki could have pegged Raymond Lamont as a blowhard, even without Rook's pronouncement. His stick-straight back; the casual way he put his hands in his pants pockets, as if he was going to be up there for a while; the slow storytelling tone of his voice laced with awareness of his own self-importance.

Rook continued. "We are about to get an entire lesson about the significant import of ethical journalism, holding government accountable, the founding fathers—" Here Rook pointed toward the ceiling, dropped his voice an octave, and launched into a dramatic speech: "'A government without newspapers or newspapers without government, I should not hesitate for a moment to prefer the latter.'"

Nikki could appreciate Rook's embodiment of one of the founding fathers of the country. "Jefferson?" she asked.

"Very good." Rook nodded approvingly. "A-plus to your high school history teacher. He—or she—did a good job."

"A-plus to me for studying hard," she amended, "but really, it wasn't that difficult to figure out. 'The founding fathers' was a pretty big clue."

"It was, wasn't it?" He leaned close to her, the sides of their heads touching. "I adore how you hang on my every word, Detective."

"Captain," she corrected.

"Right." He waggled his eyebrows. "Do captains still get to have handcuffs?"

"Oh yeah," she said. "With a key to the supply room."

"Ah, unlimited. Excellent."

The room broke into spontaneous applause, once again

drawing Nikki's and Rook's attention back to the stage. "What'd we miss?" Rook's face had fallen, making him look more like a toddler who'd dropped his cupcake than the seasoned journalist he was. Whatever had struck a chord with the crowd was in the past. Raymond had moved on.

"Fake news has been the bane of the media," he said, "but like the founding fathers intended"—Rook shot Nikki a knowing look—"the media is a check-and-balance system for our government. We must work hard, and with integrity, ensuring that the good citizens of the United States stay informed on topics of importance and of interest, presented to them with honesty and integrity."

After another round of applause, Raymond Lamont finally got to the nominees. "The Nellie Bly Award may not be the Pulitzer, but it is, nonetheless, a valuable and important award within journalistic circles. For those who don't know, Nellie Bly managed to insert herself as a patient at a mental hospital, ultimately revealing the deplorable conditions and the mistreatment of the other patients there. It was the first exposé of its kind—a true commitment to discovering and revealing the truth, no matter the cost.

"Although we can have only one winner for the prestigious Nellie Bly Award, tonight we honor four outstanding journalists." Nikki heard and promptly dismissed the first three names Raymond Lamont spoke, but then he said, "And for his revealing exposé on corruption in local government, Jameson Rook."

Rook smiled sheepishly, as if he were shy of the spotlight. He played his part effortlessly. When he graced the room with a royal wave, Nikki couldn't hold in her laughter. "You missed your calling," she said once she'd caught her breath. "You could be up for an Oscar instead of a Nellie Bly with your acting ability."

He turned his roguishly handsome face to Nikki, looking like a hurt puppy. "Are you implying that I am not sincere? I *am* honored"—he pressed his palm to his chest—"truly honored to be nominated and—"

"The winner is . . . Jameson Rook!"

Once again, the room broke out in applause; this time, however, people rose to their feet.

"I won?" Rook said with disbelief. "I won." This time it wasn't so much a question as it was a statement of fact. And then, finally, he jumped to his feet. He looked down at her, his grin gleeful. "I won!"

Nikki nodded, clapping and smiling. His enthusiasm was contagious. "Of course you won. You're the best. Now go give your speech."

He quickly withdrew a stack of notecards from the inner pocket of his suit coat, blew her a kiss, and ambled up to the stage. He and Lamont hugged, the latter patting Rook on his back. "Well deserved, you son of a bitch," he said, not realizing that his mic was still hot. "Well deserved. Sure hope I don't have to share office space at Cam U with you and your big head."

Rook stepped back and put his hands on Raymond Lamont's shoulders. Even from where she sat, Nikki could see the giddiness in her husband's smile. "Double the honor to be presented by you," he said for the whole room to hear. "And me and my big head will always make room for you, Ray."

The room erupted in applause and Lamont spun around.

"Shit," he said, then looked horror-struck. "Erm, sorry, folks." He scanned the crowd, looking for whoever was supposed to be on top of the technical side of things. Rook, for his part, brushed down his lapels and stepped up to the floor mic, not looking the least bit put off by the malfunction. "What's a little colorful language between friends and writers?" he asked to more applause. And then he launched into his acceptance speech. "Conspiracy theories," he began. "They inspired my love of investigation . . ."

Nikki crossed her legs, sipped from her glass of chardonnay, and sat back. If she knew anything about Jameson Alexander Rook, it was that this might take a while.

# TWO

Rook was 100 percent in his element at the awards ceremony. Whereas Nikki preferred to live her life privately, Jameson Rook liked to live his out loud. Screaming out loud, sometimes, if she was being honest. This fundamental difference between them made life interesting, to say the least.

He worked the room; she surveyed it. Such was their dynamic. She'd learned long ago, after losing her mother—only *not*, since, of course, her mother was back from the dead—that it was foolish to let her guard down. You never knew what maelstrom was brewing just off scene.

She kept to the perimeter to have the best view of the entire room, catching snippets of conversations as she moved. She came upon two women staring at Rook from across the room.

"Good-looking *and* smart. Quite a catch," one of them said.

"But off the market," said the other.

The first one gave a knowing nod. "Married—"

"To a cop. Have you seen her?"

"No, but he's such a hottie. I'm sure she doesn't deserve him."

Nikki's jaw dropped. She didn't deserve him? Who were these women to pass judgment on her?

"She's gorgeous, Sue," the other woman said. "They're like the perfect power couple. I heard Jameson Rook interviewed a few weeks ago. He gushed over her. 'The perfect combination of brains and beauty,' he said. You should have seen his face. That man is in love."

"Isn't she here?"

The first woman nodded. "Tall. Perfect skin. She could have been a model, you know."

"So why did she become a cop?"

They looked at each other, giving simultaneous shrugs.

Nikki left them to their conjecture and speculation about her relationship with Rook and her choice of career, shaking her head. The things people spent their time talking about.

Nikki kept on, skirting around a raucous table of journalists. "The piece was mediocre, at best," one of them was saying.

"Right!" another said, following the exclamation with a hard palm to the table. The salt and pepper shakers jumped, and the cocktail glasses rocked on their bases.

"You're just jealous," a third person at the table, a woman dressed from head to toe in black sequins, said. "That piece on Lindsy Gardner and the bribery . . . It was pretty good."

Nikki wanted to lean over the table, slam her palm against it, and say, "Damn straight, it was good." That story had it all. Greed. Power. Long-lost mother. Near-death experience. Rook had captured it all with aplomb, as he liked to say.

Nikki wandered on, picking up on other chatter. Just scattered words, mostly, that floating out there by themselves meant nothing. Finally, after a solid twenty minutes, she sidled up behind Rook, slipped her arm around his waist, and leaned in close. "Ready to blow this Popsicle stand, big boy?"

But instead of picking up the thread of her flirtatious proposition, he grabbed her wrist, yanked it clear of his body, and whipped her around until she tottered on her heels next to him. "Blow this Popsicle stand? What, are you crazy? We can't leave now. I'm just getting started. See those guys?" he asked, clutching his tumbler in his hand as he pointed to a cluster of people.

"What I see are very few women. I mean, come on, Rook. You can't tell me that women never write award-winning pieces."

He fluttered his hand in front of her. "Well, of course they do. Don't be a ninny. I did just win the Nellie Bly award. And look. Look over there," he said, and once again, he was pointing. "That's Rebecca Reisenbold. Just last year, she won the very exclusive—" He stroked his chin. "Now what was that award?"

Nikki shook her head. "You are proving my point, Rook."

His fluttering hand turned into a wave. "No, no, no. Nikki Heat, you are not going to get me all verklempt—"

She grinned, feeling it stretch the entire width of her face. She came up closer to him again, slipping her hand under his jacket and letting it snake around his middle. "Aw, but baby, don't you want me to get you all *verklempt*?"

She felt him stiffen. Oh yeah, she had him. She knew his eyes were probably rolling back slightly. If they were in a cartoon, his clutch on his tumbler would have shattered it. What were usually ordinary words coming from his mouth had turned to unintelligible gibberish. "I can . . . do . . . verk . . . now . . . coatroom," he said, his eyes now half-closed.

She took hold of his tie and pulled him into motion. "Like I said. Let's blow this Popsicle stand."

"Oh yeah," he said again, following like a tiger she'd tamed. "Let's blow *something*."

Without missing a step, she set her wine glass down on a nearby table. Rook, still her lapdog, did the same with his tumbler. They were almost at the door, where they could hail a cab to take them back to their Tribeca loft. No one had stopped them. No one had noticed. She pushed against the door. Almost there—

"Jamie, where in the devil are you off to?" The booming voice of Raymond Lamont stopped them in their tracks. He sauntered up beside them, clapping Rook on the back with one hand, a tumbler of whiskey on the rocks in the other.

*Damn,* Nikki thought. They'd been so close.

A young woman appeared from behind Lamont. Surely not his date, Nikki thought, although it wouldn't surprise her. It was the ultimate cliché for a professor to date a student.

"Thought we'd call it an early night," Rook said. Heat kept her hand on his arm, hoping she could still guide him out into the Brooklyn evening while it was early enough to walk along the waterfront when they got back to Tribeca.

He nodded his greeting to Nikki, then smiled. "Say no more. Beautiful night for lovers."

Nikki cringed. She didn't dislike Lamont, but God, he could be such a windbag. He was interesting—he was smart.

He wore an earring, and she'd glimpsed the tattoo on his inner wrist once when his long sleeve had slipped up. But he often drank too much, and now was one of those times. He was far less stable on his feet than he'd been onstage, and his words slurred.

"But before you go, my fine people," he continued, "let me introduce you to a member of your fan club. Chloe Masterson, Jameson Rook." Lamont ushered the young woman forward.

Nikki had spent half her life as an observer, trying to understand why people did what they did and said what they said. She'd learned to size up a person pretty quickly, although she also withheld judgment until she had more information. Her first impression of this girl was that she was confident and strong and knew how to get what she wanted. She had shoulder-length black hair held back with a simple thin hairband. Clear skin and a lean figure told Nikki that the young woman took care of herself. Her mascaraed eyes and pink plump lips said that she cared about her appearance, but not overly so. And her evening dress, a simple black knee-length sheath, looked like she belonged in it. She owned the dress, rather than the dress owning her.

She gave a forced smile, Nikki noticed, clearly not liking the introduction Lamont had given her. "It's very nice to meet you," she said, adding, "and I'm actually a journalism student."

Lamont thrust his shoulders back, said, "I stand corrected," and threw back his drink.

Chloe clearly had wanted to speak to Rook, and she'd gotten Raymond Lamont to give her an introduction, more evidence of her determination and strength. Nikki could see that this girl went after what she wanted. "I admire your work so much," Chloe said.

"Well. I can't say I ever get tired of hearing that," Rook answered, the quintessential twinkle in his eye. "Would you like an autograph? Or a picture? Do you have a cell phone?" Before she could answer, he turned to Nikki. "Would you do the honors?"

"No, no, Mr. Rook, I'm not a fan—" She blushed, but quickly regained her composure. "That's not what I meant. I'm sorry. Of course I'm a fan, but that isn't why I wanted to meet you."

"Do tell," Rook said, intrigued.

"Let me," Lamont boomed. "Ms. Masterson is one of Cam U's best and brightest. She's you, Rook, when you were at the university. Of course, you exceeded expectations, and her editor is not near as talented as yours." He guffawed. "But we won't go there."

"Let me guess, you were his editor?" Nikki asked, smirking so only Rook could see. Rook exceeding expectations was putting it mildly.

"Editor in chief. Perhaps the greatest experience I had. It led me down a winding path, but ultimately to become the dean of the very journalism program that produced us both," Lamont said, squeezing Rook's shoulder. "Chloe here is a go-getter just like we were."

"Are," Rook inserted. "Just like we *are*. Hide a carrot and we *will* sniff it out. Chloe, if what old Lamont here says is true, you have a bright future ahead of you. A bright future, indeed."

"What I, and everyone else, have been telling her. Saunders met with her personally. Daily's her advisor. We all have high hopes." He turned to Chloe. "You, my girl, are going to put Cam U on the map."

To Rook, he said, "This little lady is going to give you a run for your money, Jamie. I've regaled her, as well as my other students, with our journalistic antics from our time at the *Journal*. Stories we wrote, parties we crashed, the kill files—"

Nikki drew back at that. "The what?"

"Stories pitched or started, but never finished," Rook explained.

"Professor Lamont could tell stories all day long," Chloe confirmed.

Nikki detected the slightest hint of sarcasm, but it seemed to be lost on Lamont. "She has been quite determined to meet you," he said to Rook.

"Excellent," Rook said.

Nikki leaned in, keeping her voice low. "I've been on the other end of Raymond's stories," she said. "I feel you."

Chloe gave a knowing smile. "Captain Heat, I presume."

*Impressive,* Nikki thought. The girl wanted to talk to Rook—that was evident—but she'd done her homework by learning at least the bare minimum about his wife. She wondered about this meeting. It wasn't a chance encounter. She'd run across Rook's fans, both crazed and otherwise, in the past, but this one—this one was different. She wanted something.

"So Ms. Masterson," Rook said, "I see that you are more than a fan. What can I"—he swept his arm out to include Nikki—"what can *we* do to help you?"

Lamont looked at his empty tumbler and excused himself. "I'll take this opportunity to take my leave," he said. As he sauntered toward the bar, he glanced over his shoulder. "See you around campus, Rook."

Once it was just the three of them, Chloe directed her piercing dark eyes at them. "Mr. Rook. It's not what you can do to help me. It's what I can do to help you."

"That is quite an opening. You have my curiosity piqued, my dear," Rook said in his best Sherlock Holmes impersonation.

Nikki rolled her eyes, but she had to admit, her curiosity was piqued, too.

"I'm not able to take your class this term, and I'm graduating in the spring, but I do want to talk with you when you're there. If that's all right with you, of course."

" 'Visiting professor' means I'll visit with anyone who wants to pick my brain," Rook said.

Nikki stayed silent. Things were good between Rook and her. Whatever drama they'd faced in recent months had receded, and they were just living their lives. It was a rare circumstance. Nikki's mother was alive and well. Not just well, but on her honeymoon with none other than Nikki's CIA buddy Derrick Storm's dad. Love at first sight, they'd both said. She let her gaze skim over Rook. Nikki herself had fought it tooth and nail, but she knew just what her mother was talking about. None of them wanted to waste another minute.

Except, it seemed, for Jameson Rook. Two-time Pulitzer Prize–winning author for *First Press*. Ruggedly handsome investigative journalist. Her husband. He was perfectly willing to waste another precious minute. Or 172,800 minutes, which was what the four months he'd be gone added up to while he did this professor thing at Cambria University. But who was counting?

"I work on the *Cambria Journal*, like Professor Lamont said. Editor-at-large."

"Great college. Great paper," Rook said. "Worked there all four years of my attendance. I can honestly say that without the *Cambria Journal*, I would not be the award-winning author I am today."

"You're an inspiration, Mr. Rook," Chloe said. "Your work when you were a student was inspirational. My God, I bet your notebooks could be in a museum. Do you still have them? You changed the trajectory of the paper, did you know that? Raised the bar for all of us."

Nikki cleared her throat. It was possible that Chloe actually *was* president of the Jameson Rook fan club. Groupies weren't isolated to musicians. Or . . . she could just be very good at knowing how to ingratiate herself with a person. If they didn't cut this off soon, Nikki thought, they might never make their escape. "Chloe, we were just on our way out. I imagine you can talk to Rook when he's in residence—"

"Oh! Of course! I'm so sorry." She stepped back, her expression looking troubled. "I didn't mean to interrupt."

Rook flashed Nikki a look. *Cut the poor girl a break,* it said. *She just met her personal hero.* To Chloe, he said, "You didn't interrupt. I always have time for an aspiring journalist."

"I really am. I'm researching a story. I think you will find it interesting, actually. Right up your alley. Sku—"

She stopped when Nikki sighed. "I'm sorry. I don't

want to interrupt your evening any more. I'll see you in Cambria, Mr. Rook."

"I look forward to that," Rook said. "And I'm happy to share my formative experiences."

Nikki read between the lines. Chloe had hit the trifecta of capturing Rook's full attention: she'd pandered to his ego, had brought in a quick reference to conspiracy theories, à la Skull and Bones, and she'd alluded to wanting his advice on her latest piece and admiring his humble journalistic beginnings. Nikki wasn't going to let him sink into the black hole the young woman had carved out, or they'd never get back to their loft. She grabbed a fistful of Rook's jacket sleeve, propelling him into motion. "Okay, great. He'll be seeing you soon, then. Nice to meet you, Chloe."

Rook let himself be dragged out of the event room, but he turned to Chloe before the door slammed in his face. "See you in a week!"

Chloe nodded. "Counting the seconds," she called.

A few minutes later, Nikki and Rook stood outside the venue, watching cabs roll past. "Looks like the president of your fan club is all lined up and ready to go," Nikki said.

His smile widened. "You think so, too? I thought it was just me. I wonder what advice I can give to the young impressionable minds of the twenty-first century that they haven't already heard before?" he mused, stroking his chin.

Nikki had been kidding, but Rook was not. She would always be content staying behind the scenes, but Rook thrived in the limelight. No wonder he wanted to do the writer-in-residence gig. All of a sudden, it made perfect sense. For four months, Rook was going to be the expert in all things journalism, and whether or not he was aware of his need, a part of him would be fulfilled by the adulation the underclassmen at Cambria University would bestow upon him. Rook would be in seventh heaven.

And Nikki would be on her own.

# THREE

"Cap, you okay?" Sean Raley, one half of the best squad leader team in all of New York, looked at Heat, a mix of concern and curiosity on his face. She didn't like seeing either one of those emotions directed at her. She prided herself on her professionalism. On her ability to be logical, while also pragmatic.

Damn Jameson Rook. He was in her head, and she needed to get him out. She wiped away any insipid romantic notion that marriage could be perfect, resolved to deal with Rook and his writer-in-residence gig later, and turned her full attention to Raley, dismissing his question with a wave of her hand. "Yeah, of course. I'm fine. What d'ya got?"

"What we got is a dead body," he said.

The beat of her pulse quickened. Her promotion to captain had changed her. She'd taken the job rather than risk a potentially inept new captain coming in. But being head of the Twentieth had changed the primary function of her job. She'd gone from fieldwork as a detective to a job filled with bureaucracy. Most of her time was spent dealing with the brass at One Police Plaza, shuffling papers, taking reports, and all the other minutiae that came with being the head honcho of a detective squad.

Finding balance by finding a way to stay in the field was the trick. Right now, the chance to get back into it was like an itch that needed scratching.

"I'm listening," she said.

"Details are sketchy at this point." This time it was Miguel Ochoa, the other half of the dynamic duo detective team, who spoke.

"Accidental?" she asked. Not every body they came across was the result of a murder.

"Unlikely."

"Cause of death?"

"Unknown."

"Age?"

"Also unknown."

Heat dragged her hand through her hair, fingers splayed, her frustration mounting. "Is there actually a dead body, Miguel?"

He gave a noncommittal grunt. "We're pretty sure."

Raley and Ochoa were stellar cops. The best she'd worked with. But they had their quirks, namely cracking jokes at inopportune times. In the face of the violent death they were constantly surrounded by, levity was needed. Nikki herself was serious. She didn't make the jokes, but she didn't stop her crew from telling them, or from lightening the general mood of the bull pen with their antics. Instead, she did her part by playing the straight man. But right now, her annoyance was being triggered by the snail's pace with which they were parceling out information. "You're *pretty* sure? What exactly does that mean?"

"He hasn't been examined yet. It's a little bit of an unusual situation."

"Sounds like it," she said.

"We'll get to the bottom of it, Cap," Raley said.

"Oh, I know you will. But let me just get this all straight. We have what we *think* is a dead body, but no age, no COD, and presumably not an accident. And why do you think it was murder?"

"Thought you'd never ask, Cap," Ochoa said, a little too lightly for her taste. Heat rolled her eyes but kept her annoyance in check. "Our vic was found this morning on one of the sculptures in the pool at Lincoln Center Plaza."

This caught her by surprise. There weren't many firsts when it came to murder in Manhattan. Bodies in alleys. Bodies in dumpsters. Bodies in beds. Bodies in cars. There were plenty of unsavory locations, but . . . "*On* the sculpture?"

Miguel consulted his notes. Whether he was at a crime scene, hadn't gotten there yet, or had long since left, he, like every good cop, took copious notes. In truth, cops lived and died by the pen. If something wasn't in a report, it might as well not have happened. Long gone were the days when a cop's word was taken as gospel. Filing reports was the bane of each of their existences, but it was a necessary evil. Everything depended on it. A perp would walk free if there was an inconsistency or if the time line from one officer's notes didn't match those of another.

He read straight from his pad. " 'Body found on sculpture.' "

"On. Not in the water," Heat mused.

Ochoa confirmed. "Not in the water."

"So he didn't drown."

"Doesn't look like it."

"Found on a sculpture at Lincoln Center Plaza—"

"On a sculpture in a pool," Ochoa interjected.

Never a dull day in New York. She knocked back what was left of her cold coffee and stood. "Let's roll."

Navigating traffic in the city was not an easy task. Today, however, it was particularly bad. It seemed as if every personally owned vehicle, every yellow cab, every Uber, every Lyft, every Hitch, and every impossibly bad driver was on the street going the exact same direction Heat was. Her destination was only twenty blocks from the 82nd Street precinct, but it might as well have been in Chelsea based on the slow crawl of cars on the street. She was a born-and-bred New Yorker. The place was in her blood. In her bones. It had seeped into her pores and she'd never be able to wash it out. Hell, she never wanted to. She *was* New York, and New York was her.

But Christ, the traffic she could do without.

The end of summer in New York took a special kind of patience, one that was in short supply for Nikki at the moment. She was on Columbus, just past 73rd, not even halfway to Lincoln Center, when the red check-engine light appeared in the lower left corner of the speedometer of her police-issue Interceptor. In quick succession, the temperature gauge crept into the danger zone. The city was in the middle of a heat wave; her car was paying the price.

"Just great," she muttered. This had happened before. She'd barely been able to get off West Side Highway, the car slipping into limp mode by the time she'd been able to pull off the road. The ride had turned rough and, true to the name, she'd scarcely been able to limp it to the nearest service station. A new car had come with her promotion, but it was currently in the shop being detailed. Inconvenient, but there you had it. They'd let her know two days ago that it was ready, but she hadn't gotten around to picking it up. There were always more pressing issues. She pounded the heel of her hand against the steering wheel. She should have made the time, dammit. Peering outside, she could see the waves of heat reflecting off the smoldering pavement.

All she could do was inch on, rolling her window down and stretching her arm into the heavy air outside, telling the drivers next to her to make room. New Yorkers weren't known for their courtesy. Horns blared. People swore through their open windows. It took some aggressive stopping and starting—and some swearing of her own— before she finally forced her way into the adjacent lane. Miraculously, she managed to find a place to pull off the road and cut the engine. She stepped out into the scorching heat to consider her options. There were precious few. Ochoa was probably stuck in traffic somewhere ahead of her. He'd taken his own police-issued vehicle so they could each go their own way after they'd assessed the crime scene. She could call him back, but that would be a headache for him and cost them both time. Raley was already on-site and she wouldn't pull him away. She looked up and down Columbus in case a police cruiser was in sight. It was a sea of cars, but none of them belonged to the NYPD.

For a fleeting moment, she considered calling Rook. She went so far as to take out her phone, calling up his name and poising her finger over his mischievously smiling face. Why was she hesitating? Self-preservation? Since her mother's death that Thanksgiving she'd come home from college—or rather, her *supposed* death—Nikki had done everything she could to protect her heart. Rook had found his way in, but now that he was going to be gone for a school term, she already felt herself shutting down.

Instead of lowering her finger to his name, she moved to the curb. Hailing a cab made far more sense. She looked up the street. It was speckled with the traditional yellows, most with two-sided tepee-shaped taxi toppers attached to the roofs, some with wraps on their doors, most of them occupied.

She raised her arm to hail the next vacant one, but it passed her by, and once again she cursed under her breath. Then her phone rang. She guessed it would be one half of Roach, the squad nickname for Raley and Ochoa, wondering where she was, but it was Rook's name that popped up on the screen. Nikki couldn't help smiling. They had their conflicts, like any couple, but despite them, they were always in sync. They had a mind-meld thing going on, as Rook liked to call it. She pressed the green button and held the phone to her ear. "Speak of the devil."

"Only if *I'm* the devil," he quipped.

She could hear the amusement in his voice, and like a Pavlovian response, heat spread through her body.

"There's no question about that," she said.

"Ah, then you *were* thinking about me." He spoke as if he'd solved some great puzzle. "Be forewarned. This devil is dastardly, and takes no prisoners."

"Don't I know it." She could engage in innuendo and

banter with him all day long, but she had a dead body to get to. "Look, I'm stranded and trying to get to what is probably, given the heat, a ripe corpse by now. Is there something specific I can help you with?"

His voice turned serious. "Stranded?"

"Overheated car."

"Where?"

She glanced up the street again, registering what might be a vacant cab. She raised her hand as she said, "Seventy-fourth, on my way to Lincoln Center." The cab passed her by.

"So it's not the devil you need, but a knight in shining armor."

She dropped her hand back to her side, keeping a lookout for another taxi. "Uh, no. The devil is much more fun. And a cab will do me just fine. It's only, what, fourteen blocks or so. I might just walk."

"In this sweltering heat? Nonsense, wife. I happen to be en route to the Met."

"Why?" she asked against her better judgment. You never knew what crazy antic Rook was up to. Whatever it was, getting into it just now wasn't on the agenda.

"I've been in the loft all morning working on my syllabus. Needed a change of scenery. And air-conditioning—"

She'd spotted another cab so was only half listening, but then her thoughts skidded to a stop. Him working on his syllabus made the "visiting professor" thing so much more real. A trickle of sweat ran down her back. Why couldn't she get a cab, dammit?

"It's going to be okay, Heat," he said in response to her sudden silence.

"But why do you have to go?" she asked. She rarely let her emotions get the better of her, but she was hot, for Christ's sake, and she was hurt. Her husband was leaving.

"Cambria's just upstate, it's not across the country. Heat, we'll see each other all the time. I'll be back to visit. You know my mother has her opening in a few weeks. I have to be back for that."

Thank God for Margaret Rook, thespian. A horn honked from somewhere behind her. A cab. Finally! She turned— and stopped short. It wasn't a free taxi. Instead, a silver Lincoln Town Car pulled up alongside where she stood. The rear driver's side window rolled down. "Your knight in shining armor has arrived," Rook announced, his grinning face framed in the window. Just seeing him diffused the agitation bubbling inside her. He had that effect on her.

He was like Houdini, magically showing up at just the right moment. "I don't need a knight, Rook. I never needed a knight. How'd you get here so fast?"

"I told you, I was on my way to the Met. I redirected my driver, cut over from Central Park West, and came back the other way on Columbus." He placed his hand against his heart. "Knight. In. Shining. Armor."

As she climbed in beside him, the cool air washed over her, instantly improving her mood. "You do have pretty good timing," she said with a smile.

"Don't I know it." He lifted his arm, his hand closed into a fist as if he held a lance. To the driver, he said, "To Lincoln Center, my good man."

The driver didn't blink an eye. He was used to Rook's antics and eccentricities. He effortlessly merged back into traffic. Heat couldn't help grimacing. Apparently all the cantankerous New Yorkers with heavy hands on their horns had suddenly morphed into considerate drivers.

"Now, where were we?" Rook asked.

"You were telling me how you planned on coming back for your mother's Broadway opening."

"Yes, of course. And you'll come to Cambria." He put his fists on his hips—as well as he could while seated in a town car—and turned his head slightly. If he'd had a red-and-blue spandex suit, he'd have looked just like Superman. "And you might as well face it, you won't be able to stay away from this."

As ridiculous as he looked, and as annoying as he could be, he was right. She wouldn't be able to stay away. Before she could confess as much, however, he slipped his arm around her waist and pulled her closer to him. "And I certainly will not be able to stay away from you." He suddenly looked stricken, like a man who'd realized he was at death's door. "Oh my God, Heat, what *was* I thinking taking this gig? I can't possibly be away from you for an entire term. Why, why, why did I do this to myself? How could I do this to you? The suffering. The torture. The empty bed."

He was speaking rhetorically, of course, but she had an explicit answer for him. "Because the dean called and practically begged you. But there was more, wasn't there?" She tapped her cheek with her index finger, thinking, and then pointed to the ceiling. "Oh yes, and 'It's an honor,' you said. Mmm, and 'It's my alma mater,' you said."

Heat paused. "There's one more reason. Now what was it? Oh yes." She snapped her fingers. "I remember now. 'I'll be mentoring malleable minds on my former award-winning college newspaper,' you said."

He nodded slowly. "All true. I was so right! It *is* an opportunity too great to turn down. Think about that young woman we met at the awards ceremony. Imagine the impact I can have on her career. On her life! My God, there will be so many. Those malleable minds really are a powerful motivator."

"More powerful than regular sex, apparently," Heat said dryly.

His eyes clouded, but just for the briefest moment. "Ah, there's always the phone. And," he said with a devilish grin, "there's Skype. Now *that* could be fun."

The idea of it was intriguing, and it was something they hadn't tried. "I'd rather be in the same room with you," she said, "but I'm willing to try it if you are."

"Then try we shall."

With his driver's skill on the streets of Manhattan, they made it to 65th and Columbus in no time at all. She climbed out of the car, pushing the door closed, but it resisted. "Whoa." Rook thrust it open and climbed out right behind her.

She didn't bother hiding the snark in her voice. "I thought you had a syllabus to write."

He waved his driver off, then put his hand on her lower back, a familiar and intimate gesture. It sent a shiver up her spine. "The Met can wait."

Inside she was glad he was there, both for his company and for his unique insight on things. As a journalist, he saw life—and death—through a different lens, and that perspective made them a great team. She shrugged. "Suit yourself."

If he picked up on her outward indifference, he didn't comment. "Where are we going?"

"To the pool."

"Ah, Paul Milstein."

It astounded Nikki how much information Rook held in his brain. It was spongier than a child's. No matter the topic, he could spout off some bit of trivia as an aside. It was no surprise then that some background on their destination was in his wheelhouse of knowledge. A lesson in New York City history was coming. "Right. The Paul Milstein Pool and Terrace."

"Did you know that Milstein was a philanthropic powerhouse? Because of him, Lincoln Center was transformed."

"Right," Nikki said as they walked side by side. She knew him by his name emblazoned on the 65th Street plaza and bridge.

"He was a good guy. Really cared about the people who live here. It truly was his city." They rounded the corner and walked onto an expanse of green. "Ah, the Illumination Lawn. It is a sight to behold."

Heat agreed, 100 percent. "It's a fitting name. It's like a blanket of emeralds."

Maintaining a rooftop lawn in the city wasn't easy, but somehow it had been accomplished on the roof of the posh Lincoln restaurant and the Elinor Bunin Munroe Film Center. And, Nikki thought, it was nothing short of pristine. It was a brilliant expanse of vibrant green in the middle of New York.

She and Rook stopped at the top of the steps sloping down to the plaza level. Below them, Heat saw Ochoa and Raley. They stood side by side, hands on hips, staring across the pool in the North Plaza. Beside her, Rook balked and pointed. "Oh!"

Heat raised her eyebrows, nodding. There, sprawled across the bronze sculpture in the middle of the reflecting pond, was the body.

"Henry Moore," Rook said as they started down the steps.

Heat had already begun cataloguing the scene before her, but she stopped and stared at Rook. "Our vic? Do you know him?"

Rook laughed. "No, Henry Moore was the sculptor. Abstracts of the human figure. The female form. Mother and child. Reclining figures." He pointed at the sculpture in the water. "Notice the hollow spaces. They're like rolling hills. Beautiful, isn't it?"

"If you don't count the dead body," Head said.

"Right. Old Mr. Milstein probably wouldn't be too happy about that."

"No, I don't suppose he would," she said. They got to the bottom of the steps and strode across the walkway.

At the side of the pool, Raley had his notepad out, already flipping to the next page. Ochoa stroked his chin, staring at the sculpture.

"Any ideas on how he got up there?" Heat asked, coming up next to him.

"Best guess, someone—probably more than one someone—waded through the water, managed to climb the sculpture, and carefully placed him up there."

They simultaneously turned away from the water, each laying eyes on Rook. Ochoa lifted his chin in a macho greeting. Raley's head movement was friendlier. "Hey, Rook," he said.

Rook rubbed his hands together, like a kid anticipating an ice cream sundae. "It's almost as if he's part of the sculpture, isn't it? Fascinating. And no small feat to have hauled a dead body up there."

"You got that right," Ochoa said. "We've been trying to figure it out. That's some real Houdini shit."

Rook stepped closer to the pool, reaching his hand out as if there might be some invisible barrier between where he stood and the water. "I'm afraid I have to disagree with you there, Miguel. Houdini was an escape artist. A sensational one at that." He drew his hand back. "Did you know he started as Harry Handcuff Houdini, escaping from police handcuffs? Fun fact. But this, my friends, this is a case where escape did *not* happen. There is magic, don't get me wrong, but that magic lies in how our John Doe got himself sprawled out on the top of that statue."

Heat stifled a smirk. For Jameson Rook, talking magic was like commentating the Super Bowl for a sportscaster. She could sense his giddiness.

Rook stood near enough that she felt his warm breath on her neck. They both peered at the body on Henry Moore's reclining figure. "Any idea on the age of the vic?"

Raley cupped his hand over his eyes. "Hard to say from this vantage point," he said, but then he and Ochoa spoke in unison. "Probably a college kid."

The two men had been partners for going on ten years, and like an old married couple, they could finish each other's sentences and seemed to be able to read each other's minds. Heat and Rook were like that, too. They knew each other so well; understanding the inner workings of the other's mind was second nature. Would they still have that after four months apart?

"Not sure how Parry's going to do the prelim on the body," Ochoa said, looking across the pond. "She can wade out there, but she won't be able to scale that sculpture."

Lauren Parry was the medical examiner—and she was Nikki's best friend. She'd be on the scene any minute, and they'd both want answers. Heat peered into the water, then looked back at the reclining figure. "We need to get her up there." But how? They couldn't walk on water. She considered her surroundings, an idea forming. "Juilliard," she said.

The three men looked at her. "What about it?" Rook asked.

"They give performances. Sometimes they give them outside."

Rook's eyes widened with understanding. "Which means they use—"

"Platforms," they said in unison. She had the momentary hope that their impending separation wouldn't diminish what they had. It was said that absence made the heart grow fonder; in their case, she predicted that it would make them grow stronger, too.

"Och, find someone at Juilliard. Let's get a platform set up so we can get out there to the body."

"You got it, Cap." Ochoa left, heading straight for the performing arts school on one side of the plaza.

Heat surveyed the area. A crowd was gathering on the lawn, the steps, and the plaza level. Was the killer there watching? "Get Feller to canvas the crowd," she said to Raley. "Someone may have seen something."

Raley scribbled something across the page of his notepad, then pointed his pen toward the buildings surrounding the plaza. "The windows. Maybe someone saw something."

Heat nodded her approval. "Put Rhymer on that. Have him take Hinesburg."

Detective Sharon Hinesburg was not high on Heat's list. She was lazy and usually did the bare minimum, which often resulted in sloppy work. Nikki tended to give her busywork. But a murder at Lincoln Center was going to hit the news cycle with a vengeance. The brass at One Police Plaza were going to want answers, and they were going to want them yesterday. Which meant all hands on deck.

"Rales," Heat said, gesturing to the growing crowd spilling down the steps at the Illumination Lawn. "Get that area cordoned off. We need to keep those people back. And check the cameras on- and off-site. Maybe one of them caught our killer."

"On it," Raley said, and he strode off. Heat heard him giving directions to some of the unis nearby as he set about enacting her orders. Sean Raley, just like Miguel Ochoa, was someone she trusted with her life. He gave the job 110 percent. No matter what, she could depend on him to do what she asked, and to do it to the best of his ability.

A few minutes later, Ochoa returned, a team of people behind him hauling steel-framed structures, the legs folded up into the unit frames. They stepped into the pool, wading through the water. In a matter of minutes, they'd set up the platforms, making a bridge between the plaza and the bronze sculpture and dead body.

In another few minutes, the ME was crossing that bridge,

medical bag in hand. At the end of the platform, the crew from Juilliard had put up a set of steps. Heat and Rook were across the platform bridge in seconds, catching up to Lauren as she started up. "Get us something good, Laur," Heat said.

Parry didn't turn around but lifted her hand in acknowledgment. "You know I will."

Heat paced—as much as that was possible—on the platform. The temperature had climbed another few degrees. She dragged the back of her hand across her forehead, whisking away the sweat beading there. Impatience bubbled inside her. "Anything, Lauren?"

Parry spun her head around. "Geez, give me a minute, will you?"

Heat folded her arms and dipped her chin. "Sorry."

Parry went back to work. "The way he's laid out, it's like he fell from the sky. There's definitely a wound to the back of the head. If I had to venture a guess, I'd say it's the result of a drunken night gone bad, but until I get him on my table, I can't give you more."

Parry met Heat's eyes. The single glance communicated volumes. They were both baffled by how the vic had ended up dead in the middle of the Paul Milstein Pool and Terrace on the bronze statue created by Henry Moore.

Ochoa came up behind them, his notebook in hand.

"Got something?" Heat asked.

"Guy at NYU reported his roommate missing. Five ten. Dark hair. Slim. Korean. Our John Doe fits the description." He swung his arm upward. "Meet Joon Chin."

They all fell silent for a moment, and then Nikki Heat threw out a heavy sigh. She looked up at the body on the sculpture. "What were you up to, Joon, and how the hell did you get up there?"

**"Well?"** Heat asked the ME when she finally descended the makeshift lift her detectives had put together.

Lauren Parry grimaced, pulling off the nitrile gloves she'd been wearing. She was fastidious about crime scene contamination. Heat had heard Parry say it a million times: *We don't want any of the crime scene DNA on us, and we don't want to transfer any of our DNA to the crime scene. I change my gloves as often as necessary.* She closed her file and tucked it into her bag. "Well, nothing. The way our vic is positioned limits what I can see and determine on-site. I'll know more once I get a closer look."

"Do you have anything for me? Ballpark TOD? COD?"

"From what I can tell, and keep in mind, this is not an official determination, I'd say maybe a prank gone bad?"

"But that doesn't explain how he got up there on the sculpture," Rook said. "He had to have been killed somewhere else and placed here."

"Why would someone do that?" Heat mused. "If you murder someone, why go through the trouble of putting the body on a sculpture in the middle of a pool? Number one, someone could see something. It's pretty risky."

"And number two," Rook said, "is that it's a damn challenging feat. I don't think it's possible for even two or three guys to finagle a body up to that position without some help."

"What kind of help?"

Parry raised her hand, pen pointing toward the sky. "I

can help with that. There are ligature marks on his right wrist. Can't see his left side at all until he's off the rock. If I had to guess, whoever is behind this kid's death used a rope of some sort to pull him up to the top."

"Inventive," Rook said.

Heat couldn't disagree with that, but none of it answered the question of *why*? She voiced it aloud. "Why would someone go to the trouble of hauling Joon Chin up there?"

Rook cleared his throat, which was his tell. He had something important to say, and he wanted people to listen. "Killers are people, too," he said.

Parry stared at Rook. "Really? That's your big reveal? Killers are people, too," she said, "but if you're saying they deserve some sort of sympathy for whatever past wrongs turned them into monsters, you're not going to get any understanding from me."

Rook backtracked. "He doesn't deserve understanding, and that certainly wasn't the point."

"Then what is the point, Rook?" Heat sounded snappy because she was feeling snappy. And frustrated. She was hot. The baking sun hadn't abated, and there was not even the slightest hint of a breeze in the air. She could move to the shade, but Joon Chin could not, and that got to her. The breath was gone from his body. He was not coming back.

"We are all motivated by emotion. We do what makes us happy. What gives us some sense of purpose. What is satisfying. Why did you become a cop?"

He knew the answer to that, so she didn't answer.

"Joon Chin was killed by someone who knew him, someone who wanted to make a statement about the killing. This was a very personal and deliberate act. Why else would the killer go to the trouble of hauling a dead body to the top of a sculpture in the middle of a pond?"

It was a good point. "So we need to find out who Joon Chin is, who his friends are, what he was involved in, and who might have had a personal vendetta against him," Heat said. "Time to get to work."

# FOUR

Nikki Heat had defined herself as a detective for years and she'd embodied the part 100 percent. The shift in mindset from detective to captain of the Two-Oh was significant, and she still wasn't fully at ease. But each day she became more comfortable in her new role.

She stood off to one side in the bull pen, waiting to review the murder board with her squad. Her old desk was still unoccupied, and part of her wanted to walk over to what was familiar and comfortable. But she resisted. She'd quickly discovered that there was a fine line between being one of the guys and being their leader—a natural separation of state, so to speak. Over the years, she'd studied the leaders she'd worked with, as well as those who had orbited her world in one way or another. Those observations had helped her formulate her own views on the characteristics a leader should embody; fairness, consistency, and honesty topped the list. And then the ability to empower those around her.

Heat watched as her detectives came into the bull pen. Rhymer and Feller came in first, leaning back against Raley's desk, facing the murder board. Rook came next, walking straight over to her and, without a word, handing her one of the cups of coffee he'd carried in. He gave her a quick nod, then moved off to sit on the squeaky chair at the desk he'd claimed as his own.

Detectives Ochoa and Raley came in next. After her promotion to captain, she'd taken her time, but she'd eventually appointed them co-leaders of the murder squad. It had taken a while, but they had found their footing, figuring out how to work together without stepping on each other's toes.

Detective Inez Aguinaldo strode into the bull pen next. She was the newbie on the squad, but she had already proven herself multiple times over with her drive and intelligence. Heat had handpicked Aguinaldo from the Southampton Police Department to fill the void in the squad when she'd been promoted. It was one of the smartest decisions she'd made.

Detective Sharon Hinesburg scurried in last. Her tardiness and Rook's presence meant she had three choices: sitting in the old metal folding chair next to the murder board; taking up everyone's time with putting her things down at her desk and rolling her own chair up to the group; or leaning against a desk, like Feller and Rhymer. Hinesburg looked around indecisively, as if she were stuck in a conundrum she couldn't claw her way out of. Heat was just about to speak up, scolding the detective for being late and holding them up, but Rook, being the charming, chivalrous man he was, stood and offered her his chair. Nikki's immediate thought was that if she were in the same situation as Hinesburg, she would have rejected the chair. The bull pen was not the place to give in to social gender norms. Every moment, in fact, was a test for a woman working in a traditionally male job. Showing weakness of any kind was never an option for Nikki. Aguinaldo had exhibited the same sensibility. Hinesburg, however, didn't view things the same way. She gladly accepted the chair from Rook, who then stepped to the sidelines.

Out of habit, Heat started to stand, but she stopped herself when she remembered that taking the lead on an individual investigation was no longer her role. She glanced around, but only Rook, from the rise of his brows and upward curve of his mouth, seemed to have noticed her slip.

A moment later, Ochoa and Raley strode up to the front of the group, standing on either side of the murder board. They took turns being the lead on an investigation. They'd worked out their method of fair play. Raley took up one of the dry-erase markers and wrote JOON CHIN in block letters across the top of the whiteboard, while Ochoa addressed the gathered detectives. Today he was calling the shots. "What do we know about our vic?" he began.

Feller spoke up first. "My canvas turned up zilch. No one saw anything. Hinesburg got a hit, though."

Hinesburg's entire upper body moved as she nodded in affirmation.

Nikki raised her eyebrows. Wonders never ceased.

"I did," Hinesburg said. "A Juilliard girl who said she was coming home late after seeing an off-Broadway show. Said she passed a group of college-aged guys who, according to her, had come from the lawn onto Columbus. It was after midnight, so naturally, she was wary. She didn't want to pass by them—"

*Smart*, Nikki thought.

"So she hailed a passing cab, holding it off until they passed. When they were gone, she sent the cab on its way and hurried to her dorm room."

"How many?" Raley asked.

Hinesburg looked at her notes again. "Three."

Heat tried not to pass judgment against her for the fact that she'd had to check her notes to give a simple fact she'd discovered only an hour prior. It was hard, though, because three was not a difficult number to remember. It didn't instill a lot of confidence in Hinesburg; although, on the flip side, Heat was glad that the detective had, at least, taken notes.

"What was their demeanor?" Heat asked. "Any distinguishing characteristics?"

Again, Hinesburg consulted her notes. "Two wore dark clothing. The other had on a light-colored NYU sweatshirt. One was on the short end of the height spectrum. The other two were tall. Around six feet, according to her estimation."

As Raley recorded the information on the whiteboard, Ochoa addressed Hinesburg. "Were they wet?"

Hinesburg stared at him. "Wet?"

Ochoa calmly explained his thinking. "If these three were the ones who positioned Joon Chin on the sculpture, they'd have been in the water."

Raley piped up. "Right. They wouldn't have had a platform and makeshift lift courtesy of Juilliard, like we did."

Hinesburg looked like a trapped animal. "She didn't say."

"And you didn't ask," Heat said, the shoddy police work implication left unspoken.

Ochoa dipped his chin and drew in a breath. It was his typical *give me strength* move. "Anything else, Hinesburg?"

All eyes in the bull pen were on the detective as she looked at her notepad. "Um, she said they had their phones out. Scrolling or texting, she couldn't be sure. One of them said something about sending a message, so my guess is they were texting?"

"Pretty cold if they'd just murdered someone," Rook commented.

All of the detectives nodded their agreement. Feller spoke up. "First they kill the guy, and then they act like nothing happened."

Raley tapped the capped dry-erase marker against his palm. "Which would lead us to believe that, if these are our guys, they had no remorse."

"Any other leads?" Heat asked.

Raley noted the information on the board before giving his own report. "The traffic cams on Columbus. I'll get a look at those. Already have the feed from the park and the pool area. I've only given it a prelim glance. It's dark, so hard to make out much, but it does show four individuals walking down the stairs toward the pool. One of them did have on some sort of light shirt, but we only have a view from the back."

"Four go in, three come out," Rook said. "Like Agatha Christie's *And Then There Were None*."

"Agatha who-stie?" Ochoa asked.

Rook looked aghast. "Miguel, say it isn't so. Do you not know who Agatha Christie is?"

Ochoa shook his head, not looking the least bit worried about what Jameson Rook deemed as a gap in his knowledge. "Nope."

"She is only the grande dame of mystery writers. British author of some sixty-six crime novels, most featuring either the iconic Hercule Poirot or the elderly, yet incredibly astute Miss Marple."

Raley held his arm up, pointing his marker toward the ceiling. "And, if I'm not mistaken, the Broadway play *The Mousetrap*."

Rook nodded his approval. "Right you are, Sean. Which just so happens to be the longest-running play *ever*."

"Dude," Ochoa said, shaking his head in disappointment at his partner.

Raley shrugged his shoulders innocently. "What? I happen to like the theater."

"Miguel," Rook said, "a little culture, even if it comes in the bastardized form of classic books being made into mediocre movies, as is the case with several of Christie's books, never hurt anyone."

Ochoa was unimpressed. "Whatever, Holmes. I'll stick to the Yankees."

Heat would never tire of the good-natured banter between her squad leaders and her husband, but right now, they had a task at hand. "If the Yankees made a Broadway musical, we'd all be happy, but in the meantime, can we get back to the case, please?"

Rook's eyes grew large. "The Yankees in a musical. That's not a bad idea, Heat. Our own Long Islander—Billy Joel, of course—could write the music—"

Heat cut him off by clapping her hands twice in quick succession. "Rook. The case."

Rook threw up his hands apologetically. "Right. Sorry.

Got lost in my own thoughts. Carry on, gentlemen."

Raley picked up where they'd left off. "I'd lay odds that one of the guys on film going into the plaza was our vic, which, in all likelihood, makes the other three the perpetrators."

"It's the best lead we've got," Ochoa said.

"It's the only lead we've got," Raley amended.

"COD?" Heat asked.

"Yeah, call from the ME just came in. The guy drowned," Raley said, adding it to the board.

"And he went into the plaza willingly?" Heat asked, directing the question to Raley.

"Just four guys having some fun. From what I could see on the video, they were laughing and talking."

"A hazing?" Feller asked. "You know the Greek world. They can take things too far."

Rhymer nodded. "Remember they shut down Greek life for a stint, and then suspended one of the fraternities— Pi Kappa Phi, I think it was—at Florida State after a pledge died? Kids can be stupid."

"This ain't Florida," Ochoa said. "Greek life at NYU is not a thing, dude."

It might not be, but Raley wrote FRATERNITY HAZING? on the murder board anyway. They couldn't eliminate anything until they had a solid reason to eliminate it. "Maybe a challenge to see how long he could hold his breath underwater?"

"That all sounds plausible if it weren't for the staging of the body," Rook said. "If the kid drowned in a hazing, his friends would have called 911—"

"Not if they didn't want it known that they were involved in it," Ochoa said.

"Point taken, but why not just leave the body in the pool, then? Why go to the trouble of hauling the body to the top of the sculpture? They might have been caught red-handed, or they might have been seen. They took a pretty big risk doing that."

"Anything else?" Heat asked. They didn't have a lot, but at least they had somewhere to start.

When no one spoke, Ochoa gave the orders. "Me and Raley will hit NYU and the fraternities. Aguinaldo, find out where our vic lived, and if he had a roommate. Report back on what you find."

"Will do," Aguinaldo said.

"Feller. Rhymer. Find the vic's family and see what they know."

"Yep," Rhymer said, answering for both of them.

With orders in hand, the squad had started to disperse when Hinesburg piped up. "Where do you want me?"

"Good work with the lead," Ochoa said. "See if you can get anything more from your witness. Ask if the guys she saw might have been for a swim. And then check the cab company. It's a long shot, but maybe the cabbie logged the stop even though our girl didn't take a ride. And maybe he remembers something."

After everyone was gone, Rook turned to Nikki. "What about you?"

She hooked her thumb toward her office and frowned. "Paperwork. Emails to answer. No fieldwork for me."

Rook followed her into her office. "You miss being in the thick of it, don't you?"

"More than you know, Rook. While I'm sitting in here,

they're all going to be knee-deep in their investigation. Hell, I'd even take the needle-in-a-haystack job Roach gave Hinesburg."

"You need something to take your mind off things."

She picked up a file folder and waved it around. "Reports for One PP. The bane of my current existence."

Rook stepped closer to her, taking the folder from her and setting it back down on her desk, then looked over his shoulder through the slats of the blinds. The bull pen was deserted. With clear determination, he strode to the window, slapped the blinds shut, and turned back to her. "I have a few ideas," he said as he waggled his eyebrows. "Ready to break in your office?"

Oh, the trouble they could get into, she thought. But the feeling low in the pit of her stomach and the instant aching between her thighs chased those thoughts away. "So ready."

# FIVE

The forbidden midday romp in Heat's office had been followed by a slow burn in their bed that night. The next morning, Nikki had watched her husband drive away. "Thank God for video phone calls," Rook had said when he called her just an hour outside Manhattan. "Let's start tonight."

Nikki had laughed—and agreed—but after they'd hung up, the reality hit her. He wouldn't be there with her in person that night. The loft would feel empty without him.

She'd waved him off and then gone to the precinct to keep her mind occupied. The Joon Chin investigation had yielded nothing except an interview with the kid's roommate, who'd said Chin had left to go for coffee that night and had never returned. The family lived in California, there didn't seem to be any obvious motives for his death, so basically, they were nowhere. And One PP was breathing down her neck. The death of a local college student was not something the department relished. It was bad for their public image. They needed murders solved and off the books, not skulking around like vampires in the night.

She spent the day catching up on paperwork, managing to get outside to stretch her legs and walk around the block, and to get lunch at a food truck. The city heat, unusual for this time of year, emanated from the streets like steam from a locomotive. It was stifling. By the time she got home, she was more exhausted than if she'd been working the case with Roach.

Each day since he left had been the same. She buried herself in her work, and she came home to the silence of the loft echoing in her ears. It had been more than a week now, but tonight was no different than the previous evenings. She drowned out the silence with a long soak in the claw-foot tub, lightly toweling off before crawling into bed. The book on her nightstand was a Victoria St. Claire book. When she'd first found out that Jameson Rook, Pulitzer Prize–winning journalist, moonlighted as the best-selling romance novelist, she'd laughed. And laughed.

"Hey, don't knock it," he'd said. "Tori—"

"Tori?" she'd asked.

"The nom de plume for my Victoria St. Claire nom de plume," he'd explained, as if it should have been completely obvious.

"Oh, of course. Silly me, I should have known."

"Tori is a mega best-selling author, I'll have you know." He'd paused dramatically. "Mega. Best-selling. Author.

"I've been writing them for years, but they've recently taken on new life."

She remembered the conversation like it was yesterday. The angle of his head. His penetrating gaze. The movement of his lips as he said her name. "Nikki Heat, you are the inspiration for all my heroines."

She'd blanched. "What does that mean?"

"That you live and breathe in my imagination and my dreams."

"You're a writer," she'd scoffed, not all pleased to be a presence in his mind when he was writing the sex scenes that tended to come with romance novels. "You shouldn't need a real person to inspire you."

"Au contraire, my dear Ms. Heat. Every writer draws from their personal experiences. We see things through our own lenses, and the people who color our worlds become part of us. There's a mystery writer, for example, who famously shadowed a detective squad in order to write about the police in Manhattan. This fellow became indispensable in solving the crimes the team encountered. They came to count on him, in fact, and he was a de facto part of their team. He ended up writing a book about the lead detective—one incredibly attractive woman, if I'm remembering correctly. She was his muse, just as you are mine."

It had taken Nikki a while to accept that she had feelings for Rook, and even longer to come to terms with the fact that little moments that happened between them often ended up in his Victoria St. Claire books. There was almost always a harrowing adventure his hero and heroine had to finagle themselves out of, whether it was being trapped together in an elevator in an old remodeled factory or in a Brooklyn bar after hours. Art imitated life in Tori—aka Rook's—books.

Now she liked to unwind by reading the paperbacks and searching for the Easter eggs about her—and them— that she knew he hid in the text. The smell and feel of the pages had a soothing effect on her. Knowing that Rook had penned a book she held in her hands brought him closer to her in some inexplicable way. And finding signs of them between the pages was like their personal sexy secret. She slid the bookmark out and started reading where she'd left off. Eventually, her eyelids began to feel heavy and her brain started to shut down.

She put the book down and let her thoughts wander. Seeing the humanity in the victims she worked for was the thing that kept her sane. It was also one of the hardest parts of the job. Knowing that a person was alive one second and dead the next was often hard to wrap her brain around. Why would someone take a life?

It was this last question she always came back to. Who had wanted Joon Chin dead? She pondered the answer as she turned onto her side and pulled up the covers of the bed she and Rook now shared. Moving to Rook's Tribeca loft had taken a monumental leap of faith—and courage. To give up her own place—the apartment that had filled her with both childlike joy and debilitating pain—*that* had been a feat. Leaving it, and all she'd gone through there, behind was something she'd never thought she'd do. But, as her therapist was wont to say, letting go was the surest way to heal.

Giving up the apartment had always felt tantamount to leaving behind the memory of her mother. It was the last place Nikki had seen her before she'd disappeared. Nikki knew from experience that this was what the families of kidnapped or missing children frequently went through. So often they couldn't bear to leave the homes they'd been in when the event happened for fear that the child would show up again only to find the family gone.

Nikki hadn't thought her mother would show up again,

but she did feel as if leaving her childhood home would be like closing the door on her memories. And she could never bring herself to do that.

But Cynthia was alive and well. She'd been in hiding all those years, but now she was back and Nikki had her mother in flesh and blood to hold on to. All those years of unanswered questions hadn't vanished, but they'd started to fade away. Her mother's return from the dead had let her reframe them. For so long she'd asked herself why anyone would want to kill Cynthia Heat. But now that question had shifted: How had she never picked up on her mother's secret life? And the way she'd wondered if she would ever feel anything even remotely resembling love again when it had been ripped from her had turned into the question of whether she could handle the feelings coursing through her now that her mother was back.

A child's love was too simplistic, wasn't it? What she felt now was complex: joy mixed with shock mixed with confusion mixed with anger. No one, not even Rook, could know the extent of her circling emotions. After her mother had "died," Nikki had built a solid brick wall around herself. Piece by piece, bit by bit, Jameson had been tearing it down. But then something would happen—something about a murder vic would hit home or spark a memory, stuffing mortar back into the hole, filling it up again.

Rook would make her laugh, charm her with his dry wit, show her affection in inconsequential ways, each act chipping away again at the cement.

Throwing himself in the line of fire to take a bullet meant for her—well, that had been like a sledgehammer to the bricks. Trust didn't come easy to her, but Rook had managed to free her from the stifling mistrust and caution she'd carried with her like a ball and chain.

Suddenly her old apartment wasn't as crucial a part of her makeup as it had been. And now she was in this room. Hers and Rook's bedroom. It was as familiar as it was foreign; it was hers as much as it wasn't. She was alone in a bed that should have held her husband, too.

She'd get used to it. Eventually. And this "visiting professor" thing was only temporary.

Her thoughts fused together, becoming thin and filmy as sleep finally descended. But then her phone rang. She knew it was Rook by the ringtone. He'd programmed it without her knowing, connecting his roguishly handsome face and phone number to a few lines from Prince's "Little Red Corvette." *"A body like yours oughta be in jail / 'cause it's on the verge of being obscene / move over, baby, gimme the keys / I'm gonna try to tame your little red love machine . . ."*

She'd chastised him for his high school humor, but whenever she'd gone in to change it back to something normal, she stopped just short of pressing the save button. She hated to admit it—and wouldn't ever to his face—but hearing Prince's voice and knowing that her insatiable desire for Rook was the implication gave her a thrill.

She rolled over, reached for the phone, and pressed the speaker button. "I was thinking about you, too," she said, her voice groggy even to her own ears.

"Sorry to wake you." His voice was altogether too serious. No playfulness. No flirtatious undertones. No, *Why, hello, Captain Heat. Have your handcuffs nearby?*

Years of police work had trained her to pick up on the subtext. To register every nuance in voice—especially in Rook's. She sat up, instantly alert. "What's wrong?"

He didn't respond with some witty remark about her knowing him so well. Instead, he cut right to the chase. "There's a bit of a situation here."

There was the barest lightness to his tone, as if he were trying to infuse at least a small bit of levity into a situation that didn't warrant any. But Nikki saw right through it. She peered at the red illuminated numbers projected onto the ceiling: 1:43. Time for a booty call for the drunken twentysomething set. Maybe some sex talk for the night owls. But Rook didn't fit either demographic. The way Nikki's mind worked gave her several possibilities. He'd done something idiotic, like snapping pictures of someone or something off-limits for a story, and had ended up in a local holding cell. He'd stupidly driven under the influence and had ended up . . . in a local holding cell. Or worse, he had wrapped his car around a tree. But no, Rook was far too cautious to do any of those things. He could have wrapped his car around a tree without any alcohol, but she dismissed that option, too.

"Tell me," she said.

"Let me preface this by saying that I had nothing to do with it. I'm being framed."

Her heart dropped to the pit of her stomach. "Being framed for what?" she asked, although at this point, she wasn't sure she actually wanted to hear the answer.

"For murder, Nik. I'm being framed for murder."

It took her a good five seconds to register what he'd just said. "Murder? As in—murder?"

She felt the heaviness of his sigh through the radio waves. "Remember Chloe Masterson?"

How could she forget the young and enthusiastic journalism student they'd met at the Nellie Bly Award ceremony? "Of course. The president of your fan club."

"She's now the former president of my fan club. Because she's dead."

Nikki closed her eyes, drawing in a deep breath, holding it as she counted to five, and then exhaling. Her heart pounded, sending the throbbing beat to her head, but she kept her voice even. "Tell me everything, Rook," she said. "And don't leave anything out."

# SIX

Apparently Nikki and Rook couldn't even manage a few uncomplicated days, let alone their whole lives. Her head was still spinning. She paced back and forth in the bull pen, stopping, running her hand through her hair, muttering to herself.

Miguel Ochoa side-eyed her as he walked in. "You beat the chickens this morning, Cap. What's up?"

Nikki had debated how much to tell Ochoa and Raley. In the end, she decided that she really couldn't keep it from them. "Rook's in trouble," she told Ochoa.

"What kind of trouble?"

She knew her expression was as grim as she felt. "The homicide kind."

Ochoa peered at her, one eye pinched in confusion. "He's only been there, what, a week, and he's already stumbled on a murder?"

"Stumbled isn't the right word." She somehow buried the uncertainty taking root in her gut. She loved Jameson Rook. She trusted him. So where was this doubt coming from?

Ochoa folded his bulky arms over his chest. "What *is* the right word?"

Nikki didn't think there was a word to describe any

of what Rook had told her. Or the thoughts careening in her head.

Sean Raley, Ochoa's other half, came up to them. He took in their faces. "What did I miss?"

Ochoa answered for Heat. "Something about Rook and a murder."

"He's only been there a week. How does that even happen?" Raley said, proving that he and Ochoa were basically one person. The mash-up "Roach" fit to a T.

"'Stumbled' isn't the word, dude," Ochoa said, as if he hadn't just asked her the exact same thing.

"So what's the right word?"

The conversation was déjà vu. "There's no word, guys," Nikki snapped. "What there *is* is a dead woman and, unfortunately, she was in Rook's bed."

Ochoa stuck his finger in his ear as if he were clearing it of water after a swim. "Come again?"

Raley's lips parted in bewilderment. "In his bed?"

It was shocking, but she had to move them along. "Yes, okay? Yes, the dead girl was in my husband's bed. Can we get focused now?"

Nikki caught the look the detectives shot at each other. They were typical men. A woman in a man's bed could only equate to one thing. But they were wrong. Rook was . . . Rook. He loved her with every fiber of his being. Cliché, yes, but also true. She trusted Rook. He said nothing had happened between him and Chloe Masterson. He said he was being framed. She believed him.

"The brass isn't going to like it, but I'm taking a few days off to go up there," she told them. "Which means more pressure on you down here, guys. I'll need you to pick up the slack. The Joon Chin case needs to be put to bed."

Neither one of them hesitated. "Sure thing, Captain," Ochoa said.

"Anything we can do to help?" Raley asked.

"Here's what we know. Chloe Masterson was a senior. She called Rook several times, but he hadn't had the chance to talk to her before she was killed—"

Ochoa stopped her. "Uh, Cap."

She looked at him, waiting for the shoe to drop.

"You're talking like you're going to work the case."

There were no ifs, ands, or buts. "I am."

"Cambria isn't our jurisdiction."

And there it was. "I'm aware of that, Miguel. But if you think I'm going to let the fate of my husband, not to mention justice for the victim, rest in the hands of some inexperienced college town cops, you're wrong."

"So you're going down there—" Ochoa started.

"Over there?" Raley asked.

Ochoa scratched his clean-shaven head. "Where is Rook, anyway?"

Raley cocked one eyebrow. "At his alma mater."

Ochoa smirked. "No kidding, bro. But what college is that?"

They turned to her and all she could do was stare. "Really? You're the best detectives in the Two-Oh, Rook has been planning this for months, and you don't know where Rook is? Do you pay attention to the world around you?"

Ochoa tapped his temple with his finger. "I do not need to cloud this with unnecessary information. And

Jameson Rook's college background definitely qualifies as unnecessary information."

"Not anymore it doesn't," Raley said.

Nikki wanted to hit her head against a wall. "He's at Cambria University. Upstate. Visiting professor."

"Right. Because he's got that Pulitzer Prize—"

Raley interrupted. "Two. Two Pulitzer Prizes."

Ochoa shrugged. "So he's got *two* Pulitzer Prizes, which qualifies him to teach impressionable young coeds. Makes sense to me."

"He probably has a *lot* to teach them," Raley said with a smile. Ochoa was the more cynical of the duo, while Raley usually tried to put a positive spin on things. They were trying to be lighthearted, but their expressions belied their true feelings. They were both grappling for understanding. Nikki got that. Taking the job home took a toll. Ochoa and Raley both dulled their senses; they just handled it differently. When it was one of their own—as Rook was— coping was that much harder.

"Moving on," Nikki said. "Here's what we know." On one side of the bull pen was a murder board for Joon Chin. A picture of the plaza, pool, and sculpture with Joon atop it was pinned to one side. Other facts and questions about the open case were also noted. Pictures of Joon's roommate, his closest friends, and his mother. They were in the thick of that investigation, but now Nikki had rolled in a second murder board. A picture of Chloe Masterson hung in the center at the top. And a picture of Rook was off to the left. The name of the college's newspaper where she was an editor-at-large, the *Cambria Journal*, was written on the other side. And that was it.

"So basically we know nothing," Ochoa remarked.

"Which is why I'm going to Cambria. And you're staying here to work the Chin case."

Raley was a clean-cut man with neatly trimmed hair, a perfectly knotted tie, and a sweater vest. He was also the go-to tech guy of the Two-Oh. "If you need our help up there, let us know," he said.

Ochoa chimed in. "Right. Plenty of us to go around. If Rook's in trouble, we're there."

Nikki swallowed the lump that had suddenly formed in her throat. These guys were her family, and they considered Rook part of theirs. "The best thing you can do for me is figure out what happened to Joon."

"You got it," they said in unison.

"And guys? Thank you."

Heat moved on. Before she left, she needed an update on Joon Chin and the squad's other active cases. "Got an update for me?"

"You know we got spread kinda thin, what with Feller taking that fall," Ochoa said. Feller had been repairing some loose shingles on his roof in Brooklyn. He'd taken a tumble, but he was damn lucky. The statistics hadn't been in his favor. She'd heard from a friend who worked the emergency room at Mount Sinai West that 20 percent of injuries from falls were from ladders. Feller had broken an arm and busted a rib. He was going to be laid up for a while, but otherwise, his pride was more injured than anything.

"Have you checked Joon Chin's phone and computer activity?" she asked Raley.

"Looking for patterns, regular calls, and sites visited. Anything out of his normal patterns, but so far nothing's hit."

"Keep at it," she said. "There's something we're missing that'll blow the whole thing wide open."

Detective Raley took the Expo marker from her hand, putting the cap on it. "We will, Heat. Now go. We can handle things here."

She looked at him, grateful in the knowledge that she didn't have to say anything more to them. They both understood what she had to do. She nodded, grabbed the navy blazer she'd draped over the back of Ochoa's chair, and slipped it on. "You can reach me anytime by cell," she said, already heading out. "I'll check in with you . . ."

Her voice trailed away from them as she left the precinct, her mind already focused on Rook and the very dead Chloe Masterson.

# SEVEN

N ikki drove on autopilot, taking the West Side Highway to Henry Hudson Parkway, and finally crossing the George Washington Bridge. The route had tolls, but it was shorter than the alternatives and she wanted to get to Cambria, east of Lake Placid, as quickly as she could. The nearly five-hour drive meant she had plenty of time to think, which meant plenty of time to contemplate exactly what to say to Rook when she saw him. She would be out of her jurisdiction, but she decided not to register—at least not yet—with the local police department. Under normal circumstances, and in most states, it would be unlawful for her to arrest anyone outside of a municipality's geographical boundaries. It would jeopardize the prosecution. The defendant would get off because the arrest was unlawful.

But New York was different. If she had a reasonable suspicion that a crime had been committed, she could arrest anyone at any location in the state. Which meant she had free rein in Cambria to figure out what in the hell happened to Chloe Masterson.

Rook hadn't been arrested yet, but that could change any second. He couldn't stay at his on-campus housing, so the university had moved him to a local three-star hotel. It was decent, but he preferred the five-star variety, so he'd upgraded to what he considered a more suitable location. He met her outside, taking the suitcase she'd hurriedly packed before leaving the city from the trunk of her car. "You travel light," he said.

When she spoke, she heard the aloofness in her own voice. Her wall of self-protection was forming again after Rook had worked so hard to help her break it down. "I didn't have much time to plan a complicated travel wardrobe. What does one wear to investigate the murder of a young woman found in her husband's bed?"

Rook looked hurt. Truthfully, he looked like a five-year-old whose lollipop had just dropped in the dirt. "Ouch."

Heat held back her response. That comment had come out of left field. In her heart, she believed Rook was innocent. But she was also a highly competent detective, so until she had examined the facts and looked with new eyes at the situation, she wanted to keep some distance. Thus her mildly passive-aggressive sarcasm. She regretted the comment, though.

"I'm innocent, Nik, remember?"

"I know," she said, but did she? "And I'm sorry. This is a new situation for me."

"Yeah, for me too. Let's see, framed for murder. I believe that calls for casual pants, one of the classic button-down blouses you're so fond of, and, mmm, three-inch heels. Two would be better for chasing down a suspect, but three puts your lips right against mine. Yes, let's stick with three."

Heat had stepped out of her car half ready to keep

Rook at arm's length. She thought she needed to maintain perspective. She'd pressed the button, shooting up the protective wall that was always just a moment away from encasing her, but as usual, Rook had a way of disarming her. All it had taken was the mischievous smile on that devilishly handsome face of his, and the wall was down.

He stepped closer to her, set down her bag, and slid his arms around her. "I *am* innocent, Heat," he said, looking directly into her eyes. "You know that, right?"

"Of course I do. Half the time you can scarcely stand to look at a dead body—forget about actually taking a life. You don't have it in you."

"Now that's not entirely true," he argued. "If you were in mortal danger, I'd most certainly do my very best to take the life of whoever was threatening you."

"You did take a bullet for me," she conceded. It was a sacrifice she wouldn't have asked of anyone, but the fact that Rook had done it was something she would always feel a little guilty about.

He grinned, not the least bit of sheepishness in him. "I did, didn't I?"

He leaned down to kiss her, and she let him, but only briefly. "Simmer down, tiger. We have a murder to solve."

"That we do." He picked up her bag again and led her into the lobby of the hotel. Two blazer-clad people, one a middle-aged man, the other a twentysomething woman, manned the registration counter. Dark wood abounded, from the base of the counter to the paneling of the walls to the low coffee tables in front of the leather armchairs that dotted the luxurious lounge area. It wasn't the Ritz, but it was pretty nice.

It had been nearly ten days since they'd seen each other. Ten days since Nikki had felt her husband's arms around her. Once they were in the elevator, the time they'd spent apart created a tension between them that was thick. Palpable. They had a history with elevators.

The woman with the suitcase riding with them was oblivious, thankfully. Nikki's tongue snaked out from between her lips as she watched Rook. He stepped backward, making sure he was completely out of the other passenger's line of sight. Nikki followed suit. They stood side by side, silently watching the buttons on the elevator control panel light up as they passed each floor.

Rook let his fingers find hers, taking hold of them enough to pull her closer to him. He angled himself behind her, moving her hair to the side, bending his head to let his lips brush over her neck. At the same time, his hand slipped around her, his fingers finding their way between the buttons of her blouse until they touched bare skin.

She drew in a breath, but stifled the moan hovering in her throat, moving her body back until she was pressed against him. And then the elevator slowed and came to a stop. Nikki and Rook froze. Would the woman turn around and register what they'd been doing? Would there be people waiting to get on?

The doors slid open. The woman picked up her suitcase. Without a backward glance, she stepped out, turned right, and disappeared. The corridor was empty. Nikki and Rook stood completely motionless until the doors slid closed again and the elevator began its upward climb. The second the car was in motion, Rook's fingers danced against her skin. She watched the car's buttons as they lit up. Twenty-five. Twenty-six. Twenty-seven. The bell dinged, the doors slid open, and they practically stumbled down the hallway to Rook's room. He dug his room card from his pocket and held the QR code to the mechanism on the door. The lock clicked and they were inside, the suitcase forgotten just inside the threshold.

The tension of the elevator morphed into a rushed, almost desperate frenzy. Nikki kicked off her heels while Rook hopped on one foot as he pried off one shoe, then switched his hopping to the other leg and removed the other loafer. They both shimmied out of their pants. While Rook reached behind him to grab the neck of his shirt and yank it over his head, Nikki undid the buttons of her blouse and slipped out of it. Two seconds later they were making up for the lost time.

It took a while to make up for ten days.

Eventually Rook rolled onto his back, blowing out a fatigued—but contented—breath. "Good to see you, Heat," he said.

She couldn't help smiling at how his voice cracked with exhaustion. She turned onto her side, propping her head up on her bent arm. "Good to see you, too, Rook."

He spoke between heavy breaths. "Out. Of. Practice."

She danced her fingertips over his chest. "We should do something about that."

That was all the prompting he needed. He wrapped his hand around her wrist, gave a gentle tug, and just like that, she was straddling him. "You sure you're up for round two?" he asked, his breath suddenly back to normal.

She pressed her body against his, playfully nipping his lower lip with her teeth. "Are *you*?" she asked.

Without the slightest bit of effort, he flipped her onto her back. Now *he* was straddling *her*. "Detective Heat, dare I ask, is that a challenge?"

She waited a beat, letting him relax just a touch. And then, before he knew what hit him, she had wrapped one leg over his hips, angled her bottom leg under him, and flipped them both. Once again, she was on top and in the dominant position. "Are you *up* for a challenge?"

He sighed, his mouth curving into that infernally adorable smile. "You win, Detective. Take me."

So she did.

# EIGHT

A row of well-kept brownstones lined both sides of the street on what the university called Faculty Row. Each house had a postage-stamp square of grass and a short stack of steps with heavy black railings leading to the front door. A few had window boxes. One had small terra-cotta pots with colorful draping geraniums climbing the steps on either side.

"Turns out Ray Lamont knows just about everyone," Rook said. "He pulled some strings and got me the best of the town houses. Or maybe it was Saunders. Either way, old school chums coming through for me backfired in the worst way."

"What's the university saying? Do they still want you to teach?"

"So far they're operating on the innocent-until-proven-guilty platform. Not so for the police, I'm afraid. Asshole detective would have thrown me in jail if he had any actual evidence that I was involved. I had to remind him several times that I had no motive to kill that girl."

"He's doing his job. You're the obvious suspect. Being a hard-ass as I interviewed you is exactly what I would have done."

Rook had nothing to say to that. It looked bad for him. There was no escaping that fact. The best they could do was work the case. The best she could do was tamp down any niggling uncertainty she felt. Betrayal in her past didn't equal betrayal in her present.

Nikki hadn't known which brownstone was Rook's temporary housing, but it didn't take long to deduce that it was the third from the end. The caution tape crisscrossing in front of the door was a dead giveaway.

Rook stroked his chin, considering the entrance. "Yellow and black, just like the movies," he said. "Which would have been pretty cool—if it wasn't in front of *my* house."

She held out her hand. "Key?"

"We can't just go in." He tilted his head, his brow furrowing. "Can we?"

She repeated what she'd said to Ochoa and Raley. "I'm a homicide detective—"

"Captain," he corrected.

She ignored him. "You can't possibly think I'm going to leave this investigation to local law enforcement. Why do you think I'm here?"

"Moral support?"

"Sure, that, but we have a murder to solve, Rook. I can't do that from an armchair. I'm not Miss Marple."

"Okay, but Nik, you don't have jurisdiction here."

"That's the beauty of New York," she said. "I can slap cuffs on a criminal anywhere."

He looked at her for a beat. "I did not know that."

"It's a special state."

"That it is," he said. He unlocked the door and pushed

it open. She took a breath, feeling like Bruce Wayne as he transformed into Batman. She wasn't Nikki anymore; she was Detective Heat. This was wrong in so many ways. She was not officially working this case. She was bringing Rook, purportedly the prime suspect, right back to the crime scene. But she wasn't going to think about either of those things right now. She couldn't. Instead, she gloved up, handing Rook a pair.

He took them, but hesitated. "I've been living here. My prints are all over the place."

"Do it anyway," she said, and Rook complied.

Heat crouched under the caution tape, crossing the threshold and standing upright just inside the door. Rook did the same, closing the door behind him. She held her arm out at ninety degrees, stopping him from continuing. She needed a moment to take it all in. She catalogued every detail of the space. Small foyer. Mid-quality occasional table with a dark wood-framed mirror hanging above it. It reflected the light, making the space feel just a little bit bigger.

"Nice furniture," she commented.

Rook shrugged. "It's not the Tribeca loft, but it's serviceable."

"Nothing is like the Tribeca loft," she said. It was true. Rook's place was special. Rustic, yet refined. Spacious and well-appointed. He was a man who lived lavishly. It had taken some getting used to, but she had to admit that she'd grown fond of the luxuries Rook shared with her.

Once she passed through the foyer, she could see straight through to the back of the house. Like all brownstones, the house was a shotgun. A staircase straight ahead led upstairs.

To the left, a small beige couch and two armchairs formed a conversation area. "No TV," she commented.

"I assume the university thinks professors don't deign to watch television. Clearly they have never seen *Conspiracy Theory with Jesse Ventura*."

"Really?" She would never understand Rook's obsession with conspiracy theories and secret societies and biblical prophecies.

Rook shrugged. "Hey, it was a good show." He dropped his voice a few notes. " 'I've been a mayor. I've been a governor. Now I get to be a detective and seek the truth.' " He grinned. "That was a damn good Jesse Ventura impression."

She raised her eyebrows. "If you say so."

"I do."

"What is it with you and conspiracies?"

He pressed his open palm to his heart. "Um, hello? Roswell?"

She walked through the living room to the kitchen with its rectangular dining table, granite countertops and island, and French doors leading to the small backyard. "I'm not going to talk about aliens right now."

"I agree. Now is, perhaps, not the time. But file it away in the back of your mind. Roswell is real. The government has many secrets."

Heat only half acknowledged him. She was busy looking at the house. There was no evidence of her husband in this place. It was like a model home. Perfectly appointed, but no evidence of any actual living person. She backtracked through the living room, put her hand on the railing, and headed upstairs.

"It's three bedrooms," Rook said from behind her. "The master is in the front of the house. The other two are in the back."

"And Chloe was found in the master." A statement, not a question.

"Heat . . ." Rook started.

She held her hand up. "Don't say it."

"We haven't talked about it—"

"We don't need to."

"I think we do."

She stopped and turned to face him. "Oh, believe me, we will, Rook. But later. Right now we need to focus on the crime itself. There was a dead girl found in your house. In your bed. Which means you're going to be named a person of interest. Hence the lead detective being an asshole, as you mentioned. We need to figure out what happened."

She knew he wanted to say something. To argue with her and direct the conversation. She saw the struggle on his face. And then she saw his resignation. Rook liked to talk things through. To push through her barriers. She was impressed that he recognized now was not the time to press her.

She hiked up the rest of the stairs, took a right turn at the landing, and walked straight into a sitting room connected to the master bedroom. A good part of the wood flooring was covered with a medium-pile area rug. A dark brown leather armchair angled out from the corner. Next to it, a window overlooked the park across the street. A floor lamp sat to the left back of the chair. On the right was a round accent table with a burnished oak top. The style of the room was masculine, but comfortable.

The master bedroom was to the right. Heat stopped. In a typical scenario, she would put herself in the mind of the victim. The minute she stopped thinking about them as people, who just minutes or hours or days before had been living and breathing, was the minute she'd hand in her badge. The fact that Chloe Masterson was found in Rook's bed made it too close to home, but she wouldn't let that deter her from being Chloe's strongest advocate.

As she did with every crime scene, Heat examined the room with beginner's eyes. She catalogued every detail of what she saw, actively fighting against the blind spots veteran detectives often developed. Their observation skills became dull. Anesthetized by habit.

But Nikki didn't succumb to even the slightest level of complacency. She was in the moment, often going so far as to imagine the murder happening right in front of her, watching it as if it were a movie so as not to miss even the slightest piece of information. The same type of medium-pile rug was under the double bed. The brown-and-gold paisley bedspread was pulled back, the sheets beneath rumpled. She took a step forward. The bedsheet had been pulled up. Even so, the blood had seeped through. A lot of blood, she thought. She knew Chloe had been stabbed. Her body had been removed, but experience told Heat that she'd bled out fast. She heard Dr. Lauren Parry's voice in her head: *The average adult body holds five liters of blood. A stab wound to an artery will cause rapid blood loss. Exsanguination will happen fairly quickly under those circumstances.*

She moved closer to the bed, reaching her hand out. There was something about the blood—

"Wait!"

The urgency in Rook's voice made her whirl around. She looked past him, half expecting to see a bevy of uniformed officers, guns drawn, charging up the stairs toward them.

She didn't. "God, Rook, don't do that. What is it?"

He nodded his head toward the corner of the bed she'd been reaching for. "Should you touch that?"

A crime scene officer had the most basic task of discovering, collecting, packaging, and marking the evidence found at a scene. There wasn't a hard-and-fast rule as to what evidence marking looked like. Case numbers, dashes, numbers, and letters were usually combined to form a system for keeping evidence organized. One person was typically responsible for the master list so as to avoid inconsistencies.

Different jurisdictions might have their own method of marking evidence, but as long as there was consistency with the process across multiple crime scenes, confusion would be eliminated. Detective Heat knew the crime scene in front of her had already been processed. Knowing this eliminated any qualms she might have had about disturbing things, even if she wasn't officially investigating. "The body's been removed. The scene is cleared."

He didn't look entirely convinced, but deferred to her, gesturing toward the bed. "Carry on."

Her hair, its usual waves a bit mussed from their earlier romp at the hotel, draped down the left side of her head as she leaned in and grabbed hold of the sheet to pull it back. The epicenter of the bleed was darker than the surrounding area, and it wasn't red like most people likely imagined. With this much blood—this much saturation—it was almost black.

"Where was she laying?" Heat asked Rook, noticing an oddity.

"What do you mean?"

"Did she look like she was sleeping? Head on the pillow?"

"Oh. Yes." He pulled his cell phone from his pocket. "I have a picture."

She stared at him. "You have a pic—?"

"I knew you'd want to see—"

She gave him a look that said *You've got to be kidding me*. "You couldn't have mentioned that before?"

"I'm mentioning it now. When we're at the bed where her body was. Seems like the right time to me."

Sometimes Rook made her crazy. She held out her hand. "Let's see it."

He pulled up the photos on his phone, selecting the one he was after before handing it to her. He stood beside her as she looked at it. Chloe Masterson's eyes were closed. The sheet and bedspread were pulled up over her, almost to her chin, but from the shape of her figure, Heat discerned that her arms were by her sides and her legs together. "She looks peaceful. Like she's Sleeping Beauty."

Her gaze shifted to the bed in front of them. There was something . . . She felt Rook's attention follow hers. "The bloodstain—" she began.

"It's low," he finished.

"She wasn't stabbed in the heart. Or even in the abdomen." She pulled out her phone. Lauren Parry answered after the second ring. "What's up, Captain?"

The ME was a busy woman, so Nikki cut to the chase. "Stab wounds. If a person wasn't stabbed in the neck, heart, or abdomen, where else would cause a quick bleed-out?"

Lauren didn't need to think about it. The answer came as if she'd been expecting the question and had prepared her response. "The femoral artery in the groin. A wound there would cause exsanguination pretty damn quickly." She paused, then spoke again, her voice tinged with curiosity. "Why?"

Instead of answering, Nikki asked her next question. "How well would you have to know the human body to make a fatal stab wound there? I mean, most people aren't going to go for the groin."

"True," Lauren said. "You'd have to have a decent understanding of anatomy. More than your high-school biology class everyday person would."

"Got it. Thanks, Lauren."

Heat was about to end the call when her friend's voice stopped her. "Oh no you don't, Nikki Heat. You are going to tell me exactly what's going on. Where are you, and who was stabbed in the femoral artery?"

Nikki sighed. Heavily. "I'm upstate at the brownstone Rook's been staying at during his 'visiting professor' gig."

"O-kay," Lauren said. "Go on."

"A student was murdered—"

"Stabbed in the femoral artery?"

Heat lowered her chin, cupping one hand at her forehead and massaging her temples. "That's my guess."

This time Lauren did pause before asking, "What aren't you telling me?"

The two women had known each other a long time. Theirs had started as any professional relationship did. Polite conversation at the scene of a crime while Dr. Parry examined the body and Detective Heat examined the crime scene. But over time, polite conversation had turned to lengthy talks, first over coffee, then over drinks. Lauren was one of Nikki's few true friends, and probably the woman she trusted most in the world. "She was found in Rook's brownstone."

Rook leaned in next to her, talking loudly enough so Lauren could hear. "It sounds bad, Dr. Parry, but the real story is under the surface."

Nikki put Lauren on speaker so Rook could be part of the conversation.

"What are you talking about?" Lauren asked. "What story under the surface?"

Nikki answered. "The young woman was stabbed in his bed. He'll be a person of interest, but he's—"

"I'm innocent, of course," Rook said. "Heat's going to help me get to the bottom of what lies beneath."

"What the—"

Heat picked up the narrative again. "The thing is, he knew her—"

"Barely," Rook said. "I *barely* knew her."

"She worked for the college newspaper and was a fan."

"Oh boy," Lauren said, which about summed it up. "Let me know if you need anything else, and good luck. Sounds like you're going to need it," she said, before signing off.

Nikki tucked her phone back into her pocket. To Rook she said, "How well do you know the human body?"

One eyebrow quirked up. "I know *your* body—"

"Rook, be serious."

He put his hands up, palms facing her as if she had a gun

pointed at him and he was surrendering. "Okay, okay. I did an article for *First Press* on a New York doctor working in the trenches of the city. I shadowed Dr. Randall Schultz for several weeks. Saw a lot of blood, a lot of GSWs, a lot of stab wounds. A lot of foreign objects in places they did *not* belong."

"So if the police dig around, they'll determine that you do, in fact, have enough of a working knowledge of the human body to have targeted the femoral artery," she said, making sure he understood the gravity of the situation and the reason for her question.

He fell silent and considered. And then, with a heavy sigh of acknowledgment, he nodded. "Sadly, I suppose they will."

# NINE

**H**eat and Rook left the bloody scene in the master bedroom behind them and sat across from each other in the brownstone's living room. Two-inch faux wood blinds covered the windows, the slats rotated horizontally to let in light from outside. Heat wouldn't have described the house as particularly warm when she'd first entered. She might have said it was comfortable, although utilitarian. But now, after inspecting the crime scene, it felt cold and unwelcoming. She didn't want to be wrapped up in this murder. Didn't want her husband to be involved.

Yet here they were, unable to avoid it.

"So. Where should we start?" Rook asked. Under normal circumstances, meaning at the beginning of a normal murder investigation, he might have rubbed his hands together in anticipation of the cerebral exercise that lay ahead. Knowing he was going to be looked at—and looked at hard—as a murder suspect had deflated his ego.

She wanted to start alone. She wanted to not see Rook so she could keep the doubt at bay. But she couldn't do that. They were a team. If she didn't believe him, didn't trust him, what was their relationship based on?

"We have to start at the beginning," she said. Always start at the beginning. "Tell me what you know about the victim. About Chloe Masterson." She said the victim's name, and would repeat it as much as necessary to remind herself that a life had been lost. Chloe had been someone's daughter. She'd had friends. She'd loved and had been loved. Nikki would never forget those things.

"I can do that," he said. He ticked the points off on his fingers as he relayed them to her. "She was a senior at the university. She wrote for the *Journal* and won an award last year for excellence in journalism. She spent a lot of time at the paper. She seemed very passionate about her work."

"That's it?" she asked after he stopped.

"I've only been here a week and a half, and she wasn't in any of my classes."

"If she wasn't in any of your classes, then how do you know anything about her?"

His face lit up. "She reminded me of me. Everything was about the story. You know how committed and singled-minded I get when I'm in the thick of a story?"

Heat had firsthand experience with that side of Rook. When they'd first met—when he'd shadowed her for an exposé on the NYPD—that commitment and single-mindedness had turned into an in-depth piece about her. She'd wanted to ditch him every chance she got, but that, it turned out, was impossible, and he'd been instrumental in solving the murder of Matthew Star. She never would have guessed that they'd end up married. "I do know," Heat said.

"She was the same way."

"Okay, but again, how do you know that?"

"Because one of the first things I did once I was settled into the brownstone was go visit my old stomping grounds."

"The paper," she said, remembering. He'd called her that night, barely able to contain his excitement.

"The paper," he confirmed. "For a minute, it actually felt like I was in *The Time Machine*. H. G. Wells's book actually coined the term 'time machine,' did you know that? Of course, my experience is nothing like the actual protagonist of the book, who is known only as the Time Traveller. He went forward in time to AD 802,701 and witnessed the end of the world. Going to the past to experience something again, now *that* is exciting. I'd definitely go back to the first time I saw you, for example. You were in the bull pen, standing in front of the murder board. You had your hair up, but a few strands had fallen and framed your face. God, you were—are—the most beautiful woman I'd ever seen. Took you a while to warm up to me, but my charm eventually wore you down," he said with a grin.

She was irritated by his flippancy, even though she understood it. At the moment, it was his coping mechanism. If he could joke, or pull them back to a better time and place, they could get through this. But she had to stay focused. "As much as I want to go down memory lane with you, we need to stay focused. This is serious."

His smile vanished in an instant. "Right. Where were we? Oh yes, the paper. On one hand, it was like taking a time machine to the past, but on the other, it was a reminder of how things have changed. The newsroom is the same. Frantic phone calls, copy being sent last second for edits, the buzz of worker bees all working towards a common goal—original, truthful, and relevant content.

"Jennifer, Ray, and I went to the *Journal* offices. We ran into Chloe. The others went off to hold their office hours. Chloe gave me a tour. They have an entire area dedicated to online content and social media. None of that existed when I was on staff. Printed dailies are dying. The *Journal* has gone to print three times a week. The rest is online."

"A sign of the times," Nikki said. "Who is Jennifer?"

"Jennifer Daily. Awesome name for a journalist, right?"

"Right," she said, although it was just another name to her. "Did Chloe say or do anything unusual?"

"I didn't know her, so I couldn't say. She seemed fine to me. Normal. Except . . ." He paused, looking up at the ceiling.

Heat leaned forward expectantly. Rook was a people-watcher. An observer. Just like her years on the police force had trained her to look at the details, and to see things and make connections that weren't obvious, Rook's years in journalism had trained him to read people and situations. "Except what?" she prompted.

"She showed me the different areas of the building and introduced me to some people. When we got to the editor in chief's office—also a senior—he asked to speak to Chloe for a minute. I stepped out and Michael Warton—"

"The editor in chief?" Nikki asked.

"Precisely. He closed his office door so their conversation would be private. I walked around the room, chatting up a few of the students, you know. Getting a lay of the land."

*And enjoying every second of it,* she thought.

"When I looked back at the office, I could see the two of them—Michael and Chloe—through the window. From my standpoint, their conversation looked heated."

"As in they were arguing?"

Rook shook his head, considering. "I wouldn't say that, exactly. I mean, yes, it looked like there was some back and forth, but I got the impression it stemmed from Michael saying something that Chloe didn't want to hear."

Already, Heat knew they needed to talk to this Michael fellow, editor in chief of the *Journal*, but she pushed Rook to see if he remembered anything else. "Like what?"

"Who knows? Could have been anything. The editor in chief is the big cheese. The big kahuna. The boss man. He could have killed an article, assigned a story Chloe didn't want to do, cut an inch from Chloe's copy, or told her the coffee she'd made earlier tasted like mud. No way to know, but when Chloe rejoined me, she was definitely agitated."

"But she didn't say anything about what had her worked up?"

He shook his head. "Not a word."

Heat stood and started toward the front door. "Seems like we ought to pay a visit to the *Journal*."

He scooted ahead of her and held the door open. "You read my mind, Detective Heat. After you."

# TEN

Nikki wanted to get a feel for the college town of Cambria, so she drove to the university, with Rook giving her step-by-step directions from the passenger seat. Halfway to the college, she'd decided that Manhattan was far easier to navigate. In the city, numbered streets ran on a grid plan parallel to the Hudson. They were labeled either east or west, with 5th Avenue being the dividing line. Avenues, on the other hand, ran south–north. Tell someone you would see them at West 30th Street at 11th, and you'd know you were meeting at the High Line. There was not even the slightest bit of confusion.

Cambria had decided to go another route with streets named after trees, flowers, some numbers, and Avenues A, B, and C—its own mini version of Manhattan's Alphabet City. Some were named after people. Still others were centered on the university: College Street, University Avenue, and Dormitory Road were just three examples. Nikki scratched her head as she tried to make sense of it. "How does anyone remember where to go or how to get anywhere?" she mused as they waited at a red light.

"You get used to it," Rook said.

She doubted that. "After ten years, maybe. Beam me

back to Manhattan, Scotty," she said.

Rook laughed. They were fellow sci-fi nerds, complete with a few different cosplay outfits. You never knew when you might need one, Rook liked to say. Star Trek, Star Wars, Firefly, Guardians of the Galaxy. Whatever the occasion, they were prepared.

"I'm afraid we're stuck on this planet. But you will prevail. Now, carry on," he said, thrusting his arm forward like a knight with a lance as the traffic light turned green.

She hit the gas pedal. "Yes sir, Captain Tightpants."

"Ohh, role reversal. I like it when you call me Captain. Do it again."

"Captain Tightpants," she said again, this time flicking her eyebrows up and snaking her tongue out between her lips.

He let his eyes roll back. "Oh my lord, you are my angel. Let's turn around right now."

"No can do," Nikki said. "You're going to have to put a pin in that . . . idea."

He shook his head, looking forlorn, but it was all just for show. He knew they had a job to do. They'd have playtime again later.

They parked in one of the visitor parking lots and followed the main path into the heart of the university. Amidst the curves of the path and the surrounding fall foliage, Nikki felt a bit like Dorothy Gale following the Yellow Brick Road. Without the Munchkins—or the literal yellow bricks.

Rook knew the way, so Nikki followed, taking in the campus as they walked. The buildings looked to be of varying ages. Some appeared to be original to the early twentieth-century founding, while others looked more mid-century with their modern sensibility. It created a discord in the feel of the campus, as if it didn't know which era to cling to. As they walked farther, she understood which way the university wanted the identity of their buildings to go. A mundane mid-century building was completely cordoned off. Scaffolding clung to its sides. From what she could tell, the nondescript beige facade was going to undergo a transformation. One entire section of the building's outer layer had been removed, revealing the framing beneath. The structure itself wasn't bad, per se. It just wasn't particularly interesting or inspiring.

"That," Rook said, noticing where her attention was directed, "used to be the English building. I took many a class there. How well I remember. British lit with Dr. Brindle." He chuckled, stopping dead in his tracks and throwing up a theatrical arm. " 'He who repeats a tale after a man / Is bound to say, as nearly as he can, / Each single word, if he remembers it, / However rudely spoken or unfit, / Or else the tale he tells will be untrue, / The things pretended and the phrases new.' "

Her English background occasionally came back to her in bits and pieces, usually because Rook triggered something that made her remember. "Chaucer," she said. "Right?"

"Right you are. It's a passage that always stuck with me. The simplicity of the idea that minor changes will render a tale new, thereby meaning it will no longer belong to the original author, struck me as ludicrous. This was, of course, before intellectual property rights. Now those minor changes would not equal a new tale. Now it would be plagiarism."

Over the years, Nikki had learned that Jameson Rook's

brain held untold amounts of random information. He could pull facts and tidbits as if from thin air, which often annoyed Nikki, but also never ceased to amaze her. "Kudos to you for remembering something like that from college. I don't remember any of my professor's names, let alone the material they taught."

The moment passed and they stared up at the building. Rook tilted his head as he looked at the facade. "I kind of liked the old 1950s look."

"But it'll be much nicer when it matches the look of the original structures," she said. "It'll make things look more cohesive."

He shrugged. "I guess."

She tilted her head, considering him. "You're usually gung ho about anything historic. What gives?"

He gestured toward the remodel construction. "That *was* original. It might not have matched the *original* original buildings, but to pretend that it wasn't built sometime in the middle of the 1900s is a lie. I am gung ho about authenticity first and foremost. Just like you, I'm always after the truth, whether that means seeking justice for Chloe Masterson or maintaining the integrity of a building even if it doesn't *fit*," he said, doing air quotes on the last word.

Nikki stifled a smile. "Well, okay, then. I had no idea you were such a stickler for a piece of architecture's provenance."

Rook swept his hand in the air from his head to his torso. "Untold depths, Heat. Untold depths."

They walked on, spotting another cordoned-off building. This one looked ancient and, from the looks of it, the university was working to restore it to its original grandeur.

"I guess I can see your point," Nikki said. "It would feel different living in a 1900 Victorian versus a brand-new house with a Victorian look. The history would be gone."

"Exactly. No creaky floors. No shiplap walls. No double-hung windows. It would be like lipstick on a pig."

That sounded like a down-home southern saying. Another random thought in Rook's endlessly fascinating mind.

They finally ended up in front of a nondescript square six-story red-brick building. A double glass door entrance was cut into the center. Windows ran across the front in symmetrical rows. A few trees peppered the green lawn, and a plain cement walkway led to the entrance. It was disappointing. It was the home of the *Cambria Journal*, but the heart and soul of the university looked soulless. Rook, as so often happened, seemed to read her mind. "Not much to look at, I know. But it's what's inside that matters."

She ran her hand over his back, letting it slide up under his tweed sport coat. He was embodying the professorial look with gusto. "That is most definitely not *your* problem. You're pretty nice to look at and have the insides to go with the package."

His mouth quirked up on one side and he waggled his eyebrows. "I do have quite the package, don't I?"

This time she didn't hold back her laugh. "Uh-huh."

He held the door open for her and she passed through. They rode the elevator to the fifth floor. As the doors slid open, they were greeted by a flurry of activity. Young adults speed-walked or jogged this way and that, talking into Bluetooth earpieces or turning and walking backward to talk to someone they'd just passed without actually stopping to have a conversation. Directly across from the elevator doors was a wall with THE CAMBRIA JOURNAL emblazoned across the paneling in large gold letters.

Once again, Rook led the way and Nikki fell in beside him. Heat had always prided herself on being prepared for anything, but as they rounded the corner and entered the lion's den of the college newsroom, she was thrown. The cacophony that greeted her was unexpected. She hadn't been in the *New York Times* newsroom, or the *Washington Post*'s, or any other major—or minor—newsroom, for that matter, so she had nothing to compare to, but the level of activity was intense. She stopped to absorb it all. The university, or whoever had designed the newsroom space, seemed to have done it with post-millennials in mind. They'd eschewed traditional offices and cubicle farms, opting instead for an open design. People were working at standing desks, and the low walls, while defining spaces, allowed people to talk to one another. To collaborate. On the periphery, Nikki noticed a few small rooms. For the times privacy was needed, she guessed. They'd considered everything.

She would have thought that each workspace would have its own printer, but it looked as if the office was primarily paperless. With email and Dropbox and Google Docs and the cloud, there was no need to print drafts for red ink. "It's very team-oriented," Rook said. "Very different than it was in my day. And my day wasn't so long ago."

"I bet."

A young man strode toward them. His blue oxford button-down tucked into his Dockers gave him a dressed-down casual look, which seemed appropriate given his student status, yet he carried himself with an authority that belied his age. He had his shoulders thrown back, his chin up, and a serious, but not off-putting expression on his face. "Mr. Rook. I didn't expect to see you—"

"Just Rook is fine," Rook said, interrupting him. "The Mr. thing . . ."

"It makes him feel old," Nikki said, finishing the thought for him.

Rook lifted his eyebrows and gave an affable shrug acknowledging Nikki's assessment. "No need to age faster than necessary. It's Mike, right?

A feathery lock of hair fell onto the young man's forehead. "Michael, actually. Warton."

"Michael Warton. That is a very Upper West Side name."

"Given to me by my very Lower East Side parents," he promptly quipped, and then added, "Before the gentrification, that is. Can I help you with something, Rook?"

"I always get a thrill coming round my old stomping ground. Things have adapted to the times, but a newspaper's energy never fails."

"So true," Michael said, affecting a wizened tone. "Especially the fact that the editor in chief has a very full plate—"

Rook hooked his thumb at Michael, but he looked at Heat. "That's him, editor in chief," he said, in case she hadn't put it together.

"Sounds like you are a very busy man," Nikki said, reading between the lines. This guy, this Michael Warton, didn't want to be spending his time with them. She gently ran her hand down Rook's arm. "We don't want to take your time.

My husband just wanted to show me his humble beginnings."

Rook picked up the thread. "Everyone has to start somewhere. This is where I paid my dues." He laughed. "The first payment, anyway. Michael, my good fellow, get ready. Journalism, especially in this new era, is no picnic."

Apparently Michael Warton didn't want to discuss the future dues he'd have to pay in his chosen career. He did, however, have something else on his mind. "We're all in shock about Chloe," he said. He looked pointedly at Rook. "You must be devastated."

"It's a tragedy, but why would Rook be devastated?" Nikki asked.

"Because they were working on a story together," Michael said. "Chloe was very excited to have him as a collaborator."

Nikki looked at Rook. To Michael, or to anyone who didn't know him well, it wouldn't seem as if his expression had changed; but Nikki noticed the infinitesimal shift. It wasn't an *Oh shit, I'm busted* movement. It was more *You don't know what you're talking about*.

Rook cleared his throat. Loudly. "You do both know that I am standing right here, don't you?"

Michael looked chagrined, but he stayed the course. "She *was* excited to be working with you, sir."

Rook was mollified. Slightly. But he shook his head. "Here's the thing. I was not working on anything with Chloe."

"That's not what she said. Or thought. She said you had information that was going to help her bring it home."

"Bring *what* home?" Nikki asked. So far, there had been no specific connection between Chloe and Rook. Michael might be the one to provide one.

"Her article. She was incredibly stubborn about it," Michael said, shaking his head. His feathery hair flopped down over his forehead. "Normally I don't tolerate that sort of thing. I need to know what my people are working on, but Chloe was stubborn. She wouldn't tell me what it was about, but she assured me that it would be worth it. Now that she's gone, the paper would like to honor her memory. I'd like to publish her last piece posthumously. As a tribute to her."

"A nice idea," Rook said, but Nikki looked in his eyes and saw the wheels turning. Her mind was racing, too. If what Michael Warton was saying was true, whatever story Chloe Masterson was working on could have led to her death. That still didn't explain Rook's connection to it all, however. Why was she found in his house, in his bed? Why would she say she and Rook had been working together?

Michael gave Rook a pointed look. "So, do you have her notes? Or the file with her article? She said it was almost finished—"

Rook cut him off. "Why would *I* have her notes?"

"She didn't leave anything here, and from what I understand, it wasn't found in her apartment. Her laptop hasn't been found. But she said you had some information that supported her research and that was going to help prove everything."

Rook stared at Michael, complete bewilderment on his face. "Prove what? I met Chloe Masterson exactly three times." He ticked them off on his fingers. "Once at the awards dinner in Manhattan. Once right here. She showed me around. And once in the lecture hall."

This last one was news to Nikki. "Why in the lecture hall?"

"She caught me after class."

"When was this?" Nikki asked.

"Day before yesterday."

"Which was the day before she was murdered," Nikki said. "Kind of important information, Rook."

Rook's face fell. "Right."

"What did she say?"

He closed his eyes for a beat, thinking back. "It wasn't a big deal. She wanted to know if we could get together for a drink. She said she had an idea that needed rekindling."

*Odd choice of phrasing,* Heat thought.

Rook continued. "I told her I'd be happy to meet her for coffee sometime."

Heat mentally thunked Rook's head. How could he not have told her this? She wanted to berate him. To tell him he should know better. Instead, with Michael Warton still looking on, she asked, "Did you make a plan to meet?"

"No. She came up after I dismissed the class. There were a few other kids there, too. She flagged me down. I must have zeroed in on her amidst the throng because I remembered her."

*Makes sense,* Nikki thought. When faced with the known or the unknown, the majority of people would choose the known entity.

"She said she'd love to talk, and could we get a drink. I had no reason to think it was anything more than a student admiring a professor. You saw her," he said to Nikki. "She was googly-eyed. Starstruck."

She couldn't disagree with him. "So you talked to her that night."

"There were a bunch of kids. I remember she said something, but I couldn't hear her. Then she left."

"And you have no idea what she said?"

He moved his mouth, muttering. Scratched his head, thinking. Then he snapped out of it. "I couldn't hear her, but I saw her mouth move."

"Could you tell what she was saying?"

He closed his eyes, his face clenching as he tried to recall. "The shape of her mouth—"

"What about it?" Nikki prompted.

"Lip reading. There are only a few letters in the alphabet where your lips press together, did you know that? The shape your mouth forms when you speak can reveal what is being said even when you can't hear it."

"I never thought about it."

"It's true. Try it. Say the alphabet and see how often your lips meet."

"Rook . . ." Nikki didn't hold back the irritation in her voice. Rook rarely gave a simple response to a question. Usually it came with some long-forgotten historical fact, or a grammar lesson, or, as was the case at this moment, information on the alphabet. Which was something neither of them had time for. "How does this help us?"

He tapped his temple. "I'm thinking. Or more accurately, I'm remembering," he said. Then he snapped his fingers. "Yes! She put her hand up to the side of her head with her thumb up and pinkie down—"

Now they were getting somewhere. "Like she was making a phone call?"

"Exactly. And she mouthed something. *I'll call you.* Wait. No. Her lips pressed together at the end. I'll call you *tomorrow.* That's it. It didn't register at the time, what with so many people around, but now, looking back, I'm pretty sure—no, I'm positive—that's what she was saying."

Nikki said the words aloud. "I'll call you. I'll call you tomorrow . . . That would have been yesterday—"

"Which was the day she died," Rook said.

From behind Nikki, Michael Warton cleared his throat. "In your house."

For a moment Nikki had forgotten the editor in chief was there. He'd unobtrusively stepped back so he was behind her field of vision.

"She may have wanted to call me. Or even intended to," Rook said. "But she never did."

"Maybe she decided she didn't want to talk about whatever was on her mind over the phone," Nikki suggested. "If that was the case, she'd just show up. Wait for you if you weren't there."

"Which I wasn't."

"So she'd waited."

"Looks like someone else showed up to wait with her," Michael commented.

"Showed up, yes, but not to wait," Rook said. "To kill."

"How did she—or they—get into your house without a key?" Michael asked.

Nikki knew the type. He was playing it casual, but he was in reporter mode. "This is off the record, by the way, Michael," she said. The last thing she wanted was for the *Cambria Journal* to print something about Chloe planning on calling Rook. A story like that would ignite the community and Rook would be guilty before he had a chance to be proven innocent. "This is an ongoing investigation into the death of Chloe Masterson."

She waited for acknowledgment, but he didn't say anything.

"Nod if you understand," she said.

Finally, he did. "Off the record."

"To answer the question, I have no idea how anyone would get in without a key," Rook said.

It was what Nikki expected, but it was a question that still needed answering at some point.

Michael broke the ensuing silence. "Feel free to show your wife around, Rook. Let me know if you need anything."

"I have a question before you go," Nikki said. Michael stopped and waited, so Nikki continued. "Rook said he witnessed you and Chloe have a heated conversation in your office the day she gave him a tour. What was that about?"

"I remember that very clearly," Michael said. "Chloe was, mmm, single-minded, shall we say? When she got something in her head, she was like a dog with a bone."

"A good quality in a journalist," Rook commented.

Michael nodded. "Sure, but you have to have your editor's blessing—"

"How well I remember. I had my own stories killed thanks to an overzealous *Journal* editor. Not that you are overzealous," Rook said, realizing he might have offended Michael. "My point is that, while it can help, you do not have to have an editor's blessing in the real world. Writers write on spec all the time. No prior approval needed."

"Chloe didn't like having to answer to anyone. She wanted to write what she wanted to write."

"And what exactly did she want to write?" Nikki asked.

"It's not that I killed whatever story she wanted to write," Michael said. "It's that she refused to write what I needed her to write. I told her she had to get with the program or I couldn't use her anymore."

"That's rough."

Michael shrugged. "Look, Mrs.—"

"Captain," Rook corrected.

"Captain Rook—"

"Heat," Nikki said. "Captain Heat."

He dipped his head. "*Captain Heat*. This is a cutthroat business."

"And you're still students," Heat murmured under her breath. "Imagine what it'll be like after graduation."

Michael and Rook both looked at her. Her muttering hadn't been as quiet as she'd thought. "So you told Chloe she had to do the stories you wanted her to do, and she refused?"

"She dug in and argued. Said she had something hot and I'd be sorry if I passed on it."

"But she didn't tell you what it was about?"

"I asked her, believe me. That's probably the discussion you saw. Me asking her about this major story, and her refusing to share."

Rook paced the lobby. "Why was she so against telling you?"

"There's no secret. She told me straight-up."

Nikki stared. "Chloe told you why she wouldn't come clean about the story she was working on?"

"I had to practically beat it out of her—not literally, of course—but she finally told me. She said some high-level people were involved and she had to have absolute proof."

Rook balked. "And that wasn't enough for you to give her some leeway? Jesus, Michael, you're going to have to loosen the reins if you're going to make it. Your writers have to have some autonomy. If it weren't for supportive editors, Nixon might still be president, we'd all still be smoking cigars and not worried about blue dresses, and, well, there's plenty more that we probably shouldn't talk about."

"I get it," Michael said. "But this is a college paper and she wouldn't give me any information. I can't work with that."

*No, what he can't work with is having someone challenging him*, Nikki thought.

Michael turned, ready to leave them to their own devices, but he stopped, facing them once more. "Don't take this the wrong way," he started.

Rook barked out a laugh. "Which is a surefire way to make sure we do, in fact, take it the wrong way."

"I'm just wondering. Why you?"

Rook's good humor was slowly evaporating. "Why me what?"

"Why did she pick *you* to share her story with?"

That was the very same question Nikki had.

"First, she didn't share anything with me," Rook said, repeating himself. "And second, if she wanted to, it is most likely because I have a reputation in the field in which she strove to succeed."

And he didn't try to keep her under his thumb like it seemed Michael wanted to. But to Michael, Nikki said, "Pulitzer Prize."

Michael pressed on. "But she never even mentioned a story to you?"

Rook shot him a frustrated look. "As I already said, she told me she wanted to talk. She did not elaborate."

The sharpness of his tone was out of character for Rook. He was pissed off at his integrity being questioned.

"I'm a journalist, Mr. Rook. And there was a dead girl in your house. She said people in high places would be implicated. Were you one of those people?"

"If I am, it's news to me," Rook said. He wasn't falling for whatever trap Michael was laying. Nikki just hoped the local police didn't go in the same direction with their investigation. Too often, cops tried to make the facts fit the hypothesis they had rather than letting those same facts lead them to the truth.

Michael gave that infernal shrug again. Clearly he was not enamored with Rook's journalistic fame. "My job is to ask questions."

Rook met Michael's gaze head-on, his jaw tightening with aggravation. "Then my answer bears repeating, as well." He spoke slowly, emphasizing each word. "Chloe ... Masterson ... never ... mentioned ... her ... story ... to ... me."

Michael nodded, but Nikki could read between the lines. The wheels of his brain were turning. For whatever reason, he didn't believe Rook.

The two men squared off in a vaguely challenging manner. "If you say so," Michael said.

From the corner of her eye, Nikki saw Rook's hands clench into fists. "I do say so."

Heat put her hand on Rook's arm to bring him down from the ledge he was on. To Michael, she said, "I assume the police have checked her desk area?"

He nodded. "They didn't find anything, as far as I know. If Chloe had her research or article with her, whoever killed her would have taken it."

Nikki was impressed. Michael had hit the nail on the head. "I agree," she said. "If it had anything to do with her death, it's long gone."

# ELEVEN

The hotel exceeded Nikki's expectations. Rook never did anything halfway, his choice of accommodations included. He'd anticipated being here a while, what with his university housing now a crime scene, so he'd gotten himself a suite. The king-size bed was almost as comfortable as the one they shared in the loft, this one all the better at the moment because Rook was next to her.

Nikki found that she could compartmentalize. The Rook she loved and trusted was by her side. When she thought about it logically, there was no way in hell that he could have killed Chloe. He was compassionate. He stood up for those with no voice. He was Jameson Rook, not a killer. She had left the doubts trying to invade her mind at the door and now she rolled onto her side. She propped her head on one hand, dancing her fingers across Rook's chest with the other.

"Are you toying with me, Heat? Round two?"

"I'm buttering you up. There's a difference."

"Do tell. For what am I being buttered?"

"I need a murder board."

He didn't miss a beat with his response. Rook was like that. He was quick on his feet, and even quicker with his mind. "I'm one step ahead of you."

Before she could ask him what he meant, there was a rapid knock on the door. "Speak of the devil," he said. He quickly rolled out of bed, slipped on his boxers and a gray T-shirt, grabbed a twenty-dollar bill, and was answering the hotel door all before she'd started and finished yawning. The person he was having a conversation with spoke too quietly to hear, but Rook's voice carried. "This way," he said as he reappeared into her line of sight. Right behind him was a bellhop. He averted his eyes, never even glancing her way as he wheeled in a whiteboard. It was almost identical to the ones the department used at the precinct.

After Rook slipped the twenty into the bellhop's hand, the young man smiled broadly. "Let me know if you need anything else, sir. I'm glad to help."

Once he was gone, Nikki bolted to a sitting position, holding the sheet to her chest with one hand, brushing her tangled hair away from her face with the other. "Jameson Rook," she said. "You didn't!"

"But I did."

She was constantly amazed by him. "It's as if you can read my mind sometimes."

"I know your every need," he replied suggestively, climbing back into bed next to her.

As he started to slide his arm around her, she scooted to the edge of the bed. The blue button-down shirt Rook had worn earlier lay discarded on the chair next to the bed. She reached for it, slipped it on, quickly buttoned it, and stood up. "I don't know about that, but you certainly hit the nail on the head this time."

"You're starting now?" he said, but then he nodded,

more to himself than to her. "Of course you are. I would expect nothing less."

Nikki had already uncapped a black Expo marker. With neat print and in large letters, she wrote CHLOE MASTERSON across the top of the board. She turned to Rook, ready to begin organizing what they knew, but then raised her eyebrows instead. She had long ago learned to read people. The way they held their mouths; what they did with their hands; where their eyes shifted to. Rook wore a lazy smile. His gaze was on her, sliding down to her legs then up again. Instantly, she knew what was on his mind. He'd been serious about the "round two" he'd proposed. She'd put on his shirt, and nothing but his shirt. Raising her arm to write on the whiteboard had given him a pretty good view of what was missing underneath. "Jameson Rook," she said, saying his full name for the second time in less than ten minutes. The first had been in amazement. This time it was scolding. "Pace yourself, big boy. It's time to get serious."

"I'm perfectly serious," he said. He ran his hand down his face, wiping away the smile to prove it. "What do we know so far? Chloe Masterson was a senior. She had something to show me, although I have no idea what that something is. Michael Warton, editor in chief of the *Journal*, says he also has no idea what Chloe was working on."

Nikki listened as Rook spoke, then turned and started writing notes on the left side of the whiteboard. "Did you believe him?"

Rook thought about this, stroking his chin. "I don't know. Did you?"

"Why would he lie?" she asked. She didn't expect Rook

to give her an answer. He didn't know anything more than she did. It was simply a question that needed answering. A question that allowed them to speculate. To hypothesize.

"We don't know if he's lying," Rook said.

"But what if he is? What could Chloe have been working on that Michael would want to keep close to the vest?"

They fell silent for a minute, both considering this question . . . and the possible answers. Rook spoke first. "What if the story was about him?"

"He looked like a straight-arrow kid to me," she said. They often took turns playing devil's advocate. It was how their collaboration worked. They bounced ideas off one another, each making the other think about something that hadn't occurred to them before. *No bias in journalism and no bias in police work,* Rook often said.

"Looks can be deceiving. That's at the core of every murder investigation, isn't it? The murderer is hiding, often in plain sight. They can be the best friend. Mom or Dad. A coworker. The murderer can be anyone. They're always lurking behind an innocent facade. Michael Warton might very well have killed Chloe Masterson—if she'd discovered something that he wanted to keep buried."

"So we dig into Michael Warton," she said, circling his name on the board. "What else?" She thought about meeting Chloe at the awards ceremony a few weeks before. "What did she say to you when we first met her?"

His brows pulled together as he thought. "She said she had an article that I might find interesting."

Nikki drew a vertical line under Chloe's name and wrote: *What was she researching?* "Her notes are missing.

I think we were on the mark earlier. If she had them on her when the killer got to her, they're long gone."

"But if she didn't have them on her, they're somewhere. If the story was as hot as she seemed to think, she probably hid them away somewhere."

Nikki added the heading CHLOE'S NOTES to the board. Without access to the crime scene photos, the forensics, the ME's report, and all the other details she'd have if she were privy to that information here in Cambria, her hands were tied. There was only so much she could do. There was only one logical next step. "It's time to visit the police station," she said.

# TWELVE

Nikki Heat's entire career had been at the Twentieth Precinct. The jurisdiction ran from 59th to 86th Streets with the precinct building on 82nd and Columbus. As the first female captain of the Two-Oh, Heat had had to establish herself as strong and capable, willing and able to delegate. She'd had some good role models—men who represented the shield in the best possible way. Men who had been committed and honest and had always fought the good fight.

But if she was being honest with herself, it was the not-so-great role models she'd actually learned the most from. Those were the men who had caught a lucky break and landed in the position because they'd been in the right place at the right time. They hadn't earned it. They were the ones with questionable ethics; the ones with less than stellar intellect; the ones who hadn't made it long in the position. Over the years, Heat had been on the receiving end of their leadership. She'd observed and catalogued and knew exactly what *not* to do as a leader. She would never belittle her team. She would always speak with respect. At the same time, she would never let one of her detectives get away with anything that went against her core belief system.

She wouldn't let them disrespect the dead. She wouldn't tolerate racism or sexism or any other negative-ism.

It had taken her a while to adjust to delegation and to removing herself from the crime scene. Zach Hamner, the senior administrative aide to the NYPD's deputy commissioner for legal matters, had been instrumental in her ascension to captain of the Two-Oh. He'd sung her praises at One Police Plaza. She hadn't known at the time that his support, at least in his eyes, meant she was beholden to him. She'd realized too late that she'd made a deal with a Machiavellian devil. The Hammer, as he was not-so-affectionately known, had helped her win a position that he proceeded to take great pleasure in disrupting. In short, he often made her life at the precinct hell.

All that being said, Heat had learned how to play the game from The Hammer. She listened to him, but then usually did the exact opposite of what he recommended. He was out for himself, while she was about helping others.

She often heard The Hammer's voice in her head: *Do you have anything remotely resembling a lead? Does your team have a clue about what they're doing? You're clearly out of your league, Heat.* But in the current moment, she heard him saying, *You'll kiss ass, Heat, because that's what is required of you at the moment.*

It was not in Heat's DNA to brownnose, which made what she was about to do put a bad taste in her mouth. But she had no choice. She'd dropped Rook off at Murchison Hall, where he had a class to teach, and had driven her car the short distance to the local police station—ready to kiss some small-town law enforcement booty.

As Heat approached the desk sergeant, she dialed down her tough-as-nails homicide detective attitude. Being from Manhattan wouldn't do her any favors in an upstate municipality. She knew from experience that they'd dismiss her as a know-it-all city cop who had nothing but disdain for them. It wasn't true. The simple fact was that she had more experience than they did, particularly when it came to murder.

She smiled at the woman sitting behind the bulletproof barrier that separated her from everyone on the other side. She looked to be in her late twenties. Her chestnut hair was wound up in a severe bun, pulled completely away from her face. Female recruits in the academy were not allowed to wear makeup. From the evident blemishes and short eyelashes, it looked like the officer continued with that expectation into her career. The gray color of her department-issued uniform and its plum-colored tie only served to emphasize her sallow skin tone, but her clothes were crisply pressed and she looked neat and professional. Nikki admired that. It wasn't easy being a woman in law enforcement, which meant you had to go the extra mile to not "be a girl." No tears. No emotion. Nothing that jeopardized how others saw you.

"Can I help you?" the sergeant asked, her eyes scanning Nikki up and down. Heat knew the drill. It took a police officer about five seconds to make a judgment about the person standing in front of them. As a homicide detective, she actively worked against that tendency. She needed to have an open mind so she didn't color her investigations with preconceived notions and biases. The officer in front of her, however, didn't have the experience or the need to stay neutral.

Heat's initial instinct was to press her badge against the glass to gain the upper hand against the younger woman, but she resisted. *You catch more flies with honey,* Rook always said. Cliché, but true. Heat read the placard with the officer's name printed on it and applied that advice, brightening her smile and making her voice overly pleasant. "Good morning, Officer Breckenstein. My name is Nikki Heat. I'm on the job in Manhattan. Twentieth Precinct." She paused, waiting for acknowledgment. None was forthcoming, so she continued. "I was wondering if you could tell me who's in charge of the Chloe Masterson investigation?" She added a lilt to the last word, heightening her amiability.

There was a beat before the officer answered, "You're a little outside your jurisdiction."

Her voice had a huskiness to it. An additional challenge for Officer Breckenstein, since it held a sensual undertone. "I am," Heat said. "I came up to visit my husband."

The sergeant gave a knowing nod. "You're married to Jameson Rook, then." It was a statement, not a question. She was confident and didn't need Nikki to confirm what she'd surmised.

"How do you know that?" Nikki asked.

Another smile. "It's a small town, ma'am. You're police, you're here and asking about the investigation, and we heard about the professor getting a visitor at his hotel. I assume that visitor is you."

"It is," Nikki confirmed.

"What can I help you with, Detective?"

Despite the fact that she was mildly impressed with the young officer, Heat grimaced inwardly. This wasn't going to be as easy as she'd hoped. She thought about what tack to take, quickly deciding on the straight-arrow approach and deciding against giving her rank. She didn't want to give the officer a reason to resent her. "I'm sure you know about the murder . . ."

Officer Breckenstein started to roll her eyes, catching herself and schooling her expression. "Yes, I do know about the murder. It's a rare occurrence in Cambria."

Unlike in Manhattan, where people were animals and murder was ingrained into the fabric of the city, was her implication. "Right. Of course." Heat drew in a breath and started again. "Can you tell me who's leading the investigation?"

Now the officer's eyes narrowed suspiciously. "Why do you need to know?"

Heat's voice started to lose some of the friendliness she'd tried to maintain. "The victim was discovered by my husband at his temporary housing. I'd like to see what's happening in the investigation." *Obviously,* she added in her head.

Officer Breckenstein paused to consider, irritating Heat even more. The woman had no cause to withhold the name of the lead detective, and there was such a thing as professional courtesy, something Breckenstein didn't seem to understand. But finally, after a solid thirty seconds, she picked up the phone and punched in an extension. "There's a detective here from the Two-Oh in Manhattan, sir. She's asking to see you."

Whoever was on the other end of the call said something to Officer Breckenstein, who then eyed Nikki through the glass. "Detective, yes. Nikki Heat. The wife of—"

"Yes, sir. Right away," Breckenstein said after being cut

off, and she hung up the phone.

Heat saw Breckenstein's hand slip down beneath the desk. There was a buzz, followed by a click, which meant the officer had pressed a button to let Heat into the inner sanctum of the Cambria Police Department. Heat didn't waste any time. She slipped through the door, moving quickly in case the investigating officer called Breckenstein back with a change of heart.

The interior of the station was nothing like the Two-Oh. Where the building on West 82nd Street had a slightly grungy city feel to it, the walls of Cambria's single-story offices were painted a bright white and had only a fraction of the desks Heat's department had. And she ran Homicide at the Twentieth. Each precinct also ran Vice, Special Victims, and Robbery divisions, among other things, which meant the workforce at each of the seventy-seven Manhattan precincts was at least ten times larger than the one here. There probably wasn't a Raley or an Ochoa. Or a Feller, Aguinaldo, Rhymer, or Hinesburg. There might not have been *anyone* particularly qualified to investigate Chloe Masterson's murder, which would mean Rook was in trouble.

A man's voice bellowed her name from down the hall. "Well, well, well. If it isn't Detective Nikki Heat. What a surprise."

Her insides coiled into a tight mass. She hadn't heard that voice since she'd been in the police academy. And she hadn't thought about the man it belonged to in years. She turned. "Ian Cooley," she said, forcing a smile into her grimace. She was looking at the face of her first husband.

# THIRTEEN

Nikki knew the past could come back to haunt a person. She'd seen it firsthand too many times to count. It was often the motivation for murder, after all. What she didn't know—had never suspected—was that she'd be staring at the face of her own tempestuous past.

Ian looked the same as he had back at the police academy, but older. He was lanky and rail-thin, standing six foot six. His dark sideburns were peppered with gray. Silvery strands wove through the rest, which he combed to the side. Very mature. Very conservative. Very much the Ian she remembered.

Three things ran through her mind as she took stock of him: What were the odds of running into a man she hadn't seen in more than a decade, and here in Cambria where a murder had happened in her current husband's house to boot? Was he going to be a help or a hindrance to her off-book investigation? Was she going to tell Rook about her past with the man who could very well be investigating his involvement in a murder . . . and how would she explain why she hadn't told him before now?

There was no provable response to question one, so she

discarded it from her mind. Question three she'd have to deal with later. Which left question two. The answer was yet to be determined. "The surprise is mutual," she said.

"I hear you've been in Manhattan," he said, giving a low whistle. He ushered her down the hallway from the direction in which he'd come, leading her to what amounted to the local precinct's bull pen. She automatically surveyed her surroundings. Smaller than the Two-Oh. The room was brighter. More windows, which translated to more light. The old building that housed her precinct had multiple stories. Her department, in particular, had fewer windows and a dark interior that seemed to capture the mood of a homicide division.

Ian moved around one of the several desks in the room, gesturing to a chair on the opposite side for her to sit. She did, noting how it felt strange to be on the opposite end of an investigator's desk. Especially when that investigator was Ian Cooley.

He leaned back in his chair, folding his arms across his chest as he considered her. "I heard this Jameson Rook guy was married to an NYC detective. I sure never expected it to be you."

She didn't believe him for a second. Rook had to be a person of interest, which meant one of the first things a lead investigator would do was check out the background of said potential suspect. In this case, that simple background check would have revealed Rook's marriage to her. There was also the added fact that their wedding had been well catalogued in the local papers and media, thanks to Margaret Rook and her flair for drama. With her and Rook's blessing, Margaret had sent in announcements wherever she could. Nikki remembered every line.

JAMESON ALEXANDER ROOK, ONLY SON OF
TONY AWARD–WINNING BROADWAY ACTRESS, MARGARET ROOK,
IS TO MARRY NIKKI HEAT, DAUGHTER OF CYNTHIA AND JEFF HEAT.
THE WEDDING WILL TAKE PLACE AT UNION CHAPEL,
MARTHA'S VINEYARD, AT THREE IN THE AFTERNOON.

RECEPTION WILL FOLLOW.

THE COUPLE WILL HONEYMOON IN EUROPE.

"How long have you been with the Cambria PD?" she asked, skipping over Ian's obvious lie.

He leaned back and intertwined his fingers. He let his eyes drift up to the ceiling as he silently counted.

She laughed. "As long as I've been with the Twentieth, sounds like."

"I came here after the academy, then left to work in Hoboken for a bit. Couldn't stay away. And since I'm chief of police, I'll probably never leave. This place is off the beaten path, but I swear, it gets in your blood," he said, giving her a look that said Cambria wasn't the only thing that got in his blood. "You've been in Manhattan since graduation?"

"At the Twentieth the entire time."

"And now you're . . ."

He trailed off, letting her fill in the blank. "Captain."

"Captain Heat," Ian said, as if testing it out. He let out another low whistle. "That's an accomplishment, Nik."

She bristled at the familiar nickname. She could count

on one hand the people she was close enough with to have them call her that. Ian Cooley was not one of them. She was done with the small talk. "Can you tell me what's going on with your investigation on Chloe Masterson?"

It was clear that he sensed the shift in her. He kept his hands clasped, his two fingers steepled, but his body stiffened. He was keenly aware that their brief trip down memory lane was over, and he responded accordingly. "I'd like to, but you're a bit out of your jurisdiction here, Captain. Not to mention the fact that your husband has been questioned about his involvement in this murder."

She tensed, but she forced her voice to remain calm and light. "Right. My hus—Rook, he's been pretty upset, obviously. I'd like to help. You know, alleviate his concern."

"I interviewed Mr. Rook," Ian said. "He has good reason to be concerned."

Heat swallowed hard. "He's innocent, so why would you say that?"

Cooley had kept a mild expression on his face, but at her question, he dropped his hands to his desk and rolled forward in his chair. "Surely you see what a precarious situation this is. A journalism student was found dead. Naked. In your husband's bed. That doesn't bode well for him."

She bristled at his choice of words. "Very descriptive, thank you for that."

"Can't sugarcoat the facts," he said. "And those *are* the facts. Your husband is in trouble, Nikki. If I were you, I'd be spending my time with him before it all goes south."

She didn't let him rattle her. "What do you have?"

He shook his head. "It's an ongoing investigation. I can't—"

"Sure you can. We're both on the job. Professional courtesy. Come on."

"Maybe under normal circumstances, but he's your husband. That puts you a little too close to be objective."

Still working to keep calm, all doubt she'd had about Rook completely obliterated, she leaned forward, matching Cooley's body language. "Actually, it gives me all the reason in the world to get to the truth."

"You're biased," he said.

"Ian, you don't know me—"

"Of course I know you—"

She wagged her finger at him, her eyes narrowing. "Uh-uh. The Nikki Heat you knew was damaged and broken. That was a long time ago. I'm not that person anymore. I'm a detective first. I'll follow my leads wherever they take me. But I also know, with absolute certainty, that Rook did not have anything to do with that girl's death."

Ian sat back in his chair again, crossing one leg across the other, ankle on knee. "See, that's the problem. You know in your heart that he didn't do it, but what if the clues tell you that he did? Two divergent paths. They aren't going to cross in the woods."

She rolled her eyes at the Robert Frost reference. "A play on words from one of my favorite poems. You have a memory like an elephant."

"I do indeed."

Once again, she matched his body language, leaning back in her chair and crossing her ankle to the opposite knee. "See, where you see divergent paths, I see a man who's not guilty of anything at risk of losing everything."

"That very sentence strikes me as a pretty big conflict of interest. I'll say it again, Nik. You can't be objective."

She balked. "I am a trained detective. Objective is what I do." This conversation was underscoring that fact, but it also reinforced her certainty in Rook's innocence.

"You forget that I knew you pretty well once upon a time. And I know from experience that you make things personal."

Once again, the mystery of Cynthia Heat rose, circling around Nikki's memory like hot steam rising from the ground. "My mother died in my arms. That *was* personal. This is different."

"If your husband goes down for this, he won't come back from the dead."

"If you let me help you, it won't get that far."

He looked affronted. "Why, because our little precinct can't handle a high-profile murder like Chloe Masterson's?"

"That is not what I said. Don't put words in my mouth, Ian."

"You need to back down and let me do my job."

She considered her next move. She could push Ian, or she could let him have this win. She really had no choice. Pushing him was only going to make it worse. She had to retreat, review, and come back in when she had something to offer him.

**Nikki answered her ringing cell phone with a clipped "Heat."**

"Hey, Captain. How goes it in Timbuktu?" After the unsuccessful conversation with Ian, Nikki had wanted to bang her head against a wall. Miguel Ochoa's voice was a welcome distraction.

"Not great," she said. "Local law enforcement just shut me out."

"Nah. They won't pony up anything?"

She shook her head, still in disbelief herself. "Not even the tiniest scrap of hay," she said, not able to mask her frustration.

Ochoa was silent for a beat before speaking again. "How's my man Rook? Hanging in there?"

"I don't think the gravity of the situation has hit him yet. I don't know where the cops stand with him. Person of interest, definitely, but that's it. There's no motive."

"Does he have an alibi?"

That had been one of the first things she'd asked him, but the answer was inconclusive. "Without the ME's report, I don't know TOD, which means we're not sure. He was at a lecture on campus, but then he left, alone, and headed to his place. That's when he found her. Before the lecture, he was at a coffee shop."

"Did the police try to corroborate?"

She threaded her fingers through her hair in frustration. "I have no idea. I'm giving the detective here some space before I hit him again."

"So what's your plan?" Ochoa asked.

"Going to talk to the roommate next. What's going on there? Anything new with the Chin case?"

"That's why I called."

God, she hoped it was good news. "Tell me."

"Have you on speaker now, Captain," Ochoa said. "Raley's here."

The other half of Roach greeted her, then launched into the update on the Lincoln Plaza case. "Our vic was squeaky-clean," Raley said. "We've followed up every lead and they've all come up dry. Model student. No girlfriend. Roommate and he got along. No drugs. Parents he liked, and who liked him. He was on the reserved side. Not much of a partier, but also not a recluse."

From Ochoa, "In other words, this kid should not have been murdered."

"But he was, which means there's something hidden. He had to have had some secret; we just don't know what it is yet."

"Parry has an update," Ochoa said.

In addition to being Nikki's best friend, Lauren Parry was the most competent ME Heat had ever worked with. Their friendship had begun slowly. Lauren spent most of her time with the dead, while Nikki spent most of her time thinking about the dead. These facts together made them both overly cautious about forming real connections with the living. Over time, their friendship did evolve, however, and eventually they both realized that they were each other's "person." Lauren had been Nikki's maid of honor at her wedding to Rook. Now, hearing Ochoa mention her name make Nikki wish she could talk to her friend about Ian and the situation she was in. But that would have to come later.

"Nothing earth-shattering," Ochoa continued. "He drowned, which we knew. No alcohol or drugs in his system, which goes along with what the people who knew him had to say."

"Like we said, squeaky-clean," Raley said.

"Anything on the three suspects seen by our witness?"

"Nothing," Ochoa said. "It's a needle in a haystack. We've got a few more avenues to pursue, though."

She nodded with satisfaction. She had faith in Roach. If anyone could get to the bottom of a tough situation, it was them. "Keep me apprised," she said, and she went back to her own needle and haystack.

# FOURTEEN

Nikki had taken the long way back to the hotel. Part of that had been unintentional. The lack of a grid pattern in Cambria's streets meant she'd missed turns or gotten off track more than once, even with her phone's GPS. The other reason for the scenic route, however, was that it provided her time to think. Generally speaking, she spent as little time as possible ruminating about the past. The here and now, and the future—those were the only things that mattered.

But after seeing Ian Cooley, she needed to think—about the past and the present, and how to reconcile the two. The fact that her former husband, a man her current husband knew nothing about, was in charge of the investigation complicated personal matters. It also made the investigative matters more difficult. She couldn't have an antagonistic relationship with the man. He'd had one opportunity to step up and be helpful. He'd opted not to be. If the occasion presented itself again, she had to get him to opt for helpfulness.

The fact was that without Ian's help, Nikki and Rook were on their own without any resources, and that didn't bode well for an investigation they needed to bring to a close.

She couldn't succumb to fear. Even contemplating the possibility of Rook being charged with Chloe's murder was unthinkable. If he were found guilty, she didn't know what she would do. Rook incarcerated? She had no doubt he'd put himself in a penitentiary—maximum security, even—to do an exposé on the prison system. But to be put there after being declared a murderer? Could he survive that? The very idea sent her into a panic, but she couldn't give in to it.

Years on the force had taught Nikki how to compartmentalize. She could flip a switch and turn off her emotions, which is what she did now. She couldn't get sidelined worrying about what *might* happen if they didn't prevail.

She made it back to the hotel suite and found Rook already there, reclining on the couch, laptop open, fingers tapping away. "Working on a story?" she asked.

"Writing a narrative of everything that's happening as we investigate this story. I like to chronicle things, as you know."

That she did. He had an entire cupboard in his office filled with his chronicles.

"Which got me thinking," he said. "Did Chloe chronicle things, as well? Diaries, perhaps?"

It was quite possible. Heat herself had kept a journal for years. It was something one of the therapists she'd gone to after her mother's death had suggested. Writing down her emotions made them tangible. Real. The process of putting words to paper turned out to be cathartic. It didn't take her pain away, but it redirected it somehow.

Rook looked up at her suddenly. "Any luck at the station?"

"We're not going to get any help there," she said. "The police chief was not inclined to cough up any information."

"What happened to 'you scratch my back, I scratch yours'?"

"Guess the Cambria Police Department doesn't work that way."

"We don't need them," Rook said.

She knew he was trying to keep a stiff upper lip, for both their sakes. "Sure, but it would be helpful."

"Guess you'll just have to prove your salt sans databases and forensics."

"Guess so."

Rook set his computer off to the side. "Whatever story Chloe was working on has to be connected to her death."

"Sometimes the obvious path isn't actually the right path. Maybe she had a stalker. Or a disgruntled boyfriend. There are a lot of other scenarios that could materialize."

But Rook was far from convinced. He shook his head. "You don't understand. She was a *journalist*."

"*You're* a journalist. You're not always following a lead."

"Oh, but that's where you're wrong, Heat. I am *always* thinking about my work. If I'm not actively working on a story, I'm formulating ideas, observing everything around me in case an idea sparks, or reading other journalists' work to hone my skills or get new perspectives. I just don't always talk about it."

Nikki supposed he did always have a story in the back of his mind—in the same way she always had one case or another on her mind. "I believe that about you," she said, "but Chloe was a college student—"

He stopped her with a wag of his finger. "Oh no, she was a newshound. She was out for the story. I've been thinking about the argument she had with Michael Warton. She was willing to go down for this story. To risk her job at the *Journal*, which is a really big deal. Whatever she was working on was huge in her mind. Which means it probably *was* huge. Which means someone very well might have wanted to keep her from writing it. Maybe she'd been too overt in her investigation."

"She tipped off the murderer that she was digging around. But let's hypothesize. If she *was* following some sort of lead, why not tell Michael Warton? He's the editor in chief. If the story was that big, why wouldn't he want to run it?"

Rook's eyes gleamed, and he gave a satisfied smile. "Because I think she was a stringer."

Nikki waited for more, but more wasn't forthcoming. She sat back, shrugging. "I give. What's a stringer?"

"Aha!" His face lit up as if he'd just made a terrific discovery of some sort. "I thought you might ask that. A stringer is someone selling their work to a variety of sources, but not on staff at those publications."

She failed to see what his excitement was about. "Okay, but she *was* regular staff."

"That's true. But let's play the 'what if' game. I'll start."

Rook had invented the "what if" game recently when they'd been working a case and had hit a wall. They'd gone back and forth posing "what if" questions. Finally, the game led them to a new idea, in a new direction, and ultimately, to solving the case.

Rook's eyes shone. Give the man any type of cerebral activity and he was on cloud nine. "What if Chloe thought she had the story of a lifetime?"

"What if she thought the story would be a game-changer for her career?"

"Good one," Rook said. "What if she decided she wanted to go bigger than the Cambria University newspaper with the story?"

"What if she tried to sell it somewhere else?" Nikki posed. Was that even how it worked?

The sound from Rook clapping his hands made her jump. "Exactly! She had a story and she thought it was too big for the *Journal*. She was trying to be Deep Throat."

"You think she was shopping it around to other papers?"

Rook nodded. "I think she was moonlighting. She worked on the *Journal*, but she was doing her big story on the side." He paused for dramatic effect, lowering his voice. *"She was investigating off-book."*

As Nikki's mind processed this idea, another "what if" came to her. "What if the argument with Michael wasn't about him telling her that *he* didn't want her story? What if it was *her* telling him that he couldn't have it?"

Rook jumped off the bed. "Good thought."

He grabbed the dry-erase marker and held it out to her, but she shook her head. "You do the honors."

"Are you sure? You're usually possessive about your murder boards."

"I'm trying to let go of the control a little bit," she said. It was a small thing, but giving up the small things that had given order to her life when she was a detective allowed her to create new order as captain. She had made room for sifting through emails, filing reports, meetings at One PP, requisitions, and all the other minutiae that made up the job.

Presiding over the murder boards had gone by the wayside.

He uncapped the marker and wrote two questions on the board.

DID MICHAEL WANT CHLOE'S STORY?

DID CHLOE REFUSE TO GIVE HER STORY TO MICHAEL?

He paused, then added a third: WAS CHLOE A STRINGER?

Nikki considered the questions. "So the theory is that if she refused to give the story to Michael, then she had someone else who wanted to publish it?"

"Exactly."

"Which would make her a stringer?"

"Yes. Working for the *Journal*, but also writing for someone else. My bet, though, is that she was writing on spec."

"Why do you think that?"

"If you're on staff, you pitch a story and the editor either gives their blessing or they say no. If you're not on staff, unless you have a reputation and clippings to prove yourself, an editor might like the idea but isn't going to commit until they've seen the piece."

She cocked an eyebrow at him, in part because of his dramatics, and in part because he'd surprised her with a tidbit of information about himself that she hadn't known. "Sounds like you've been a stringer. Rook, have you been holding out on me?"

"I could never hold out on you," he said with a wink.

"You didn't tell me you were a string—" She stopped. The hypocrisy. Rook neglecting to tell her that he'd investigated stories "off-book" didn't compare to the marriage she had never mentioned.

"Let me clarify," he said. "A stringer is just a journalist who freelances and gets paid for individual pieces rather than receiving a salary. I still do it. Anything I write that isn't for *First Press* is freelance."

"So it's not a bad thing?"

"Not unless you have a contract that stipulates no freelancing, or a relationship with your editor that would be compromised if you withheld a potentially great story in favor of another avenue."

"That works with our theory, then. If Chloe had a great idea and Michael got wind of it, he might have gotten pretty angry."

"Very likely. He wants to put out the best paper he can."

"Maybe that's what she wanted to talk with you about. She may have needed your advice on how to handle her story and the conflict between the *Journal* and wherever she wanted to sell it."

Rook sat back on the edge of the bed. "Right. And here I am, a visiting professor at her college. It was an opportunity for her. But wrong place and wrong time for the killer."

"Which led to her death and you being framed." Unbidden images of Chloe Masterson came to Heat's mind, first at the awards ceremony and then in Rook's bed—blood pooling around her.

Rook continued with his train of thought, taking her on the verbal journey he relished sharing. "I got to thinking about my time with the *Journal*. Some of the best years of my life, I must admit."

"I bet," she said. Rook's college experience had been so vastly different from hers. While he'd been living every young adult male's dream, she'd been holding her mother's apparently dead body in her arms. While he had been learning the tools of his trade and developing a love for 1930s-era Blackwing pencils, she had been learning how to assess risk and handle weapons. She'd developed the mental preparedness necessary to face potentially dangerous situations. In short, she'd done what it took to become a highly competent New York City police officer. She'd learned how to put the good of the many above the needs of one person. Rook, on the other hand, she was quite sure had been all about his individual needs during college. She couldn't say she blamed him. At some point, he'd decided that helping people through his reporting aligned with what he wanted.

Rook realized his mistake. He reached his hand across the table. "Best years of my life until I met you, Heat. Everything pales in comparison."

She smiled at him and intertwined her fingers with his. "It certainly does."

Her life before Jameson Rook had been like a black-and-white movie. After meeting him, it had turned to Technicolor. Had she never told Rook about Ian Cooley because Ian had been part of the monochromatic life that came before Rook?

"I became a stringer when a story I was working on for the *Journal* was killed before I was even done with it," Rook said, moving the conversation along. "It happens. You move forward, that's all."

"The great career of Jameson Rook. That's how it all started?"

"That's my journalistic origin story. Snapped up out of college by the *Times*."

"Ohhh, the *Times*. My, my."

"Of course. It's just like you bringing in Detective Aguinaldo. You saw her value and brought her to the Two-Oh. Any organization worth its salt will snap up the standouts before someone else does. They'd seen one of my pieces and hired me on an article-by-article basis—"

"As a stringer," she said.

"As a stringer."

Nikki backed up to the beginning of their conversation. "How do we get proof that Chloe was a stringer?"

"We live in the era of the Internet. We search. Maybe she's had luck with published pieces and we get a hit."

"But maybe she hasn't and we don't," Nikki said, finishing the thought. She stared at the sketchy information on the murder board, her frustration mounting. Damn Ian Cooley for not cooperating with her.

As Rook followed her gaze, he seemed to remember something. He suddenly jumped up and pulled an eight-by-ten photograph of Chloe Masterson from the leather satchel that lay resting on a nearby chair. "I got you a present," he said.

"How did you get that?" she asked, taking it from him. She took the magnets he offered and immediately added Chloe's likeness to the murder board.

Rook tapped his finger against his temple. "Journalist. Resources."

She turned back to him. "Can you be more specific?"

"A journalist never reveals his sources, Heat. You know that."

She arched a reproachful eyebrow at him, and he sighed. A flirtatiously resigned sigh. "God, you drive a hard bargain, Heat. Fine. I'll tell you."

"I knew you would," she said, flashing her own smile.

"I talked with someone at the *Journal* and asked for Chloe's professional photo. They were happy to oblige. As soon as I got the image, I sent it to be printed."

Having Chloe's amber-rimmed brown eyes staring back at her—eyes filled with life—brought a lump to her throat. With or without the help of the local authorities, she and Rook would get to the bottom of her death.

So many thoughts circled through Nikki's mind, but she landed on the first night she'd spent with Rook. Manhattan had been in the midst of a heat wave and a citywide blackout. He'd made his attraction to her very clear since he'd begun his ride-alongs, and when he showed up outside her apartment that night (to protect her, of all things), she'd only heard a noise behind her and felt a hand on her back. Instinct had kicked in and she'd whirled around and given him a swift kick to the jaw. That same night, they'd sat side by side having margaritas, and then she'd taken him to her bed.

She didn't know what she'd expected, but Rook turned out to be unlike any man she'd ever been with. Playful. Energetic. Attentive. And he brought out a playful side of her that she'd thought had been long forgotten.

Whether it was pouring a glass of wine after a long day, drawing a hot bath, wheeling in a murder board, or pinning up a picture of the victim—strange as it was—he always knew exactly what she needed.

"Nicely done, Jamie," she said, and she pulled him down onto the bed.

**Maple Village Apartments, where Chloe Masterson had lived** with Tammy Burton, was not at all what Heat had been expecting. "More upscale than I thought it would be," she commented as they approached the redbrick building.

"Parents," Rook said, echoing exactly what she'd been thinking.

They found the apartment and knocked. And knocked again. As Rook raised his hand to rap his knuckles against the door one more time, the door flung open. He stumbled backward. Heat put her hand on his back to steady him. They raised their gazes. A young woman Heat presumed was Tammy Burton stood in front of them. She was red-eyed and gaunt-cheeked, clutching a box of tissue against her stomach. From the wrinkled gray cotton pajama pants and the equally crinkled Henley to the bleeding cuticles around her nails, it was clear the girl was struggling.

Nikki held her badge out. "Tammy Burton?"

She nodded.

"I'm Detective Heat," she said, downplaying her Captain title. "This is Mr. Rook. We have a few questions for you about Chloe Masterson." She looked over Tammy's shoulder. "Is it okay if we come in?"

Tammy wiped her nose with the back of her hand. She hesitated, shooting a furtive glance at Rook. Her eyes clouded with wariness. Clearly she recognized the name.

"Can I see your badge again?" she asked, her voice trembling.

"Absolutely," Heat said with a smile. It was rare that someone wanted to get a close-up of her badge. Usually a quick flash, just like movie and TV cops did, was enough to gain people's trust. Tammy earned a few brownie points with that simple question. Heat held the NYPD badge out. Tammy leaned down to peer at it, strands of her dark hair falling over her face like beaded curtains in a doorway. She nodded, satisfied with its authenticity. Not that she'd know if it were a fake. Still, at least she'd asked. That was more than most people did.

She stepped aside and let them pass, shutting the door behind them. The bolt slid closed with an audible click. "Straight ahead," she said from behind them. "The living room is on the right."

Rook led and Heat followed. The first door on the right was wide open. Bedroom one. The sheets were rumpled, the bedspread half off the bed, an excess of the heavy fabric pooling on the ground at the foot. Mounds of clothes dotted the carpeted floor. Clean and dirty, Heat guessed. A stack of books perched haphazardly on the nightstand, already crowded with a lamp and who knows what else. From the quick look Heat got passing by, she couldn't make out any more details. Whichever roommate lived in the room didn't have a high regard for organization.

The next door was cracked open, but not wide enough for Heat to see anything. "That's Chloe's room," Tammy said. "Her mom is coming . . . over the weekend to . . ." She stopped, her voice cracking with emotion. "To clean it out."

Heat turned to Tammy. "I'm so sorry, Tammy. I know what you're going through."

Tammy's face contorted in pain. "How could you possibly know what I'm going through? What Chloe's family is going through?" Her gaze flicked to Rook. "She was murdered!"

Heat swallowed, feeling this girl's agony pulsing through her own body. "I *do* know," she said, meeting Tammy's pained eyes. "I know the pain will lesson, and I know the horror of it never goes away."

The color drained from Tammy's face and her gaze dropped to the floor. "I can't believe she's gone," she said hoarsely.

Their positions changed and Heat ushered Tammy the rest of the way to the back of the apartment. It had an open floor plan, with the kitchen and eating nook on the left and a living space on the right. Blue, white, and gray chevron-patterned pillows adorned either side of the light gray upholstered couch. The two armchairs had the same color scheme in a striped pattern. Heat made a point of circling around the couch so she could walk near the black bookshelf that stood against one wall. The shelves held mostly textbooks, a few novels, and a pile of magazines. Rook ran his finger over the titles. Looking to see if one of the Victoria St. Claire novels was there, Heat thought. She was always amused at how excited he got if he spotted his books someplace, even if he never publicly admitted it.

She scanned the book spines, as well. There were compilations of horror stories, books on journalism, hot-topic books covering things like terrorism, conspiracy theories, charter schools, and global warming. Rook nodded with approval. "Quite an impressive collection."

"Most of the stuff in here is . . . was . . . Chloe's," Tammy said. "She wanted things to look a certain way."

"She liked to decorate?" Nikki asked.

"Totally. Home decor here is low on my priority list. I can barely pay my tuition. She footed the bill and got the stuff she wanted. I'm going to have to get another roommate and hit Craigslist once her stuff is all gone," she said wistfully.

*Another downside of Chloe's death,* Heat thought. She looked around at the high-end furnishings, wondering how a college girl could afford such nice things. "Family money?"

"I don't think so," Tammy said. "Her parents aren't together. She's estranged from her father. She has—oh, God—*had*. She *had* a younger brother, so I don't think there's ever been a lot of extra money, you know? She wasn't very open about things like that, though, so I don't really know. She would sometimes just come home with something new."

*Money earned from her external writing jobs?* Nikki wondered as Tammy's voice broke again and fresh tears spilled from her eyes. "I'm going to miss her."

"What about a boyfriend?" Rook asked.

Heat shot him a warning look. Tammy Burton clearly knew that Chloe's body had been found in Rook's house, and she was suspicious. Rightfully so, thought Nikki. She didn't have a reason to trust that the visiting professor wasn't involved in her friend's death. Nikki didn't want the girl shutting down on them, which meant she needed to take the lead—which meant Rook needed to become part of the scenery.

Rook dipped his chin in acknowledgment. He turned

his attention back to the shelves as Heat followed up on his question. "Did she? Have a boyfriend?"

Tammy shook her head. "She used to date some, but not anymore. She was too busy for that. She was obsessed. All she ever thought about was her research and her articles."

No boyfriend. Heat crossed that possibility off her mental list, turning to the framed photos on the shelves. The first one she zeroed in on was one of Tammy and a man about the same age. "Your boyfriend?"

Tammy followed her gaze. "My brother, Todd," she said.

"And this one?" Heat asked, pointing to a photo sitting atop the pile of magazines. In it, bikini-clad Tammy and Chloe held up margarita glasses as if they were toasting the camera.

"We went on vacation to Cancún last year," Tammy said. "She was way more relaxed back then."

"When did her obsession with her work start?" Nikki asked.

"I don't know. Maybe six months ago? It wasn't all at once. It kind of happened over time."

Heat remembered what Tammy had said a minute ago about every penny she had going toward her tuition. "It must have been hard to save for a vacation," she commented. "Traveling is expensive."

"I saved forever for it. Chloe helped a little bit." Tammy sniffled, clutching another wad of tissue to her nose. "It was the best vacation I've ever had."

Heat scanned the rest of the photos displayed, stopping when her gaze landed on a group photo. She looked carefully at each of the fifteen or so people that looked to be gathered in front of the campus building that housed the college newspaper. Chloe was in the front row. She wasn't frowning, but she also wasn't smiling.

Moving on to the other faces, she recognized one of the young women from her visit with Rook to the newspaper, and Michael Warton, editor in chief, stood to one side of the group, but the others were unfamiliar to her.

"The newspaper staff," Tammy said, shaking her head. "I worked there my sophomore year, but I couldn't take it. The stress got to me."

"Not to Chloe?" Nikki asked.

"No way. She couldn't get enough of it."

After another minute spent looking at the contents of the shelves, Heat moved to the sofa. Rook followed suit, sitting next to her. Tammy perched on the edge of one of the chairs. She tossed a used tissue onto the floor next to her and plucked another from the box she still held.

Heat wasn't sure how long Tammy was going to hold it together, so she cut to the chase. "Is there anything you can tell us, Tammy? Was Chloe worried about anything lately? Do you have any ideas about what happened to her?"

Tammy's eyes snaked to Rook, but she quickly looked away. "Do I have to go through it again?"

"It could really help," Heat said, softening her voice. "We want to find out what happened. We want the truth."

Once again, Tammy turned her attention to Rook. "Ask him."

Rook scooted up to the edge of the couch. "Ask me? Ask me what?"

"She worshipped you—"

Heat leaned forward, elbows on her knees, hands clasped between them. "Why? Why did she worship him?"

Tammy threw up her hands. "Something to do with some story she was doing? Or wanted to do? Or was in the middle of. Honestly, I don't know. It was 'top secret.'" She heaved a sigh. "That's what she always said. 'I can't tell you, Tammy. It's for your own good.'"

Heat looked to Rook before she answered. "She never talked to Mr. Rook about anything she was working on," Heat said after he drew his brows together and shook his head.

"Never?" Tammy asked Rook, clearly surprised.

"Never," he confirmed. "She talked to me once after my class, and she wanted to meet with me about something, but it never happened."

Tammy looked baffled. "But she was in your house . . ."

"We believe someone might have brought her there to make Rook look guilty."

"You mean someone's trying to frame him? God, I thought that only happened in movies."

If only that were true—but life imitated art. "Unfortunately not."

Tammy directed her gaze at Rook. "So you didn't talk to her?"

"No," he said, shaking his head.

"And you didn't have anything to do with . . . with what happened to her?"

Again, he said, "No."

Heat's gut told her that Chloe's death had nothing to do with her personal life, and everything to do with whatever story she had been obsessed with. But her gut wasn't proof, and in order to get a solve, proof was what she needed. She had to explore all avenues until there was only one clear path to follow. "Did Chloe have any enemies, Tammy? People she'd wronged or who held a grudge?"

Tammy's expression turned indignant. "No way. Everyone likes—liked—her. If you needed help moving furniture, she'd be there. If she couldn't lift it, she'd get some guys to help out and buy the pizza. If you were short ten dollars, she'd foot the bill. She was a good person. A genuinely good person."

Heat had no doubt that Chloe Masterson was exactly who her roommate said she was. But everyone had skeletons in their closets. She just had to keep shaking the tree to see what would fall out. "All right if we take a look in Chloe's room?" she asked Tammy.

Tammy tossed another crumpled tissue on the floor before hauling herself out of her chair. "They've already scoured everything," she said.

"I know, but I'd like to have my own look around. Form my own opinions. If it's okay."

Tammy led them back to the hall, stopping at the first door. She pushed it open and then stepped aside. "Help yourself," she said and then left them alone, retreating to her own room.

"Her emotions seem real," Heat said quietly.

"Definitely grief-stricken," Rook said, his voice booming compared to hers.

Heat held a finger to her lips to shush him. Who knew how thin these apartment walls were. His eyebrows shot up and he nodded, putting a finger to his own lips, then clasping it to his thumb and turning it like a key in a lock.

"It also looks like she's been to hell and back since those pictures were taken." Heat stood in the center of the room, hands on hips.

"Not surprising," Rook said, much more quietly this time. He came up beside her. "I know I'd be a shell of a man if I lost you."

She slipped her hand under one side of his brown leather jacket, patting his taut stomach. "We can't have that, now, can we?"

He draped his arm across her shoulders, pulling her close. "No, no death and no wasting away. That would never do. Carpe diem, even in the face of adversity."

"We have a truckload of adversity at the moment," she commented.

He looked at her with an intensity he didn't normally have. "We should seize the day, Nik."

"We should," Nikki agreed, reading his intention. She needed him. The precariousness of this situation had her spooked. She needed to feel him. Taste him. Touch him. But first they had to finish the task at hand. She gently pushed him away. "After we do everything else we need to."

He straightened up and squared his ruggedly handsome face. "Then let's get to work. What first, Captain?"

"See if you can find anything about the story Chloe was writing that the police might have missed. Notes jotted on a scrap of paper. A source's name. Anything that might help us figure out what she was writing about."

They spent the next ten minutes scouring every inch of Chloe's bedroom. Just as Heat had suspected, Chloe was neat and organized. Unlike Tammy's room, in which the bed was rumpled and unmade, books were precariously stacked, and clothes were strewn everywhere, Chloe's was the epitome of order, pattern, and arrangement. The clothes in the closet were grouped by color. Her books were lined up, spines facing out, and organized by type: textbooks, nonfiction, and a smattering of fiction. Shoes lined up like soldiers at the front. Even in her dresser drawers, her underclothing, T-shirts, yoga pants, and such were folded and neatly stacked.

Heat opened the nightstand drawer, riffling through its contents. Underneath a sleeping mask, a scattering of lip balms and pens, and a small package of tissue was a notepad. She took it out and flipped through it. Page after page was filled with various sketches and doodling. Eyes, noses, and lips. Feathers. Squares and circles and triangles. Chloe had drawn some of the shapes one-dimensional. Some were three-dimensional, with shading and depth. A square held an eye, or a triangle held lips. Chloe had mixed and matched the different designs as if she were seeing what fit best, and where.

"Look at this," she said, holding it out for Rook to see.

"Not bad," he said as he flipped through the pages, just as she had.

She turned in a slow circle. "I don't see any other drawings or sketches. No art supplies, either."

"People doodle, Heat.

"True," she conceded. Something about the sketches bothered her, but she put the pad back.

They spent another fifteen minutes poking around every nook and cranny of Chloe's room before Heat gave it up.

Chloe hadn't left any clues about what she was working on. She'd been fastidious about it, in fact. This told Nikki the most important thing she needed to know: that Chloe had recognized what she was researching could put her in danger.

# FIFTEEN

Heat didn't bother with niceties when she answered her phone. It rang, and invariably she answered with a short "Heat."

"Nik."

Ian's voice was the last thing she'd expected on the other end of the line. Several scenarios ran through her mind: he could be calling to tell her to leave Cambria, that her presence was not wanted; he could want to reminisce about the old days, although she couldn't imagine why he'd want to rehash their breakup; or he could pony up something that would help her. "Ian."

A silence hung between them for a long beat before Nikki spoke again. "What can I do for you?"

He cleared his throat. "Look, I, uh . . ."

She read the tone of his voice as he trailed off and knew he was trying to apologize for being such an ass. She could've made it easy for him, but instead she let him sweat by remaining silent.

"I, uh . . ."

"What is it, Ian?" she finally asked, letting him off the hook.

"I gave it some thought after you left the precinct and,

well, we would be okay with you helping out on the Chloe Masterson case."

This was a surprising turn of events. "Is that right? Who is *we*?"

"The mayor, actually." He'd sounded tentative at first, as if he was having trouble saying what he'd called to say. Apologies had always been hard for him. But now, with just the slightest pushback from her, his tone was slightly indignant.

"Give him—"

"Her," he corrected.

"Give *her* my thanks."

"Nikki, all bullshit aside, the mayor wants us to work together on this. I'm the chief and I want a solve. We talked and she thinks your experience as a homicide detective can help us get there faster."

"What about the fact that Rook is my husband?"

He paused before answering, as if weighing his words. "I cannot take him off the persons-of-interest list. The girl was in his place and he found the body. There is a connection. If he doesn't know anything, then why was she killed there? That is a big unanswered question. I know you want to believe him, but it's too damning to just ignore."

As much as she wanted to, she knew she couldn't argue with him. If she were in his shoes, her thought process would be the same.

"I know you want to be involved, so I'll cut right to the chase. Turns out Chloe Masterson's father went to college at Cam U," he said, referring to the university by its shortened moniker.

"You just learned that?" Nikki bit her tongue as soon as

the words were spoken. Criticizing Ian's investigative skills wouldn't endear her to him. He was willing to let her in, and she did not want him change his mind. Just because the mayor wanted it didn't mean he couldn't fight it. She backtracked. "I just mean that I usually check next of kin first thing."

"We did that, Detective. We may be upstate, but we're not imbeciles. We're just not New York City. Our limited manpower only goes so far."

Heat chastised herself for being so careless with her words. "Of course you're not. You don't have to be. I—"

"Don't placate me," he said, cutting her off. "I get it. You're used to being the one in charge."

The comment gave her pause. He was 100 percent right. She didn't take instructions or orders from someone else; other than the brass at One Police Plaza, she called the shots.

Rook came into the hotel room, a white cardboard cup of coffee in each hand. She mouthed *Thank you* as he handed one to her.

"Who's that?" he whispered, pointing to the cell phone at her ear.

She covered the base of the phone. "Ian Cooley," she whispered.

Rooks eyebrows shot up. "New information?" he whispered back.

Nikki shrugged just as Ian started talking again. "Let's get to it. Turns out Masterson is Chloe's mother's maiden name. Mom and Dad were never married. The mother didn't give Chloe her father's surname."

This was interesting. "Masterson is on her birth certificate?"

"Yep."

Tammy had said that Chloe didn't see her dad. Nikki had assumed divorced, but now that narrative was changing. A lesson that she shouldn't jump to conclusions. "Who's the father? Have you talked to him?"

"Not yet. But Chloe's cell phone log shows that *she* had been talking to him. For five months now."

Nikki swiveled around, looking for a pen and piece of paper. Rook saw her searching and quickly grabbed both from the bedside table. She nodded her thanks and jotted down what Ian had just told her. "And before that?"

"Nothing. It's like he suddenly blew into her life from out of nowhere."

Five months ago. Multiple questions came to Nikki. It explained why Chloe had her mother's name, but why hadn't her father been part of her childhood? Was that his choice, or had it been orchestrated by her mother? And what brought him back? Lots of questions. Far fewer answers.

Rook waited impatiently, gesturing at her. She turned her back to him as she listened to Ian. "There were no calls from Chloe's phone to her father on the day her body was discovered," Ian continued. "The day before there were four calls from her phone to his. Three lasted for less than ten seconds. The fourth call connected and lasted several minutes."

"Sounds like we need to talk to Chloe's father ASAP."

Behind her, Rook drew in an interested breath. This was the best development they'd had to date. Heat and Rook had already learned that Chloe could keep a secret. She'd proved it with whatever research she was doing. It was not a surprise, then, that she'd kept her father a secret, as well.

"I'm going to interview him," Ian said. "I thought you might want to tag along."

She had to swallow her eagerness. "Of course. Where and when?"

"Right now. I've been to his house. Not there. I'm heading to his lodge. I'll pick you up."

"Where and when *what*?" Rook said, his whisper louder.

She looked at Rook. "No, I'll drive myself."

"Sure, suit yourself."

Heat scribbled down the address he rattled off. "I'm on my way."

**The streets of Cambria were calm** compared to those in Manhattan. There were no blasting sirens, no blaring horns, no continual street noise like in the city that never slept. Heat was getting her bearings and figuring out the lay of the land, but she missed the cacophony that was New York. "It's too quiet," she said.

"It does have its own appeal, though," Rook said from the passenger seat.

She could enjoy a slower pace for a while. A long weekend in the Hamptons, definitely. A week on Nantucket, without a doubt. But permanent residence in a suburban town would have her yearning for the energy of the city and all its boroughs, for the eclectic people, for the variety of food to be found no matter where you happened to find yourself. "I suppose, but it's nostalgic for you," she said.

"I can't deny that," he said. The smile she loved crossed his lips, this time with a hint of sentimentality. "There's

nothing quite like one's college days, is there? It's the place
you discover who you are. Your authentic self, so to speak.
New knowledge. The excitement of young love." He looked
at her from the corners of his eyes. "Of course, not all of us
have the best luck with early romance."

He was referring to Petar Matic, the boyfriend she'd
had in college who'd later turned out to be involved in the
conspiracy to kill her mother. And then there was Ian.
She'd been giving it a lot of thought. She had to come clean.
It might as well be now. "Rook, I want—"

"Me?" he said with a grin. "I know. I'm hard to resist
now that I'm a professor."

She gave him a sideways glance, letting her eyes roam
over him. "I do like the tweed jacket with the patches on
the sleeves look. Very professorial."

"I'll give you private office hours."

"Promise?"

"I'll grade your papers anytime," he said, cringing the
minute the words left his mouth. "Scratch that."

"Yeah, that didn't quite work."

He shrugged nonchalantly. "Can't win them all."

They drove in silence for a few minutes before she came
back to what she wanted to talk about. "There's something I
need to tell you, Rook."

He glanced at her, a mixture of wariness and concern
suddenly coloring his face. "Nothing that follows that
sentence is ever good, you know."

He had a point. It was a phrase that set people up for
bad news. "Depends on your perspective, I guess."

"Should I be worried?"

"No, not worried."

"Then what?"

"Mmm, you might be mad," she said, leaving out that he might also feel betrayed that she hadn't told him about Ian early on in their relationship. A marriage was a pretty big deal.

He was quiet for a few seconds before he said, "I don't think you could say anything that could make me too mad."

She hoped.

He swiveled slightly in his seat to face her. "Lay it on me, Nik."

And so she did. "I kind of, um, know Ian Cooley."

Rook drew back, surprised. "I'm not sure what I expected, but it wasn't that."

"We were in the academy together."

The worry dissolved from his face. "That was a lot of buildup for—" He broke off as realization hit. "Oh. You *know* him."

She swallowed, her guilt at having kept something so important from him expanding like a balloon about to pop. She tightened her hands on the steering wheel. "There's more."

This time he swiveled his head to look at her. The mood in the car had changed, but Rook was still Rook. He had a light in his eyes that showed he wasn't taking this too seriously. They both had pasts, after all.

He nodded sagely. "Bear with me as I do a little deductive work here. I mentioned the young love one can find in college, adding that it's not always good. Case in point, Petar Matic, but of course he's best left in the graveyards of our minds. That topic, however, seems to have sparked a memory for you. A memory that involves our intrepid Cambria police officer. Which leads me to conclude that whatever went on with Mr. Ian Cooley was, in fact, short-lived. Memorable for some reason, but in the end, inconsequential."

Nikki's eyes pinched together. "Maybe not *that* inconsequential."

Rook had that smirk of a smile and she could see his eyes dancing with amusement, even from the side. What she said next might well wipe that mirth clear off his face. "Do tell, *mi amor*," he said.

A deep breath might not help bolster her nerve, but she drew one in anyway. "He was my . . . husband," she said.

Rook's eye twitched. He poked a finger in his ear, wriggling it around. "Sorry, I don't think I heard you. What was that?"

She spoke louder this time. "We were married."

This time his eye twitched in a series of spasms. "I'm sorry, did you say you were m-m-married to this sheriff?"

"He's the chief of police," she corrected.

"Of podunk Cambria."

"Now it's podunk? You just got done telling me how much you love this place. New knowledge. New loves. Finding your authentic self."

"Well, yeah, but that was before. My authentic self eventually wanted to get the hell out of Cambria and move to Manhattan. This is a great place to visit, but I wouldn't want to live here." He rubbed his hands on his trousers. "Married?"

She nodded.

"To a guy named Ian Cooley?"

"I was still undone at that point. A little broken and lost."

He knew she was talking about the years following her

mother's apparent death. Sometimes, looking back, she was amazed she had recovered at all.

"Ian Cooley was your—"

"Husband." She spoke the word he couldn't. "He was my husband."

The silence that followed felt thin, as if it were deprived of oxygen like the Colorado air high up in the Rockies. Finally, after a solid minute, maybe two, Rook glanced at her. "Who's more handsome, him or me?"

Classic Rook. She laughed. "You are, Jamie. No contest."

He seemed satisfied with the sincerity of her response. "So marrying Barney Fife was a fleeting moment of you being young and dumb, as they say."

"I suppose that's one way to put it," she said, not bothering to take umbrage at the "young and dumb" comment.

He waved his hand as if he were casting a spell. "Once this mess is finished, your former husband will be banished from our minds."

While she probably couldn't completely eradicate his memory, the truth was that she hadn't really thought of Ian in at least ten years. After she and Rook left Cambria, there would be no reason to think of him ever again. "You're not mad?" she asked, a little surprised but greatly relieved.

He responded without missing a beat. "Why would I be mad? I win in the handsome category. There is no question that I have superior intellect and am the better catch—"

She smirked. "And how did you come to that conclusion?"

He turned his head and arched a brow at her, then put both hands out, palms up, as if they were the scales of justice. He lifted his left hand so it rose higher. "Chief of police in Cambria, New York." He lowered it, and then raised his right hand. "Pulitzer Prize–winning journalist."

Finally, he moved both hands up and down, up and down, ultimately letting his right hand claim victory by raising it high above the other. "Ding, ding, ding! We have a winner."

She laughed. "Okay. I see your point. You are brilliant, and before I snagged you, you were quite the eligible bachelor."

"Thank you. Now, if you will, I do have a question, Heat."

She watched the road, glancing at him for just a moment. "Okay."

"Why didn't you tell me?"

She'd been asking herself the same question. The answer was complicated, but she whittled it down as concisely as she could. "I guess because I don't think about it. It's a part of my past I wish I could forget." She paused before asking her own question. "Can you forgive me for not telling you?"

He took her hand. "Nik, there's nothing to forgive. I get it. The past is the past. I've loved you since the moment I laid eyes on you. Through thick and thin, for better or for worse, and whatever other English idioms you can think of. We're in this thing together."

The way he squeezed her hand sent an unspoken message. They were a team, even in the face of murder.


Nikki hadn't gotten around to telling her husband where they were meeting Chloe's father. She finally filled him in when they were less than a quarter of a mile away, and then she braced herself for what she knew was coming. "A Freemason? How perfect! And how serendipitous." Rook spoke with unbridled enthusiasm. He was a conspiracy theorist of the highest order, and the Masons had a reputation. He suddenly looked like a kid on a free shopping spree in Willy Wonka's factory.

"Why is it serendipitous?" Heat asked, almost afraid of the answer.

Rook rubbed his hands together. "Because, my dear wife, an insider's look into fraternal organizations, including the Freemasons, has been something I've wanted to do for a long time. I'm taking this as an omen. *Now* is the right time to revisit the idea."

"Great, but Rook. That is not why we're here. You have to stay focused on the investigation. Do your research later."

Rook scoffed. "I am the world's best multitasker."

She had to disagree. Vehemently. "You are so *not* the world's best multitasker. In fact, you may be the worst. I used to read my niece, Sarah, a book called *If You Give a Mouse a Cookie*. After the cookie, the mouse wants milk. Then he has to check the mirror for the milk mustache, but he's sidetracked and has to trim his whiskers. Etcetera, etcetera, etcetera. In this scenario, you're the mouse," she said.

He clutched his chest as if his heart were breaking. "Heat, you wound me deeply, comparing me so callously to a mouse with a cookie."

She shrugged apologetically. "Just calling a spade a spade."

"Heat, a young woman lost her life and I know full well that the police are looking at me. I want to find out what happened to Chloe more than anyone. That is my priority."

She sensed a "but" coming.

"But if I get a little insight about an interest of mine along the way, who am I to turn a blind eye?"

"Just focus on the case," she said.

"The case, and nothing but the case."

Ian was sitting in his cruiser in front of the Masonic Temple of Cambria. It was a nondescript building with pink bricks, a white triangle roofline, and four white pillars, but Rook did not look disappointed. "It's what's happening inside that's important," he said, as if he'd read her mind.

Heat pulled in along the curb behind Ian and parked. They all opened their car doors and stepped out like synchronized swimmers emerging from the water in perfect unison. The two men instantly moved toward each other. Not only did Ian consider Rook a potential suspect, but their current encounter also had a personal twist to it. Rook extended his hand. Ian stepped forward, grasping it tightly. "You'd better watch yourself," he said, "because I am. Your wife may believe your little stories, but I don't."

"Enough," Nikki said. They were behaving like two territorial preening birds, sizing each other up and thrusting their chests out. Rook winced slightly at the intense pressure of Ian's hand, but he was not going to break the handshake. "My wife's belief is all I need to get me through the night."

Ian gave his own equally tense smile. "I didn't know you were tagging along, Mr. Rook. Unusual, given the circumstances." He spoke through his teeth, the veins in his temples pulsing.

Heat answered before Rook could pop off with a flippant remark that might piss off Ian. Right now they needed him. "Rook is invested in finding the truth."

Ian answered her, but he didn't cut the intense stare

he held with Rook. "Or burying it."

"Come on, guys," she said briskly. "Cut the pissing match." To Ian, she said harshly, "Objective, remember? Are you capable of that?"

For a moment, neither man broke eye contact, but finally, after she touched Rook's arm, he released his death grip.

Instead of answering her question, Ian worked to get under Rook's skin. And hers. "Guess you know that Nikki and I were married once upon a time." He clenched his hand into a fist—to mask the pain he had to be experiencing.

Rook, she noticed, didn't try to hide his discomfort. He stretched out his fingers, then curled his knuckles, rubbing his right hand with his left to work out the strain and to un-crunch the bones. "Tragically short-lived, from what I understand."

Ian shrugged. "Some things are fun while they last, but aren't meant to be."

Nikki felt Rook's biceps flex beneath her hand. "Some things are fun *all* the time, *and* meant to be."

And so the pissing match continued. Heat left them at the curb and walked up the short wide path to the front door. A moment later, she heard their rapid footsteps behind her. Ian quickly moved in front of her and pushed open the door to the lodge. "After you," he said, stepping aside. Heat moved past him into the building. Before Rook could follow, however, Ian cut in front of him. He let go of the heavy door. Without a pneumatic closer attached to it, the door swung quickly. Rook caught it with his hand before it slammed in his face, grumbling under his breath.

Heat chose to ignore Ian's passive-aggressive actions,

instead absorbing the lodge's interior. It was as plain on the inside as it was on the outside. She'd imagined it would be more like a church, but it reminded her more of a simple town hall.

Rook saw her expression. "Don't be fooled," he said. "I hear the ceremonial rooms are heavy with symbolism."

A middle-aged man wearing an ill-fitting gray suit appeared from a hallway off to one side. "That they are."

Rook pumped his proffered arm as if in victory. "Yes! I knew it."

The man smiled congenially. With his gunmetal hair, a pronounced gap between his two front teeth, and sagging jowls, he looked like someone's frumpy grandpa. A Grand Poobah à la *The Flintstones* rather than a grand master, Heat thought.

"What can I help you folks with?" His gaze dropped to Rook's hand, and then to Ian's uniform, giving her only a cursory glance. She had heard that women were not welcome in the order, but the overt exclusion seemed to validate that rumor. And it riled her up.

"I'm Chief Cooley, and this is Detective Heat," Ian said. "We're looking for Christian. Is he here?"

The man gave a quick glance at Rook, whom Ian had omitted from his introductions. "And you are . . . ?"

"Jameson Rook. Writer and interested party."

The man paused in thought before recognition dawned. "*The* Jameson Rook? With *First Press*?"

Heat watched her husband with amusement. He had a sensitive disposition and could get his feathers ruffled pretty easily, but that mildly neurotic nature meant the slightest unsolicited compliment could make him preen like a peacock. "That's right. You've heard of me." He turned to Heat, hooking his thumb at the Mason. "He's heard of me, Heat."

She nodded, stifling a smile. "So I see."

The man took Rook's offered hand again and shook vigorously. "It's a real pleasure. I'm a big fan of your work. That article you did in *National Geographic* on the Romani in France was fascinating."

Rook nodded. "It is a national tragedy for the Roma."

Ian's irritation at the man's attention to Rook was obvious. "Hate to break this up, but we need to talk to Christian Foti about his daughter's murder," he told him.

Heat bristled. Even that little bit of information was more than she would have given, but she had to remind herself that she was not leading the investigation.

"Of course, of course. They'd only recently reunited, but he's taken it hard."

Heat noted on her pad that he'd corroborated what Tammy had told them about Chloe and her father.

The man focused on Rook. "I read about what happened. You found her, didn't you?"

"I did," Rook said, his demeanor instantly morose. He was as good as she was at compartmentalizing when it suited him, but one could not erase the image of a dead body. The people she'd seen over the years, the life drained out of them, haunted Heat sometimes. Rook had seen his share, too, tagging along with her, but this one was personal, and she knew it would stick with him forever.

The Mason seemed to understand the trauma of it. "Chris

was in a bad way when he first found out. It's a real tragedy."

"I can only imagine," Rook said.

Heat met Rook's gaze and kept quiet. Even Ian withheld comment. The man was engaged with Rook, which meant they needed to take a backseat for the time being.

"I didn't catch your name," Rook said, and Nikki thought, *Finally.*

The man threw his shoulders back. "Bill Holz, at your service. I'm one of the lodge officers with the Order."

Heat jotted down the man's name as Rook continued. "I've always wondered what it would be like to be part of a fraternal order like the Freemasons. The ancient orders were fascinating."

"Rook," Heat said in a harsh whisper from behind him. She didn't want him to go off on a tangent, but he batted his hand behind his back and she stopped. She could give him a minute to get his fill.

"It's an inclusive organization," Holz said. "Our members are from all walks of life. I have to say, we'd welcome a man of your caliber . . ."

Holz rambled on, but Heat rolled her eyes. Rook's head was bloated enough without this guy blowing it up some more.

"The ceremonies and the insignia, of course," Rook was saying.

Holz agreed. "Exactly."

"Is the Worshipful Master here?" Rook asked, his voice reverent.

Holz was clearly impressed. "For an outsider, you do know your stuff."

Rook looked sheepish. "I admit, I've always wanted to be an insider."

Heat stared at her husband. Had he? He'd certainly never mentioned his desire to be part of a more than two-hundred-year-old group like the Freemasons, although, if she was honest, if didn't surprise her. The lore surrounding almost all fraternal organizations was exactly the type of thing Rook lived for. To be part of one had to be on his bucket list.

Before they launched into another discourse on fraternal orders, Heat jumped in. "Mr. Holz, where can we find Mr. Foti?"

"Right, the reason you're here. I told him he should stay home, but he wanted to come in." The Mason flipped his wrist, reading the time on his watch. "He should be on duty now, actually. He's just running late." He gestured to one of two benches along the left wall of the lobby. "Feel free to wait."

Heat opted to remain standing and Ian moved to sit down, but Rook wasn't done. "Mr. Holz, you said Mr. Foti is supposed to be on duty. I'm curious—is he, by any chance, a Tyler?"

Heat was pretty sure Rook wasn't referring to Stephen Tyler or Tyler Perry. His enthusiasm—and apparently his knowledge of the Freemason member hierarchy—was boundless. How he held so much random information in his head astounded her.

"You know our internal structure. My God, but you are good," Holz said.

The way Rook smiled and hung his head, he might as well have said, *Aw shucks.* "I was just talking to my . . . to

Detective Heat, here, telling her that I've always wanted to do a piece about fraternal organizations. The Freemasons, as you know—I'm a fan—are at the top of my list. What a civic-minded group!" He lowered his voice, once again infused with reverence. "Could I . . . Could we . . . Would you show us your ceremonial room?"

Holz hesitated, but only briefly, before giving Rook a gap-toothed grin. "This is highly unusual, Mr. Rook, but because you're you, I will give you a quick look."

Rook lit up like a Christmas tree, but Heat had to give him credit for the modicum of restraint in his reaction. "Excellent." He looked at her, nodding enthusiastically. "Excellent," he repeated, and then held out his arm in a broad gesture that encompassed both of the two hallways leading out of the lobby. "After you, good sir," he said to Holz. "After you."

Ian, who looked decidedly disgruntled, followed Holz. Rook winked at Heat as she passed, and then he brought up the rear. He was like a kid in a candy store. Sometimes she loved Rook just a little bit more than she had the moment before. This was definitely one of those times.

A moment later, Heat, Rook, and Ian stood at the threshold of the first-floor temple, Ian's own temples pulsing from anger at Rook's presence. But Rook was his mother's son, which meant he could act his way out of a paper bag if need be. He was aloof, completely ignoring her ex-husband. "This is where all the ceremonies take place," Mr. Holz said as he ushered them into the gathering room.

The space was eclectic. Chairs ran around the perimeter. Medieval-looking tools hung on the wall in the front of the room, where an ornate chair sat like a throne. It seemed to Heat that everything in there held some sort of significance. Rook didn't know where to look, so he looked everywhere. His gaze skittered here and there, trying to take it all in. Even the floor in the ceremonial room, with its black-and-white checkerboard pattern, demanded attention. His brain, she knew, was on overload.

"The floor makes me dizzy," Heat said, averting her eyes.

"Oh, but it's symbolic to the Order," Rook said. "It represents the dark and the light in all of us. In life."

She was noncommittal to that, answering only with a pondering "Huh." She saw plenty of the dark side of life. She didn't need a floor to remind her of it. She pointed to the ancient tools. "What's the deal there?"

Rook gently touched her arm, slowing her down so he could whisper in her ear. "Everything has meaning in the ceremonial room. Those are the tools of the Craft."

"The craft?"

"Not witchcraft, Heat. I know where you think my mind goes, but that's not what we're talking about here. I mean the Craft. Capital C. The tools of the medieval stonemason."

Neither Heat nor Rook had noticed that Holz and Ian had both stopped and were listening. "You're absolutely correct again, Mr. Rook. Everything has meaning." He pointed up at the images painted on the walls. "Those are most important symbols. The first is what we call the square of morality. The compass next to it marks what we call due bounds. And the line—"

"A plumb rule," Rook interrupted.

"Exactly. The plumb rule represents our need to be

upright at all times, figuratively and literally."

Heat pointed to two stones on a display stand in the front of the room. One was rough and bumpy, while the other was completely smooth and polished. "And what are those?"

Holz gestured to Rook. "Can you answer that, Mr. Rook?"

Rook thrived in the spotlight, and Mr. Holz was doing a fine job of shining it right on him. "They both symbolize man," he said, looking at the Mason for approval before going on. Holz nodded, just once, and Rook continued. "The one on the left, the rutted stone, represents what the Freemasons call the raw apprentice. That is the first level of membership in the order. The polished stone on the right is the improved version of man."

"Nicely put, Mr. Rook."

Ian shifted from one foot to the other, clearly irritated, but Rook ignored him, bowing slightly, inordinately pleased. "Why thank you," he said as he walked up the center aisle. "Another tidbit, if I'm not mistaken, is the fact that the Worshipful Master's throne, no matter what lodge you may be in, sits in the east."

"Absolutely right," Holz said. "The Freemasons adopted their traditions from the early days of masonry, when guilds would guard the secrets of their craft."

Rook circled around the gold and velvet throne. "Fit for a king," he said, before moving on. He walked up to the back wall. It was paneled with beveled frames divided into sections, as if each were a door to another room in a castle. Next he went up to the two stones, reaching his hand out touch them.

Holz had been walking a step behind him, but as Rook's

fingertips lowered to brush the first stone, he was next to him in an instant. "Those are sacred," he said, his polite way of telling Rook not to touch.

Rook snapped his hand back and apologized. "It's all so fascinating."

Holz had said earlier that the Masons came from all walks of life. Rook's interest was rubbing off on her. "Who are Masons?" Heat asked, curious. "Doctors and lawyers and politicians?"

Holz ushered them back out the way they'd come. "Yes, yes, and yes. But not only that. City workers. Roofers. Garbage men. We welcome the upper echelon as well at the laborer. We don't turn people away."

"It's a religion- and politics-free zone," Rook told her.

"Banned from the dining table," Holz confirmed.

"What about the secret handshake?" Ian asked. His voice was uninterested, but he was trying to get in on the conversation.

Holz laughed. "Yes and no. There are levels of handshakes and signs when you greet a brother of the Order, but they're not secret, per se."

Heat had been biting her tongue over the fact that the Order, as Holz called it, was male only. "Why aren't women allowed?" she asked.

Holz didn't hesitate and didn't have any qualms about defending the fact that women were not admitted to the Freemasons. "Our order is an allegory for the ancient male craftsman. Women did not have that role, therefore they are not part of the brotherhood. There are sister lodges or clubs in which they are more than welcome to participate."

*Hmph.* There was a reason behind the practice, but Heat still didn't like it. The so-called inclusiveness of the Order was, in fact, exclusive of her gender.

Once they were outside the ceremonial room, Rook turned to his new best friend. "Mr. Holz," he said, placing his hand on his chest. "It has been a true honor."

"For me, as well, Mr. Rook. You are welcome here anytime."

The main door opened and a man rushed in, stopping short when he saw the group. "Oh, uh, who . . . hello?"

Holz emerged from the center of the group and walked up to the man. They shook hands, gripping each other's forearms at the same time.

It looked like a special handshake to Heat.

"This is Christian Foti," Holz said to them, and then to Chris he said, "These folks are here about your daughter."

Ian spoke up, showing his badge. "This is Captain Heat, Mr. Foti, and I'm Chief Cooley."

Nikki noticed that he again omitted introducing Rook, but she left it alone.

"You can use my office to talk," Mr. Holz offered.

Without a word, Christian Foti led them down the hallway opposite the ceremonial room. Heat took the time to catalogue his appearance. He looked to be in his early-to midforties. His hair was thinning, but he kept a neatly trimmed beard, which, like his hair, was a sandy brown. His cheeks were ruddy, and his eyes were puffy, almost as if a translucent caterpillar were beneath the skin under each one. It looked as if he hadn't slept since his daughter died, Heat thought. She knew the feeling. The grave eyes; the pit in the gut; the shortness of breath, as if even the mere act of drawing air was a strain. He might not have known Chloe well, but her death had clearly taken a toll.

"Don't say a word, Rook. You are only here as a courtesy to your wife. I don't trust you, so know that I'm always watching," Ian whispered harshly.

Rook looked nonplussed, but he quickly put on a mask of indifference and ignored Ian. He wasn't going to let the guy faze him, she knew.

They entered a well-appointed office. A large mahogany L-shaped desk with matching shelving occupied a good portion of one of the walls. Two armchairs sat opposite the front of the desk.

Once the door was closed behind them, Ian shouldered past Rook. It was as if the confined space of the office and Christan Foti's presence flipped a switch in him. He took over. Interrogation was at the center of his wheelhouse and he launched right into it. "Mr. Foti, we need to ask you a few questions about your daughter."

Foti sank onto one of the chairs. Heat perched on the edge of the massive desk, pen poised over her notebook. Ian pushed the second chair aside and stood looking over Foti. Meanwhile, Rook made his way around the desk and sat in Holz's chair. He leaned back, looking more comfortable than he should. Just like a kid, he had a tendency to touch and break. Heat shot him a look that said, *Keep your hands to yourself,* and then turned back to Foti. Ian had already asked him about Chloe's childhood and if he'd been part of it.

"Her mother and me, we weren't married and it didn't work out. We were young. I left when Charlie—that's my son—was a few months old. Chloe was five. Maybe almost six." Foti cupped his hand over his forehead. "I was the perfect weekend dad for a while."

"But it didn't last," Ian said, filling in what Foti didn't say.

"I regret it. I really do. I came back home. Went to college. Got a job. Had a life. It's not an excuse, but—"

"That's exactly what it is," Heat said. She had no tolerance for people who made babies but weren't mature enough to be responsible for them.

Foti's beard didn't quite mask the trembling of his lower lip. "Things didn't work out like I planned."

"We've looked at Chloe's phone records," Ian said. "You had a lot of conversations over the past several months."

He nodded, his lips turning up in a sorrowful smile. "She was a great girl. I still can't get my head around what happened. I just found her again, and now she's gone."

Christian Foti had spun a narrative that let him off the hook, so Heat jumped in. "But *you* didn't find her. She found you."

"I suppose that's true."

"There's no suppose. It *is* true," she said, going with her gut as she pushed him. "She realized you were here and got in touch, isn't that true?"

"Yes."

"Was she upset at all about the fact that you never looked for her all these years?" Heat asked.

"She never said so," he said.

Heat studied him. Was his sorrow sincere? Did he even care that Chloe had come back into his life? It was hard to tell, and she wasn't sure she believed it.

Ian tapped the tip of his pen against his little notebook. "So Chloe got in touch with you, you talked pretty regularly, and now she's dead. Does that about sum it up?"

Foti squeezed his eyes shut for a beat, finally responding to the chief of police. "I guess so."

Ian flipped the cover to his notebook shut and slipped it into his pocket. "*That* is a tragic story."

Christian Foti's spine stiffened and he gripped the arms of the chair he sat on. "You're right, Officer Cooley. It *is* tragic. It's easy for you to pass judgment, and you're right, I didn't know her for long, but she was my daughter. My *daughter.*"

Ian opened his mouth, but Heat spoke up before he could put his foot in it. "What did you talk about, Mr. Foti?" she asked. "Once she found you, how did you and Chloe connect again?"

He ran his hand over his head. "She just wanted to spend time with me."

"And you, did *you* want to spend time with *her*?" Ian asked, apparently not able to control himself. "Because from what I can tell from the phone logs, she initiated most of the contact. I've also seen her financials. She had a pretty decent nest egg. Almost ten thousand in a savings account. Did you know that?"

Chloe's savings was something Ian hadn't shared. Heat jotted it down on her pad. Suddenly the apartment decor as well as Rook's theory about her writing for another publication that paid both made sense. The implication of his question to Foti was that maybe the guy had found out about Chloe's fund and wanted to get his hands on it. Ten thousand wasn't a lot in the big picture, but she'd seen people do stupid things for a lot less.

Foti balked. "I didn't know she had any money."

Ian scoffed. "Sure you didn't," he said, not bothering to feign impassiveness. He was pushing Chloe's father hard, but without cause.

It felt as if they were playing good cop, bad cop, only Heat didn't want to be part of it. What she wanted was to have a conversation with Christian Foti that wasn't antagonistic so that maybe he'd give something up that could be useful. Ian was acting like the guy had killed his own daughter. "Mr. Foti," she said, wanting to soften the animosity that was heavy in the room. "Was Chloe in trouble of any kind? Anyone she was afraid of?"

Foti avoided Ian's piercing eyes, instead turning all of his focus to Heat. "Not that I know of," he said. "She was always focused on her writing and the *story* she was working on." He made air quotes around the word "story," but he didn't sound irritated. Not exactly.

Heat heard a smooth sliding sound from behind her. From Rook. She chose to ignore it, zeroing in on what Christian Foti had just said. "Do you know what the story was?"

"No idea. She was close-lipped about her research." From his tone, Heat understood: he might not have been the one to reach out to his daughter, but it sounded like he would have liked to know more about who she was and what she was doing.

"She only ever wanted to talk about me," he continued. "I tried, but I couldn't pry much of anything from her. A little bit about her childhood. About my son. He's not as inclined to see me, she said. Nothing about her schooling, or even about her plans for the future. Her roommate's name was Tracy. No, Tammy. She talked a little bit about the people she worked with at the newspaper. Don't think she ever mentioned anyone's name, though. She kept it all in some mental vault."

Ian jumped in with a question. "Where did you get together?"

"Different places. Sometimes at my place. Sometimes here. There's a diner a couple blocks away. Sometimes we'd get lunch. And sometimes she'd call and just want to talk."

"Anything in particular she wanted to talk about?" Heat asked.

He shook his head. "Not really. Sometimes she would tell me about her day and I'd tell her about mine. Sometimes she'd ask about my years away from her. Nothing in particular. She just wanted to talk."

"Is there anything else you can tell us, Mr. Foti?" Heat asked.

He stroked his beard and started to say no, but then stopped. "Wait."

She and Ian both leaned toward him. "What?" Heat asked.

"I did see her calendar once."

"We haven't found a calendar," Ian commented.

"It was on her phone."

Ian spoke again. "We haven't found her phone."

Heat followed up. "Did anything jump out at you?"

"She was busy. Lots of appointments entered in."

"Nothing in particular, though?" Heat prodded.

"There was one thing. I don't know why, but it popped out. I think because it reminded me of a game."

Heat wanted to roll her hand to get him to speed up, but he stayed the course of his roundabout story. "Me and Chloe, we used to play chess. Before I . . . before I went away. She was young, but she was a smart girl. Quick learner. We played again just recently. She won both times."

Ian sighed. "What does this have to do with Chloe's calendar? Was she planning a trip to Manhattan? A little chess in Washington Square Park?"

"No, no, nothing like that," Foti said, not seeming to pick up on Ian's impatience. "She had an appointment with someone. The name was a piece from the game. King? Oh no, Bishop? No, no—"

"Rook?" Ian offered.

Foti snapped and pointed at Ian. "That's it!"

Damn. Everywhere they went, someone said something about Chloe needing to talk to Rook, but no one knew why. If only Chloe had insisted on talking to him sooner.

"Anything else you can tell us?" Ian asked, ready to wrap this up but taking a moment to shoot a shit-eating grin at Rook. To him, Nikki thought, Rook's tangential connection to Chloe gave the makings of a motive. Everything came back to him and the story Chloe was writing. How could it not be related to the murder? It was flimsy at best, but there were possibilities.

Rook needed to stop Chloe from writing her story.

Rook wanted to steal Chloe's story for himself.

Rook had an affair with a coed, and things went wrong.

None of them was even remotely a possibility in Nikki's mind, but she realized that Ian had been right on some level. She could not be completely objective in this investigation.

"Not that I can think of," Foti answered.

Heat and Ian both withdrew business cards from their pockets. "If you do," Heat said, beating Ian to the punch and offering hers to Christian first.

"Let us know," Ian finished.

A quick knock sounded at the door before it suddenly opened and Mr. Holz appeared at the threshold. Before he spoke, he noticed Rook sitting behind his desk.

"Best chair in the room," Rook said as he straightened the blotter pad and the pens so they were perfectly aligned. He patted the arm of the chair. "Very comfortable. It could take the place of the Worshipful Master's throne in the ceremonial room." He looked at Heat. "I need to get one of these. Great lumbar support."

"Of course. My lower back," Holz said. "It always gives me trouble. Everything good in here?"

Christian Foti stood, his shoulders slumped. He looked as if the fifteen-minute conversation had taken the life out of him.

"Everything is fine," Heat said. "Thank you for your time."

The two Masons stood at the main door and watched the trio until they were on the sidewalk. Heat was left with a strange feeling in her gut, but at the moment, she couldn't say why.

# SIXTEEN

Heat and Rook drove off in one direction, while Ian headed the opposite way. The collaboration, such as it was, had ended for the time being. Heat asked Ian to call her with any new information; he gave her an ambiguous nod, and they went their separate ways.

Heat had set up a conference call with her squad back at the precinct. Roach was handling the Lincoln Center investigation, but she needed an update. Her being in Cambria and wrapped up in her own murder investigation didn't absolve her of responsibility. She was still the precinct commander, and that meant staying abreast of everything that was going on at the Two-Oh, even in her absence.

"We're pounding the pavement, Cap, but so far we're coming up zero." Raley's voice was apologetic.

Nikki and Rook were back in the hotel room. She leaned back in the chair, staring at the whiteboard but not seeing. "Come on, guys. Someone killed that kid."

"The best we have right now are a few strands of hair Parry found stuck under a jagged edge of one of the vic's fingernails," Ochoa said. "She's running it for DNA, but that'll take a while, and who knows if we'll even get a hit off of it."

"What's she thinking?" Nikki asked. Parry was good at creating scenarios for the bodies that wound up on her table. Did the hair belong to one of the killers? Nikki could take Lauren's opinion on that to the bank.

"Parry thinks that the attackers held our vic under the water at the plaza. Water from the dude's lungs are a match to the pool. He gave a good fight, though. One of his nails ripped, leaving a jagged edge. Joon Chin must have been holding on to his assailant's head, fighting for his life. Unbeknownst to our killer, he left behind a calling card."

"Still nothing about where our vic was before he died?"

"Negative," Raley answered. "We've checked every coffee shop in a two-mile radius around Lincoln Center. If Chin was there, no one remembers him. I've scanned all the connecting street cams, but there's no sign of them around any of those coffee shops."

"What about—"

"Around NYU? Checked. Nothing."

If the King of All Surveillance Media had come up empty, that meant there was nothing to find.

"Sorry to say it, boys, but you're going to have to do this the old-fashioned way."

"Already have our walking shoes on," Ochoa said.

"And the knuckles are wrapped," Raley said. "We're going to knock till we drop."

There was no doubt in her mind that Roach would do whatever it took to find some kind of justice for Joon Chin. She gave them her blessing, then signed off with a resigned "Keep me posted."

# SEVENTEEN

By the next morning, there had been no significant developments in either of her open cases. Heat was frustrated beyond belief. They had to figure out what Chloe's story was about. Once they did that, she knew the oyster shells would open up.

"Are you sure you want to teach your class?" she asked Rook. "I'm sure the university would understand if you took a pass. They'd probably welcome it, in fact. They've got to be in a PR nightmare."

Rook scoffed. "Never show your weakness, Heat. I was hired to teach journalism, which is just what I aim to do. And what better way to fill in the blanks of the story than by being up close and personal with the students? If and when the university feels differently, they can tell me that to my face."

"It's bound to happen unless we keep at it."

"What better place to keep at it than with my students? The kids taking my course, Journalism in the Real World, are Chloe's people. Trust me, they'll be champing at the bit to talk to me about every single detail. And you? You'll be the icing on the cake. Investigative journalism at its best, with the lead detective there for a show-and-tell session."

"I'm not the lead detective."

"Pft. You mean your former spouse?" he asked as he adjusted his Italian leather cross-body bag. He waved away the very idea of Ian Cooley. "You could investigate circles around him. Heat, come on, get serious. The guy can't hold a candle to you."

Discussing Ian was the last thing Nikki wanted to do. She diverted the conversation. "What are you going to say to your class? Surely they all know where Chloe's body was discovered."

"I'm sure they do. Cambria's still a small town, and the university is even smaller."

"You want to face your students?"

"Heat, when have I ever backed away from a fight? I did not kill Chloe, and I'll tell that to anyone who'll listen."

She got that, but still. Frankly, she was shocked that they hadn't completely dismissed him while the investigation was ongoing. "The provost didn't try to put you on leave?"

"Saunders and Lamont are keeping the Board of Regents at bay."

She let it go, but she was still uneasy about the class. She stopped suddenly. Rook walked a few steps before realizing it and doing an about-face.

"Don't get too comfortable with this professor thing," she said. "Manhattan awaits your return with bated breath."

"I can't promise that I'll never professor again, but I can promise that if I do, it will be well within conjugal-visit range. Being apart from you is for the birds." He deftly brushed the feathered wing of his hair back into place.

"Oooh, a conjugal visit with the ruggedly handsome

Pulitzer Prize–winning Jameson Rook? I certainly couldn't pass that up."

He wagged a finger at her. "Mock me if you will, but just remember—"

He stopped as she took his hand and led him to the nearest building, to a hidden spot behind a pillar.

"Why, Captain Heat, I take you upstate and you go feral on me." He gave his Cheshire cat grin and slid his arm around her back, pulling her in until their bodies were pressed together with nary a space between them. "I like."

She flicked her eyebrows up. "Thought I'd get my piece of you before everyone else."

"You married me, which means you can have any piece you want, anytime you want."

"Mmm." She pulled away from him, just slightly, and slid her hand between their bodies, her fingers dancing over his chest. "This piece?"

"Yes."

She traced a finger over his lips. "And these pieces?"

He flicked his tongue against the tip of her finger. "Most assuredly."

"Mmm." She gave him a seductive smile as she moved her hand back to his chest, then let it slide down to his belt buckle. "What about this piece?"

"Captain, you can have—" His words caught in his throat as her hand traveled lower.

And then, as suddenly as she'd started the little game, she stopped, pulling away. "Sadly, it will have to wait. You have a class to teach."

His voice had grown hoarse, but he pulled himself

together and a wicked gleam settled in his eyes. "What cruel and unusual punishment, Captain, but rest assured, payback will be a bitch."

She took his hand and they started walking again. "Something to look forward to."

A low rumble came from behind the closed doors of the lecture hall. Nikki and Rook stopped at the entrance, stealing a look at one another. "Sounds like standing room only," she commented.

"Well, I am somewhat of a celebrity," he said.

She rolled her eyes. "I didn't think you had so many students."

"It's about seventy-five or so," he said as he opened the door, "which is far fewer than are attending *today*'s lecture. In the spirit of Batman and Robin, holy popularity, Professor Rook!"

Nikki stood next to him, both of them looking at the full house. She quickly surveyed the room, determining a rough estimate. If she had to guess, she'd say there were probably 250 people in the hall. "You think it's your celebrity. I think it could be a lynch mob."

"Looks like it is," he agreed, but with an excitement she didn't feel.

"They're here for a reason, Rook," she said.

"Of course they are. Schadenfreude."

"Schaden-*what*?"

"It's human nature, when the misfortunes and problems of others are a delight for people to observe. It's the reason we are rubberneckers, slowing to look at traffic accidents, or why we watch television show after show about serial killers or collect their memorabilia. It's sad, but true."

"In other words, it's morbid curiosity," she said, shaking her head. "And in this case, their schaden-*whatever* is all about you."

Rook exhaled. His excitement deflated like air being slowly squeezed out of a tired balloon. "Because Chloe was found in my house."

Nikki wasn't going to mince words. "She wasn't just found at your house, Rook. She was found *dead. Naked.* In your *bed.* That makes your problems and misfortunes pretty damn interesting to the general public, especially to young adults who spent their childhoods with their phones attached to their hands, YouTube videos on any and every topic at the ready, and mindless video games. Whoever framed you wants you to go down hard for this. Problem is, a body in a bed isn't enough proof to convict."

Rook side-eyed her. "You just jumped ahead a few steps. Suspicion, arrest, lawyering up, building a defense. All that comes before the trial, throwing me in the slammer, and throwing away the key."

"You understand my point, though," she said, interrupting him. All these people wanted something. The question was what.

Nikki noticed a notable shift in the room's volume. Someone called out, "It's him! There he is!"

A cacophony ensued, with people hurling questions at Rook. *Were you having an affair with Chloe Masterson? How well did you know her? Was she your long-lost daughter?*

As Rook and Nikki descended the steps, Rook held up

one arm to quiet the room, but the questions kept coming. They made it to the front and mounted the short flight of steps to the raised platform, and Rook faced the crowded lecture hall from behind the podium. Once again, he raised his arm, and this time, the cacophony dimmed and a blissful quiet fell over the room like a blanket snuffing out the light.

Rook had his serious moments. Nikki had seen him in action plenty of times. Hell, he'd flown in a helicopter over the Hudson in order to save her from a deranged killer intent on making her fish food in the Atlantic. One of the things she loved best about him was his wickedly sardonic sense of humor, but when push came to shove, he changed his mask and faced dilemmas head-on. Which was just what he had to do right now.

"Since we're well past the add/drop deadline"—his voice seemed to bounce off the walls as he spoke into the microphone attached to the podium—"I'm guessing that the majority of you are not suddenly enrolled in my class. Therefore, I respectfully request that you vacate your seats and leave, as the lecture, as they say, must go on."

"Tell us about Chloe," someone said from the right side of the audience.

"There's nothing to tell. The police are investigating her murder. In the meantime, classes at Cam U will continue. Including this one."

"Is it true she was secretly in love with you?" This time the voice came from the left side of the room.

"Of course not," Rook said, not bothering to rebut such a ludicrous claim.

Nikki debated with herself about whether she should

stop him. She didn't want him to say anything that could come back later to bite him in the ass. On the other hand, he was innocent, so nothing he said would be incriminating. Unless, she reasoned, it was taken out of context. The questions brought her out of her internal debate and back to the moment.

"But she was at your house—"

"I heard she was in your bed—"

"And she was naked."

The voices kept coming, a seemingly endless barrage of queries that for a lesser person might have caused a lot of doubt. Since her mother's apparent death, Nikki had learned how to disconnect herself from her emotions. She couldn't worry about Rook and how he felt as the questions were hurled at him. They came, one after another, like arrows flying through the air, each hitting its mark. Bull's-eye. She couldn't stop them, so she was determined to learn something from them. With each new question, Nikki searched the crowd to try to pinpoint the speaker, but each time, someone new piped up with another question. It was like a moving target. Just when she thought she had someone in her sights, bam! That person was gone.

A voice, deep and accusing, came from the depths of the hall. "Was it you? Did you kill her?"

Nikki spun to face the direction the voice had come from. Something was different about that voice. It somehow sounded more personal. Next to her, Rook shifted from one foot to the other and gripped the side of the podium with one hand, cupping the other over his eyes, peering into the crowd. Nikki had no idea who'd spoken. Rook dropped his hand to his side, giving up his search. "No. Of course not," he said, clearly affronted.

"I think you did," the voice said.

Rook opened his mouth to respond, but Nikki elbowed her way in front of him. She spoke into the microphone, loud and clear. "Who are you? Stand up."

The room fell ominously silent. Only the rustling of clothing could be heard as the students turned from side to side, looking over their shoulders, trying to see who would stand up.

No one did.

From her spot behind the podium, Nikki's anger flared. "Are you too much of a coward to stand up and face us?"

The silence in the room was heavy with the accusations of murder and cowardice. It was a game of chicken, and Nikki was going to wait it out. "Come on, be a man," she taunted.

A female voice came from the center of the audience. "Yeah, stand up."

Several others joined in, chanting, *Stand up, stand up, stand up.*

Nikki stepped aside as Rook took over the podium again. "It's easy to hide behind anonymity," he began, "but a person has the right to face his accuser. If you won't stand and face me, I can only assume that you are, indeed, afraid. Whether this is because your conviction isn't as strong as you'd like us to believe, or due to the fact that you don't want to be singled out and confront not only me, but your classmates, as well, only you can say. Really, it's immaterial. I'll answer your questions. For the record, I did not kill Chloe Masterson. It is true that I discovered her body—"

"In your house," the voice said.

Rook didn't acknowledge the interruption. "But I was not on any intimate terms with her. She was a student determined to get to the bottom of a story."

Nikki leaned close to whisper in Rook's ear. "Flush him out," she said, hoping he'd understand what she meant.

He gave her a brief nod before turning back to the audience. "She shared her research with me, and I offered only my guidance as her mentor."

*Not bad,* Nikki thought. If she hadn't known better, she'd have believed what he'd just said was the complete truth.

Rook kept speaking. "If any of you have information about Chloe, the police need to know about it. And if the killer is here"—he paused, letting the idea sink in that the person who'd murdered Chloe could be right there in the room—"if you are here, rest assured, I will be sharing everything I know about Chloe with the authorities. Make no mistake. You will be brought to justice."

A low murmur spread like wildfire through the hall. Within a minute, it was blazing, the audience consumed by what Rook had said.

"Class dismissed," Rook said, his voice booming from the speaker system, and just like that, the people scattered like ants.

"That was . . . unexpected," Rook said. "Definitely an ambush rather than the course on crime investigation I'd planned."

Nikki ran her hand down his arm and took his hand in hers. "You did a good job in a tough situation."

A young woman approached them, computer bag slung

over her shoulder, disposable coffee cup in her hand. She had the long spiraled ringlets of her dark hair pulled back into a ponytail, wore no makeup, and was extraordinarily beautiful. Chiseled cheekbones, tall and lean, clear black skin that looked like it had never seen a blemish. She wore navy yoga pants, white canvas sneakers, and a lightweight sweatshirt over a workout top. Either she'd finished a fitness class before coming to the lecture or she was heading to one now.

"Excuse me, Mr. Rook?" Her voice was smooth and velvety, too. If she had a good head on her shoulders, this young woman might have it all.

Rook turned to her. "Can I help you?"

Instead of answering, the girl addressed Nikki next. "You're his wife? A detective?"

"I am."

"I . . . I want to talk to you about Chloe."

Rook was a little gun-shy after the battering he'd just taken. "Are you an enrolled student in the course, or just here out of curiosity?"

"Both, actually. I am in the class. Which I love, by the way. You lead such a fascinating life. It's no wonder Chloe wanted to pick your brain." Her voice cracked slightly, but that was her only outward sign of emotion.

Nikki spoke up, immediately intrigued. "You knew Chloe wanted to talk to Mr. Rook?"

"Oh yes, she was determined. She would say how he was the only one who could help her. He knew her story."

"What did I know?" Rook asked, as much to himself as to her.

"She never said more than that."

"What's your name?" Heat asked.

"Jada," she said, putting her hand on her chest. "Jada Rincon."

Nikki made a mental note of the girl's name. "You must have been close with Chloe." *Closer than her roommate,* she thought.

"Definitely. It probably sounds silly to say, but she was like my sister. I could tell her anything, you know?" Jada's eyes welled and her lips quivered. The emotions were bubbling just under the surface, but she stopped and breathed, exerting control over them again.

"It's not silly at all," Heat said. She felt that way about Lauren. Different families. Different childhoods. Different everything, and yet there was no woman she was closer to.

After another few seconds, Jada started again. "I teach at the rec. Chloe took one of my classes last year. That's how we got to know each other." She looked imploringly at Heat. "Do the police know anything yet?"

"Not enough," Nikki said vaguely.

The lecture hall had completely cleared out. "Let's sit," Rook said, leading the way to the first row of chairs.

"Tell us about Chloe," Nikki said, once they were seated.

"I don't know if I can hold it together," Jada said, her voice trembling.

"Jada," Rook said in his most empathetic voice. "You don't have to hold it together. We're here to listen. Take it at your own pace."

She dragged a finger under her eye, rolling her eyes upward and stretching her lower lid down as if she had a fleck of something caught there. "I don't know anything," she said after she'd composed herself. "I really don't."

Nikki didn't believe it. If that were true, then why had she made a point to come up and talk to them? She glanced at Rook, who, from the small nod he gave, seemed to have the same thought. "Jada," he started again. "If you've been attending my classes, then you know how much investigative reporting depends on information from people who don't even know that they have valuable knowledge that can help. You may be that very person. The one who can help us learn what led to your friend's death."

Jada glanced around, registering the empty hall, before lowering her voice to a hoarse whisper. "What if they come after me?"

Nikki dropped her voice to match Jada's. "Who's *they*, Jada? If you tell us what you know, we can help protect you."

Jada shook her head, closing her eyes for a beat. "But I don't know anything," she finally said.

Rook turned sideways in his seat to face her. "I think you do, Jada, and I think you want to tell us."

A weighty silence fell. Nikki heard every little sound as she waited to see if Jada would say what she needed to. A phone buzzed. Not hers. Rook's. He ignored it, though, not wanting to break the connection with the girl. The old building settled. A chair creaked, and then the air-conditioning kicked on. The faint sound of a door closing outside the lecture hall drifted in.

Finally, Jada looked at them and spoke quietly. "She knew who it was."

"Knew what?" Rook asked.

"I think she knew her killer."

Nikki was not surprised by this. It was an FBI statistic that 80 percent of murder victims knew their killer, so the odds were good that this was the case with Chloe. "Why do you say that?" Rook asked.

Jada glanced around again, and Nikki realized the girl had been running scared since her friend's death. "I saw her the day she was killed," Jada said, her voice still low and fearful. "She came to class that morning. We went to a juice bar after. She was pretty nervous, and when I asked her why, she said she was about to get the last piece of information she needed for her big exposé. That's what she called it. An exposé."

*Okay,* Nikki thought. Jada's story gave them a time line, but also a clear motive. Someone clearly wanted to stop Chloe from getting that last bit of information and to prevent her from finishing, and publishing, her revealing story.

Just as she knew he would, Rook had come to the same conclusion. "Jada, did she tell you who she was going to meet or what she was hoping to learn?"

Jada shook her head, but she reached into her computer bag. "She didn't tell me anything else, but I found this." She handed over a composition book. It had a black background with primary-colored polka dots all over it. The choice told Nikki something about Chloe. Although she was driven and independent, and clearly not afraid to buck the system since she'd been investigating something on her own, she wasn't so utilitarian that she picked up an ordinary speckled black-and-white comp book from a local big-box store. She had a softness about her, just as Nikki herself did. Neither one of them wore it on the surface.

Nikki slipped on a pair of nitrile gloves she'd dug out of her jacket pocket, taking the notebook from Jada. Rook looked over her shoulder as she began flipping through it. "It's her notes about whatever she was investigating." Nikki looked at Jada. "Where did you get this?"

"We have lockers at the rec. She usually put her locker key in my bag."

"You don't use a locker?" Nikki asked.

"We have to bring our own music, so when I'm teaching, I keep my bag with me at the front of the studio. That way I have my backup CDs in case my phone dies or the Bluetooth won't work."

Made sense. Nikki had taken enough fitness classes over the years—before she began training in Brazilian jiu-jitsu—to know that music often made the class by creating the atmosphere or by giving motivation cues through rhythm and beat.

"She put her key in my bag, but she left her cell phone on top. It went off in the middle of class, which made me pretty mad at the time. Everyone who practices yoga knows to turn the ringer off before class."

Yoga. The breathing Jada must have used to control her emotions. Her calm demeanor. It made sense. Nikki took over the questioning. "Her phone rang?"

Jada shook her head. "Well, no. It flashed."

Nikki didn't use the LED flash setting, but her niece did. "And she noticed?"

"We were in Shavasana—"

"And that is?" Rook interrupted.

"It's usually the final pose," Jada said.

*Corpse pose,* Nikki thought. It was a grim coincidence.

"The lights are dimmed. You lay flat, completely relaxed but awake," Jada continued. "Chloe was antsy all class. She couldn't find a comfortable position and was kind of stiff. When her phone flashed, she noticed right away. I think she was waiting for it, actually."

"Sounds like it," Nikki said.

"After you found out she was dead, you checked her locker?" Rooked asked.

"No. Not right away. I didn't realize her key was in my bag until this morning. I thought I should take it to the police, but I wasn't sure. This story was important to Chloe, but she was in trouble, and . . . and now I don't know what to do. She trusted you, Mr. Rook. So here I am."

Jada had been holding herself together, but now the tears came. Her chin bunched up. She tried to talk, but the onslaught of grief hit her hard and she couldn't get the words out.

These were the moments that tugged at Nikki's heartstrings more than any other. She would never let herself forget that the victims she worked to get justice for had people who were suffering from their loss. Jada Rincon, just like Tammy Burton, was in the midst of that pain.

Rook took Jada's hand in his. "It's going to be okay."

And then, as if he, himself, were a talisman, her heaving slowed and her crying stopped. She drew in a ragged breath. Then another. After a few more, she was able to continue. "Chloe was scared."

Nikki believed that a person's first instincts were usually right. Too often, people ignored the niggling feelings centered deep in their guts; she wished Chloe had listened to hers. "If she knew she was in danger, why did she go when she got the phone call?"

Jada shrugged helplessly. "I should have stopped her—"

"Jada," Nikki said. "Nothing you could have said or done would have stopped what happened to Chloe. This is not your fault."

Jada's tears started to pool again, but she squeezed her eyes shut as if they were dams holding back an onslaught of raging water. The poor girl was racked with guilt. Nikki wasn't going to be able to change that. Jada was going to have to come to terms with what had happened to her friend on her own.

"We can take Chloe's notebook to the police for you," Rook offered

The visible relief in Jada was instantaneous. "Really?"

"Of course. You did the right thing bringing this to us. We'll take care of it," he said, but Nikki had one more question for her. "Jada, did Chloe have a computer?"

Jada nodded. "Of course. She always had it with her."

"Did she have it that day at your class?"

"It was under her phone. She took it when she left."

Nikki cursed under her breath. Chloe's computer was the golden egg they needed, but it was one they'd never be able to find.

**"Why would she lock up her notebook, but not her computer?"** Rook pondered aloud when they were alone again. Jada had left looking like a weight had been lifted from her shoulders, but their burden was still fully intact.

"We know she was scared. And she thought she was close to some crucial information, so naturally—" Nikki said.

"She'd want to keep the notebook separate from her laptop in case one was stolen."

Rook finishing her sentences always sent a stream of warmth through Nikki. In moments like this, it was crystal clear how in tune with each other they were. How perfectly they fit. If they hadn't had a hot lead, she'd have taken him right then and there. Instead, she continued with her thought process. "She was running scared. She knew she had to protect her story."

"She wasn't just worried," Rook said. "She knew she was in imminent danger. Why else would she have taken such precautions?"

They spent the better part of an hour going through Chloe's notebook. "There's no rhyme or reason," Nikki said, frustrated. It was chock-full of information, sketches, designs, but not as organized as she would have thought based on the neatness of the girl's apartment and bedroom. She'd used abbreviations and symbols. Given more time, they might be able to decipher it, but Nikki had an ethical obligation to turn it over to the police. "We're going to have to give it to Ian," she said.

He gave a mirthless laugh. "Do you really think your ex is going to be able to figure out what Chloe got herself involved in with this if we can't?"

When she didn't respond, he continued, "A lot of reporters and journalists create their own shorthand. It helps them take notes with speed, and also protects their story and their sources. Her system is not obvious.

Drawings and letters and symbols. It's like she combined them all. Unless Chief Cooley has a code breaker on staff, it's going to take a while to figure this out."

A lot of detectives used some sort of shorthand, too. Taking accurate and thorough notes was essential, but so was speed. "Look at this." Rook had turned the page and pointed at a name written in what they now knew was Chloe's straight up and down penmanship. "It's a name."

*A. Albright,* Nikki read. "Someone here in Cambria? Connected with the university?"

Rook pointed to an arrow Chloe had drawn. The point stopped at the words *July Pub Date*. "It's familiar. An editor?" Rook suggested.

"If you're right, A. Albright could be who Chloe was writing her article for. Someone with the local newspaper here? Or could it be someone big? Someone at the *Post* or the *Times*?"

Rook opened a browser on his cell phone, immediately Googling the name. In a matter of seconds, he held the phone out for her to see. Several A. Albrights came up in the search. A neurosurgeon. A CEO. An author. "Well, would you look at that," Rook said, his finger stopping on the fourth entry. "April Albright. What are the odds?"

"Features editor for *First Press*?" The very publication Rook worked closely with. Nikki might even say it was the magazine that had launched their relationship. She looked at Rook. "You've never heard of her?"

"Look at the masthead sometime. The list of editors is as long as my arm."

Nikki knew enough about the publishing world from

her experiences with Rook to know that nothing there was simple, nothing moved quickly, and there were layers to everything. Much like the bureaucracy of law enforcement, come to think about it. "Could Chloe have been writing an article for the magazine?"

Rook shrugged. "Sure. Why not? Definitely on spec, given how green she was, but this editor must have liked what she queried."

Nikki pointed to Rook's phone at the same time he pulled up his contact list. "Same wavelength," he said. "Hot."

"But later." She flicked up her brows in such a way to suggest that "later" entailed an activity worth waiting for.

Rook got the message. "Let's work fast so later will come sooner. Calling my editor," he said as he punched in the number and put her on speaker.

Nikki continued to work her way through the notebook for the second time, listening to the conversation. After an update on Rook's latest project and the investigation—because news of a murdered coed traveled fast—Rook cut to the chase. "Do you know April Albright? I believe she's an editor with the magazine."

His editor, whom Rook had taken to calling Sparky, was a fast talker. Nikki had to stop in order to catch it all. "Of course I know her. I know everyone. She's an editor-at-large. Thinks she's hot shit 'cause she's hit with a few great stories. Puts out too many calls on spec for my taste; I prefer a sure thing, like with you, Rook. By the way, where are you on the John Legend story? And what's happening with that investigation? They can't possibly think you killed a woman, can they?"

Rook could hardly get a word in before Sparky was on to the next topic.

"I have a story idea for you. Everyone's crazy over *Hamilton*, right? New York history is all the rage. We're much more than Times Square. I want a series. Three-part. Maybe four. An exploration into the history of what many people forget is a historic town."

Before she could keep going, Rook inserted himself. "How can I get in touch with April?"

"April?"

"Albright. Editor-at-large."

"I'll text you her number. Gotta go, darling. Give me some ideas on the historic New York idea, yes? Great, thanks. Ciao."

"Thanks, Sparky," Rook said, but before he even got the words out, his mile-a-minute editor had hung up.

Nikki laughed out loud. "I can see why you call her Sparky."

"She's a spark plug," he said, holding up his phone after it pinged with a new text. "And she'd true to her word. Gotta love that woman."

He immediately saved the contact and called the number, once again putting it on speaker. After several rings, it went to voicemail. "Damn," Nikki muttered under her breath as Rook left a message asking April Albright to call him as soon as possible.

A short while later, with Chloe's notebook tucked safely in Rook's bag, which he held on to as if it housed a brick of gold, they headed back across campus toward the car. "I feel for Jada. That girl is going to need a good therapist,"

Rook said. "Her guilt is going to eat her alive."

"Hey, nothing wrong with a good therapist," Nikki said, thinking about her own sessions with the late Lon King. She hoped Jada found one just as good.

Rook had a sixth sense when it came to knowing what Nikki was thinking. He took her hand, giving it a reassuring squeeze. "She'll be okay."

She hoped he was right. They turned the corner, still following the path leading them to the parking lot when someone running up from behind plowed into Nikki. The force of the blow ripped her hand from Rook's. She fell, managing to tuck her body and roll to lessen the impact. From the corner of her eye, she saw Rook spinning, and then stumbling, trying to keep his footing. "Heat—" he yelled.

"I'm good."

And then he went down hard, not as adept at falling gracefully as she was. The offender hadn't stopped to check if they were all right. Instead, he barreled through them.

"My bag," Rook said, standing and spinning around. "He got the bag!"

In a split second, Heat gave chase. She could hear Rook's feet pounding the pavement behind her. She yelled over her shoulder and pointed at the bushes along the perimeter of the building. "Go that way! We'll cut him off."

His footsteps faded, the sound replaced by her own breath and the pounding of her heart. With Rook cutting through the shrubs along the side of the building, and her following the path the thief was on, they'd be able to intercept him. And retrieve Rook's bag—and Chloe's notebook.

Heat kept her focus on the back of the runner. The gait,

the size, the height. She was sure it was a man. Probably a young man, from the way the guy dodged around the smattering of people strolling the campus. The hoodie he wore covered his head, so there was no way to tell the color of his hair. She wanted a good look at his face. She couldn't say why, and she certainly couldn't prove it, but it was crystal clear to her that Rook's bag had been stolen because of Chloe's notebook. Which meant someone had been in the lecture hall when Jada handed it over to them. She recalled the heckler challenging Rook and calling him a murderer, and then later, when the hall had cleared out, she remembered the rustling. Their thief.

This guy would *not* get away with it. Heat moved faster, gaining on him. "Stop!" she yelled.

He kept running, but he looked over his shoulder. It slowed him down just enough to give Heat the advantage she needed. Like a runner in the final stretch of a race, she gathered up every last ounce of strength she had and jetted forward. She caught sight of Rook in her peripheral vision. He was winning his own race, hurtling over the stubby shrubs like he was channeling superstar hurdler Lolo Jones. "Don't let him get away!" he yelled to her.

Oh, there was no way this guy was escaping. In one last burst, she came up within reach of him. Her hand outstretched, her fingers brushed the back of his hoodie. Then, coming in from the side, Rook hurtled through the air. They hit the ground in a tangled mass. Rook let out a loud *oomph* as Heat landed on top of them, her chest smashed against the side of his head. She worked to disentangle herself from the pile, straining to hear Rook's muffled voice from underneath her. Finally, her feet found purchase on the pavement. She leveraged her body off of his, freeing his face. "You know I love it when you're on top, Heat, but this—"

"Can't . . . breathe . . ."

Rook's hands curved around Heat's hips and pushed her up. "Is not the way I want you to get off—"

The muffled voice beneath them strained again. "Can't . . . breathe . . . !"

Rook and Heat scrambled back, freeing the thief at the bottom of the mound. The guy pushed himself onto his hands and knees, dragging air into his lungs. "What the hell, man?" he said once he caught his breath. "Why'd you do that?"

Heat grabbed hold of his hoodie, yanking him up to standing. "Why did we do what? Chase you?"

"You knocked me to the ground," the guy said indignantly.

Heat laughed. "You say that like you didn't just steal his bag," she said, hooking her thumb toward Rook.

"Yeah, but you coulda hurt me." He looked down at the torn-up knees of his pants. "You *did* hurt me."

This time Heat rolled her eyes. "Seriously? You're a thief. You ran. You didn't stop when I yelled 'stop.' We went down with you, remember?"

"Thanks for blocking our fall, by the way," Rook said. "Without you, we would have gotten hurt, too."

The guy shot Rook an unamused side-eye. "Without you, I'd be long gone."

"With my bag," Rook said, bending to grab the strap of it. "This was a gift from Andrea Bocelli after I did an article on one of his charity events." He slung it over his head, then patted the case. "This is special, and certainly *not* for grubby little thieving hands like yours."

"Want to tell us what that was about?" Heat asked.

The guy responded by clamping his mouth shut like a defiant child.

Heat stared at him. "Really? You're going to play games now?"

Rook stared the kid down. "We caught you red-handed. You don't really think you can talk—or, silence—your way out of this, do you?"

The guy still played the silence game.

"Don't want to talk, huh?" Heat said. She grabbed hold of one of his arms. Rook flanked him, taking his other arm. "He might change his mind at the police station, don't you think?"

Rook put on his best innocent expression. "You know, he just might."

The burp of a police cruiser's siren greeted them as they marched the thief to the parking lot. Nikki cursed under her breath. She usually appreciated a do-gooder, but whoever had seen their scuffle and called the cops interrupted their opportunity to interrogate the thief, and it also meant they'd have to turn over Chloe's notebook a lot sooner than she would have liked.

Chief of Police Ian Cooley and his girl Friday, Deputy Breckenstein, emerged from either side of the cruiser. Ian strode over to them, not bothering to mask his irritation. "Getting into trouble, I see."

Rook shrugged, his innocent expression tinged with smugness. "Trouble tends to find us."

That was an understatement. Nikki Heat and Jameson Rook: magnets for trial and tribulation, everywhere they went.

"Want to fill me in?" Ian said, ignoring Rook.

Heat did the honors, ending with the tackle and apprehension of the cross-body bag thief. "A gift for you," she said, shoving their collar over to Breckenstein.

The chief, meanwhile, pulled on a pair of nitrile gloves and took the notebook Rook had withdrawn from his bag. "I'm sure you were heading straight to the station to turn it over as evidence."

"Absolutely," Heat said.

Breckenstein put her hand on the perp's head, guiding him into the back of the cruiser. Just as Nikki opened her mouth to ask about sitting in on the interview, Ian offered. Rook replied, "Love to, thanks, pal."

Irritation colored the chief's face, but he'd already made the offer, so he couldn't take it back. He drove off with Chloe's notebook, leaving Heat and Rook to follow.

**The guy had a name: Joseph Hill. And young Mr. Hill looked** like death. Pale. Hollow, dark-rimmed eyes. Dark hair he'd run his hands through so many times that it stood up on its own. He jiggled one knee under the table, wrung his hands, and chewed on his lower lip. Nervous didn't even begin to cover it. Something was definitely up with this kid. Heat had seen her share of nervous Nellies in the interrogation room, but more often than not, they tried to look tough. This kid wasn't even attempting it. Whatever posturing he'd done at the scene of the theft had evaporated. Now he was clearly petrified, and his fear seeped through every pore in his body.

While Rook watched from behind the two-way mirror, Heat and Ian sat across from the kid, letting him sweat it out. The silence had to be incredibly uncomfortable for Joseph Hill. To Heat, on the other hand, it was simply a strategy. Her instincts told her that Joseph would wear himself down. She just had to wait and ride the wave.

"Aren't you going to say something?" Hill finally asked when he couldn't take the pressure anymore. There was a hefty dose of panic in his voice.

Heat glanced at her watch. It had only taken three minutes. "Oh, are you ready to talk now?"

Under the table, he jiggled one leg. The force of the action made the table vibrate. "It wasn't my fault," he said. "I swear. It really wasn't my fault."

"What exactly wasn't your fault?" Ian asked. "The fact that you stole Mr. Rook's bag, or the assault—"

Joseph's eyes bugged. "Wait, what?"

Ian leaned back, folding his arms over his chest. Intimidation looked to be his go-to in the interrogation room. "You plowed into them, knocked them both to the ground, and proceeded to hit and kick Mr. Rook. The snatch-and-grab would have been a misdemeanor, but the assault takes the whole thing up a notch. And then, dumbass, you ran from Detective Heat. Not looking too good for you, Joseph."

Joseph looked like a man who'd been beaten down by the world, not just by the Cambria Police Department, a visiting detective, and a writer.

"Why'd you do it?" Heat asked when he didn't respond.

From the way he studied his own wringing hands, Heat knew this boy was on the verge of breaking. She pushed again. "Did you know Chloe?"

He leg kept working under the table, and his left eye twitched. "I'll take your non-answer as a yes," Heat said. "Did you kill her, Joseph? Is that why you tried to steal the bag?"

"No!"

"You needed to get Chloe's notebook, right? Is there something incriminating in it? Did she write about you?"

Joseph shoved back in his chair and stood up. "Jesus Christ, are you serious? No! I didn't kill Chloe. I hardly knew her."

Ian stuck out his pointer finger then angled it down, indicating that Joseph Hill had better sit his ass back down. Joseph read the gesture for what it was and slowly sank back into his chair. "He said it was no big deal. He said it was *his* notebook."

"Who said it was no big deal?" Ian asked.

"I don't know his name. I didn't even see him."

Ian slammed his hand on the table. "Don't screw with us, kid!"

Joseph jerked back, waving his hands in front of him. "I'm telling the truth. You have to believe me. I'm not even going to get paid, and I'm—oh shit—" He drew back, looking even more terrified than he had just a few minutes before. "Am I going to jail?"

"That depends," Heat said.

"On what?"

"On you cooperating with us," she said.

Ian leaned forward. "Who's paying you, Joseph?"

The chief's stern and unforgiving approach had the desired effect. Joseph started jiggling his leg again and beads of sweat formed on his forehead. "I really don't know."

Ian scoffed. "You stole a bag to get Chloe's notebook, but you don't know who you did it for?"

Joseph looked like a bobblehead, moving his head in a random combination of shakes and nods. He laid his forearms on the table and looked imploringly at them. "If I tell you what I know, will that help me? Because I can't go to jail. They'll kick me out of school." He looked up at the ceiling, covering his face with his hands. "Oh my God, my parents'll kill me."

This time, Heat leaned forward and met Joseph's gaze. "Tell us what happened and we'll see what we can do."

The kid sucked in a shaky breath. "Okay, look. I was sitting in class today—"

"In Mr. Rook's lecture?" Heat asked.

"Right. Then that guy started talking shit."

Nikki could hear the voice from somewhere in the lecture hall asking if Rook had killed the girl. "I remember," she said. "Go on."

"Someone tapped me on the shoulder."

"The same guy challenging Mr. Rook?"

"No. That guy was in front of me somewhere."

"So someone tapped you on the shoulder. What then?"

"When I started to turn around, he told me not to. Kind of freaked me out, to be honest. Cloak-and-dagger shit, you know?"

"We don't know, which is why we need you to tell us," Ian snapped.

Heat caught his eye, patting the air with her open palm. His raging cop approach was going to shut Joseph down if he wasn't careful.

"What did he say?" Heat asked, her voice softer to compensate for Ian's angry tone.

"He said that the professor was a hack and took his notebook and he wanted it back."

Nikki balked. Rook was a lot of things, but a hack was not one of them. She shot a glance at the two-way, imagining how Rook was taking the slander against him. Not like a champ, she'd have bet. "And you believed him?" she asked.

He shrugged noncommittally. "He said he'd pay me three hundred dollars if I could get it back. I didn't think about it too much, I guess."

From behind the glass, she heard the muffled sound of Rook's voice. Again, she patted the air, but this time over her shoulder and directed at him.

"Let's recap," she said to Joseph. "You were in class, minding your own business, when a man tapped you on the shoulder and offered you three hundred dollars to steal a notebook Mr. Rook had in his possession."

"It doesn't sound too good when you put it like that."

"That's because it *isn't* too good. In fact, it's pretty bad, because it's all connected to an ongoing murder investigation."

Joseph suddenly looked like a light bulb went off over his head. "Oh man, you think this guy's involved in Chloe's death?"

"It's a very strong possibility," she said.

Joseph sat back, covering his face with his hands again. "I can't believe I fell for it."

Heat couldn't believe he had, either. "Joseph, is there anything else you can tell us about the guy?"

He shook his head. "I never saw his face."

"How were you supposed to deliver the notebook?" she asked.

"And how were you going to get the three hundred dollars you sold your soul for?" Ian asked.

The sarcasm flew over Joseph's head. "I gave him my cell number. He said he'd call me at five o'clock and arrange a trade."

Heat flicked her wrist to check the time. "That's in three minutes."

She and Ian shared a look that they both understood. It was not enough time to set up a tap. "Joseph, we're going to need you to help us," Heat said. Joseph raised his eyes and waited, so she continued. "When this guy calls, you have to convince him that you have the notebook. We need you to set up the meeting."

Joseph scraped his fingers over his scalp. "I don't know if I can do that."

Ian scowled. "Your other option is for me to throw you in jail. See how well you like that—"

Heat cut him off. They now had less than three minutes, and Ian's berating Joseph wasn't going to help the kid stay calm. "You'll be better at it than you realize, Joseph. All you have to do it say you have the notebook. He'll tell you where to meet and we'll do the rest."

Joseph's leg started up again. "What if he knows what happened?" His gaze skittered between them. "That I'm here?"

Heat had to admit that it was a possibility. If she'd been the one making a deal with some stranger to steal something for her, she'd have stuck around to make sure it actually happened. They had to take the opportunity in front of them, though. "We'll cross that bridge when—or if—we get there, okay?"

He breathed out a jagged "Okay."

Ian opted to step out, leaving Heat alone with Joseph. In theory, she thought this was a good idea. He'd shown himself to be too hotheaded. But in practice, Ian and Rook being alone behind the mirror could go south real fast. He'd jumped from the frying pan into the fire.

When Joseph's phone rang precisely at five o'clock, she didn't have to think about that particular scenario anymore. Instead, she focused only on coaching the scared kid through the mess he'd gotten himself into.

"Go ahead and answer and put it on speaker," she said, keeping her voice calm and controlled in order to keep him calm and controlled.

His eyes were wide and his hands shook, but he did as she told him, answering with a shaky "Hello?"

The man on the other end cut right to the chase. "Did you get it?"

He looked at her for direction. *Say yes,* she mouthed.

"Yes," he said immediately.

"Any problems?"

Again, his eyes sought hers. She sighed. *Say no,* she directed silently.

"No," he said, but to Nikki's practiced ear, the hesitation he'd given, and the tenor of his voice, made him sound less confident than she would have liked.

"You sure?" the guy on the other end asked. Heat detected a hint of unease in the guy's voice, which told her he'd heard the tentativeness in his mule's response, too.

Joseph gulped audibly. "Um, it was nothing. I hid in the lecture hall and saw Mr. Rook put the notebook in his bag. Then, when he was walking through campus, I did a snatch-and-grab. Easy."

Heat gave a relieved sigh. The boy seemed to have recovered, tossing out the term Ian had used to describe the theft as if it were part of his everyday vernacular.

"Easy getaway?" the man asked.

Heat listened carefully, trying to detect any bit of familiarity in his voice, but she couldn't say for certain one way or the other, and there were also no clues as to his age or education. Too few words. She rolled her finger in the air, indicating that Joseph should keep talking.

"Totally easy. Knocked him flat on the ground. Kind of felt bad for the guy, to be honest. He *is* my professor."

Heat nodded in approval. The guy was slipping right into his role.

"They didn't see your face or come after you?"

"No, not at all," Joseph said. "He was laid out on the ground."

"Oh yeah?"

"Yeah. He never saw it coming."

"And they didn't put up a fight or chase you?" the guy said, and just like that, Heat knew the jig was up. Just like she would have, it seemed the guy who'd tapped Joseph for the snatch-and-grab had, indeed, stayed around to watch it all go down.

Joseph must have sensed it, too, because he scratched his head and looked stumped. "Um, no, there was no fight."

"Jesus Christ, kid. Do you think I'm an idiot? You are at the police station right now. Are they listening? Because I have a message."

There was no point in pretending she wasn't there, so Nikki sat down, the phone face up in the center of the table, and spoke. "What message do you have for me?"

"You and writer boy need to back off."

The "or else" was implied. "Why did you kill Chloe?" Heat asked, following her gut. This guy wanted the notebook, which had to implicate him in some way. It was only logical that he had killed Chloe to keep her from revealing whatever he wanted kept under wraps . . . or he knew who did.

"Back off," he said again, and then the line went dead.

# EIGHTEEN

Chief Cooley was holding Joseph Hill for further questioning, but Nikki and Rook had gone back to the hotel and to the murder board. Chloe Masterson's notebook had helped fill in a few of the gaps, but there was a missing link. "We still don't know where Chloe went when she left yoga class," Heat said after she'd written it in the form of a question on the board.

"Or who she was meeting," Rook said.

"We know she had at least been contacted by or was in touch with April Albright from *First Press*."

"Maybe we missed something," Rook said. They'd spent what felt like hours scouring Chloe's notes, trying to decipher her shorthand. They'd managed to read some of it, but she'd been cryptic, so whatever they were able to understand was not enough to even form a lead.

"Maybe," she conceded. She'd wanted more time with the notebook, but the moment Joseph Hill had stolen Rook's bag, her time had been up. To have kept the notebook would have been unethical. And Nikki didn't do unethical unless there was no other choice and the ends really did justify the means. She had a code, and she lived by it.

"Ian said he'd let you know if he found anything else."

Rook sat down beside her on the couch in the suite portion of the hotel room. "In the meantime, let's review what we know."

They sat side by side, staring at the board. The major gap was still understanding what, exactly, Chloe had been investigating. What was her big story? Wishing that the young woman had told Rook didn't get her anywhere. "Let's backtrack," Heat said. "We know she wanted to talk to you, but why? Let's assume it was more than just you being her mentor and wanting to run an idea by you. Why you? Why not one of the Cam U journalism professors? Why you?" she repeated.

Rook jumped into musing right alongside her. "I did an article once about being a mentor and choosing a mentor. A person chooses to be a mentor to help others and to share the breadth of their experience. Think about my good friends James Patterson and Michael Connelly. They mentor other writers, guiding them on their journeys to being mystery authors."

"But you didn't reach out to Chloe, and she had other choices," Heat said. "Why did she zero in on you?"

"Other than my—"

"I know, your rugged handsomeness."

"Because I have done something that she connected to."

"Did she follow your work? But again, why you?"

Rook had a certain look when he was deep in thought. His brow furrowed. He stared off in the distance, his eyes vacant. And he stroked his chin. All three were in play at the moment, so Heat waited. Following a deep thinking session, he sometimes came up with something brilliant. Heat hoped this would be one of those times.

He snapped his fingers a second later. "Jada said that Chloe knew I'd understand."

"That you could help her because you knew her story."

"'Knew her story,'" he repeated. "I don't know what she could mean, unless Chloe was writing about something I'd already covered."

That made sense. "Think back, Rook. What stories have you done that would have piqued her interest?"

He considered for a moment before responding. "I don't think that's the right approach. If I had already completed a story, there wouldn't have been anything more to investigate. I think a better question is: What stories did I start, but not finish?"

They were on the same team, but damn, she hated it when he landed on a better question than she did. "Okay, so what have you started, but then stopped?"

He pointed his index finger to the sky and *tsk*ed at her. "Once again, there is a better question. She would not be privy to my abandoned stories, therefore it stands to reason that she was aware of something I'd talked about publicly."

Dammit again. "Are you done one-upping me?"

He bowed his head. "I do believe I am."

"Then tell me, oh smart one: When have you spoken publicly about stories you killed?"

"Not often," he confessed, deflating the entire buildup of the conversation. "My hypothesis about how Chloe learned about one of my stories is a good one, but the how-she-discovered-it part is not so easy to pinpoint. Writers don't go around sharing their ideas with other people. Intellectual property is a big deal. You never know if you'll want to come back to an idea you had ten . . . years . . . ago . . . ."

She knew him so well. He'd slowed down because what he was saying had triggered a thought. "Tell me."

"Remember the awards ceremony? Chloe said something about my old journalism notebooks."

"Right. She said she'd always keep hers, too, or something along those lines." During a murder investigation, everything was on the table. Heat dug in deeper to explore the idea Rook had brought to the surface. "From what people have said, Chloe was intentional about things in her life. Her job at the paper, her writing assignments, her apartment, her room, her shorthand. She thought things through."

Rook picked up on her train of thought. "So if she was curious about my old notebooks, it was for a reason. Her being at that ceremony, it wasn't an accident, was it?"

"I don't think so," Heat said. "She brought up your old notes, which means that is what she wanted to find out about."

"Exactly. Did you bring them?"

"I did. I planned to use them as exhibits during some of my lectures. The point is to show the kids how we keep learning, even after we leave college, and how our investigative skills develop and refine over time."

Nikki agreed with that perspective 100 percent. The details of every case she'd investigated were catalogued and filed away at the precinct, but what she'd learned through the steps of the investigations always affected how she approached subsequent cases. Her case leading to the downfall of a prominent candidate for president, Lindsy Gardner, had shown her that what happened in the past could come back to haunt you. Similarly, her own past—the trauma of hearing her mother's scream over the phone and then as she took what Nikki believed to be her last breath—always reminded her about the humanity of the victims and their families, and it informed her every action on the job.

Heat uncapped her dry-erase marker and added notes to the time line on the whiteboard, as well as the idea about Rook's old material. "Maybe she looked but didn't find what she was after—"

"Or maybe she did and wanted more," Rook said.

They looked at each other. "We need to go through my old stuff," Rook said at the exact moment Heat said, "We need to read your old notes."

"And Chloe's notebook again," they said in unison. They grinned at their symbiotic relationship. She and Rook were like Captain Kirk and Mr. Spock, and each case a voyage on their personal Starship *Enterprise*. Proving her point, Rook grabbed the car keys, she grabbed her jacket, and they headed to the door, all without a word.

# NINETEEN

The crime scene at Rook's brownstone had been completely sanitized. No evidence remained to indicate that Chloe Masterson had ever been there, let alone died there. Heat and Rook sat in the front room. She perched on the edge of the beige couch, while he sat opposite her in one of the armchairs. On the floor next to Rook was a plastic box, the lid removed. Inside, neatly lined up, was a collection of notebooks. They varied in size and color, as well as in their overall condition.

Upon closer inspection, Nikki was able to correlate the growth of Jameson Rook as a journalist, and as a person, to the type of books he'd used. Some were the inexpensive spiral-bound type a typical middle school student might use. Three were composition books, but unlike Chloe's nice polka-dot special order notebook, his were black-and-white drugstore numbers. By the time Rook had been a senior, he'd graduated to the more permanent—and more expensive— black Moleskines. She laid the array of notebooks on the table between them, sweeping her hand over them. "Here lies the evolution of Jameson Rook," she said.

"Mock me if you will, but evidence of growth is actually a good thing. Would you look at me the same if I'd not graduated to the book-bound variety?"

"You're right. I'd think you were still an immature thirty-six-year-old instead of a . . . oh, wait, you are an immature thirty-six-year-old."

He mimicked a stab to the heart. "I'm wounded. I'm an *impishly adorable* thirty-six-year-old. Semantics, my dear Heat, are everything."

"Either way, you're a—" She stopped as something triggered in her mind. "Semantics," she murmured.

"You have an idea," Rook said. A statement, not a question.

"I do," she said after she fleshed it out, "but not about this case. Remember when you did that story on the crime families, and Tomaso Fats told you about the old speakeasy the family had repurposed?"

"Sure. They used it as gambling central. We made a deal to not turn them in to Vice."

"Right. But what did they *call* it?"

He laughed. "Oh yeah, that was the best part. They called it the library. 'We're going to the library' meant going to shoot craps, or play blackjack. Pretty clever."

Without a word, she reached for her cell phone, dialing Sean Raley. "Rales, it's me," she said when he answered.

"Hey, Cap. Everything good upstate?"

"Yeah, fine," she said.

"So you got a collar? Excellent! Coming back to civilization soon? We caught another murder. Spread a little thin over here."

"Mmm, not quite yet. Still working on that. But Sean, listen. I have a thought about our NYU vic."

"Joon Chin," he said.

"Right."

"That's good, because we're dry."

She didn't know if her hunch would lead anywhere, but it was worth a try. "Remember when you interviewed the vic's roommate? He said Joon had been at a coffee shop that night."

"Right. Thing is, though, he didn't have any books or his laptop with him, so we're pretty sure he didn't go to study."

"It may be a long shot," Heat said, "but maybe 'coffee' doesn't mean coffee." She recounted the Tomaso Fats library reference. "You've tried all the normal scenarios. What if going to get coffee actually meant something else?"

Raley didn't respond. Of the two members of Roach, Sean was the more contemplative detective. They were both thinkers, but Raley did more of his thinking internally before voicing his thoughts. "It's possible," he said after he'd considered her idea. "Yeah, it's definitely possible. I'll dig around. See if 'going to get coffee' means anything else to Joon Chin's group of friends."

Heat's phone beeped. "Let me know what you find," she said to Raley, then clicked over to the incoming call.

"Captain Heat," said the snarling voice of Zach Hamner when she answered. "Your absence in New York is causing some consternation."

She cupped her hand over her eyes, wishing she'd stayed on the line with Raley. A conversation with The Hammer was never an enjoyable experience. "Big word, Hamner. Did you look that up in the dictionary just for this call?"

"I have plenty more words for you, Captain Heat," he said. "I'm happy to call you in to One PP to discuss it."

"I'll be back soon," she said, deciding she needed to placate him, at least a little bit. "They are my personal days, though."

His response was a single word. "Honeymoon."

She gritted her teeth and came right back at him. "Days that I've earned from my exemplary service with the force. Days I have every right to use. Days that are mine to use as I see fit."

Rook stopped flipping through his notebooks. "Tell him how many overtime hours you've put in but haven't gotten paid for," he said, expressing the indignation that she felt but was trying to control.

She frowned and shushed him. "Hamner, do you have any idea how many unpaid hours of overtime I've put in?"

Rook leaned forward. "Tell him that you deserve to take time off every now and then."

She waved him off, but dammit, he was right. "I deserve time off, you know."

"You're working a case there, Captain, so it's not exactly recreational time. One PP is, shall we say, concerned that you have 'mis-prioritized' your duties—"

The inanity of such a statement riled her, but she checked her instinct to cut him off at the knees. "Please tell me, how have I 'mis-prioritized' my duties?"

Rook was on his feet the second the words left her mouth. "There is not a moment in time when you've shirked your duties," he said in a harsh whisper. "*Mis-prioritized?* That is—"

He sat back down when she put her palm out to him, but once again, his response foreshadowed her own. "I have never shirked my duties. Ever. My husband is in a situation of which you are well aware, and I am taking some of my earned time to help."

"That's all well and good, Captain, but the brass expects to see you here, in person, first thing Monday morning."

"Can't wait," she said, hanging up before Hamner could say anything else to piss her off.

"Oh my God," Rook said a moment later, pushing his chair back and standing again. But this time, instead of agitated, he looked stunned. He dragged his hands through his hair, pacing the room.

"What did you find?" Heat asked.

Rook came back to the table, pushing the open Moleskine notebook toward her with his fingertips. "It's right here."

She picked it up and scanned, her eyes widening. She looked back at him. "This is what you were digging into your senior year?"

He leaned over Nikki's shoulder, his breath warm against her neck. He reached around her and tapped his finger against the page. "*This* is what Chloe was writing about."

She tilted her head back to look up at him, questioning whether it was really possible that Cambria University had a secret society and that it was at the center of Chloe's investigation. "This is a real thing, this Tektōn?"

"I thought so at the time, but I never got around to proving it. The story was killed. I wanted to pursue it, but I had an article picked up for *GQ. That* was a big deal back then. I dropped the secret society story and went all in on the other one."

Heat sat back, thinking aloud. "So Chloe knew about this Tektōn group and was trying to prove its existence. But why would that put her in danger? What's so bad about a college secret society? Don't they just drink and do stupid rituals that no one but the order itself cares about?"

"Not necessarily. There are untold facets and all is never as it seems." In typical Rook fashion, he spoke cryptically. He was going to take her on what would no doubt be a lengthy roundabout tale before he got to the point.

"Do tell," she said, knowing that he would with or without her prompting.

"They're called collegiate societies. They are usually very serious and morose. They all use mortuary imagery. Far too pedestrian, if you ask me. You'd think they could be a bit more original."

"Rabbit trail," Nikki said, and that was enough to get him back on track.

"There are far too many to count, but my God, they are incredibly interesting. Membership rolls. Initiations. Signs of recognition. They're all top secret. No one but the members themselves know about the inner workings.

"And outside the college setting? Even more fascinating. The Seven Society, for example, has a legend behind its formation. The legend says that there were originally eight men. They were to meet up to play cards. Alas, one didn't show. The seven remaining men formed their society. And then there is the Gridiron Secret Society. Most of them are connected to universities. Some, like the Seven Society, keep their memberships secret for the members' lifetimes. Only upon one's death is their membership in the society revealed—with a wreath shaped like the number seven put on the grave of the recently deceased. A wreath of black magnolias, no less." He slapped his hand on the table in delight. "Can you imagine? A wreath of black magnolias. You just can't get more poetic than that.

"So many are associated with universities, of course. And many are connected to one another. It's like a web. Gridiron is at the University of Georgia. Its first president, more than a hundred years ago, graduated from Yale and was believed to be a member of the Order of Skull and Bones." He looked at her. "You have heard of it?"

Even if she hadn't, she could put two and two together. "Yale plus secret society equals Skull and Bones."

Rook winked at her. "Quick as a whip, that why I love you, Heat."

"So you're saying that every society has their lore."

"They do, indeed. Secrets abound. Skull and Bones, for instance. Rumor has it that they had something to do with the Kennedy assassination."

"Which one?"

"John F.," he said. "And people have also said that they had were involved in creating the nuclear bomb."

"Do you think that's really true?" she asked, clear skepticism in her voice.

He stood and began pacing as he spoke. "There are rumors that the CIA used it as a conduit to their organization."

"Cambria University is small. You think a secret society actually exists?"

"So many colleges have their secret orders, you have no idea. In this particular case, size doesn't matter."

Heat had long ago learned to ignore her husband's never-ending off-the-cuff sexual references. She thought back to Chloe's notes. "Let's say Cam U has this Order of Tektōn. They're obviously well hidden. But remember Chloe's sketches? Buildings and mazes and—"

"Tunnels," Rook finished.

"Could there be some old meeting place that isn't publicly known?"

The questions brought forth another tidbit of information held somewhere in the depths of Rook's mind. He put his hands on the back of the chair and leaned forward. "Washington and Lee."

"The university?"

"They have the Cadaver Society. They've managed to keep nearly every part of their order secret. It's said that there is an entire system of passageways underground. They're used so the members are ghosts to the student body and faculty of the school. Get this: there are doors that are locked, and no one has the key. Suspicious-looking doors. A miniature door in the library. You can find their symbol, a skull with the letter C inside of it, across the campus. They leave it as a calling card when they partake in mischief."

"What if Cam U really does have some sort of secret passageways? What if those are the sketches Chloe drew?" Heat posited.

Rook considered. "It's definitely possible. Yes, Captain Heat, I think it's most certainly a possibility."

# TWENTY

**N**ikki had been in Cambria long enough to feel as if she'd worn a path in the pavement between the hotel, the police station, and the university. Rook had a meeting scheduled with the provost, as well as his old buddy, Lamont, so after their review of Rook's old notebooks, they headed, once again, to the university, this time to the administration building. "Come with me," Rook said after they'd parked in their usual spot.

"It's fine. I'll wait for you here," she said. She'd had the foresight to photograph as many pages of Chloe's notebook as she could. She'd focused on the ones that looked cryptic on the hunch that they held information Chloe didn't want easily deciphered. Some of those included sketches that might show them where to look for hidden tunnels or passageways.

Before she started scrolling through them, Heat queued up her emails. Roach had sent an update, which was that they were chasing down a lead on the "coffee" idea, and that they'd see her soon. Zach Hamner had called, gone to voicemail, said nothing, then hung up after fifteen seconds. It was meant to signal disappointment to her, but she just ignored it.

Rook got out of the car, came around to her side, and opened the door with the flair of a footman helping a princess out of a chariot. "I won't take no for an answer. It's your turn to be a visitor in my world. We'll be done in no time, and then we can search the campus from head to toe."

She looked up at him, ready to decline, but Rook's excited face changed her mind. He was right. He lived in her world far more than she lived in his, metaphorically speaking. How could she refuse? She took his proffered hand, and a short while later, they were seated around a conference table in the provost's office, waiting for the provost himself. Kaden Saunders was another of Rook's former college buddies who'd made his career at the university and had advanced quickly. Second only to the president, he'd helped secure Rook's position as a visiting professor. Saunders's secretary had showed them in, and now they waited.

The office itself was just as Nikki imagined a provost's office would look. Dark wood, bookshelves filled with journalism books, a few photographs of Saunders arm in arm with celebrities and politicians, several engraved plaques and trophies, and other miscellany.

Lamont and Rook wore twin outfits: navy trousers, tucked-in button-down shirts, and brown blazers. Jennifer Daily came barreling in, flinging her briefcase onto the table in front of her. Typed student papers, newspaper clippings, and photographs slid partway out of the case. She shoved them back in and plunked herself down. The chair creaked, more from the force of the action than anything else. She was a short woman, probably around five feet three inches, and she had a good twenty years on her colleagues, plus at least twenty extra pounds on her frame. She had the softness that came with age: loose skin around the neck, sagging jowls, and one eyelid drooping a touch lower than the other. If she felt anything like she looked, she was ready to retire.

As Daily riffled through her case, Rook and Lamont carried on a conversation about the dangers journalists faced in the Middle East. Nikki sat back and observed. Finally, ten minutes after the meeting had been scheduled to begin, Kaden Saunders entered the room. Lamont popped up out of his chair like a jack-in-the-box. They shook hands, each clasping the other's forearm with their free hands. Next Saunders came around the table and shook Jennifer Daily's hand. Rook stood and the two men embraced, the provost giving Rook a hearty clap on the back. Last, he greeted Heat. "You look well, Mrs. Rook," he said, leaning in to lightly buss her cheek.

"So do you," she said, resisting the urge to correct him with "Captain Heat." Compared to his colleagues, the dean of the Merritt School of Journalism had a strong air of leadership about him. Kaden Saunders's smoky gray suit was polished and pressed and his hair neatly combed to one side in a conservative style. After greeting Nikki, whom he'd met once before at her wedding, he sat forward in his chair, hands in front of him on the table. He cleared his throat, bringing the others to attention. Even though they'd known each other for the better part of fifteen years, Saunders spoke formally. "I understand it's been a long day, so I don't want to drag this on. Tell me what happened, Jamie."

Rook recounted the events of the day: the opening of his class in the lecture hall, meeting Jada Rincon, Chloe's notebook, the theft of Rook's bag, and the arrest of Joseph Hill. "That's about it."

"No other progress on identifying the girl's killer?" Saunders asked, directing the question to Heat instead of Rook.

"We're chasing down a few leads," Heat answered.

"But nothing you can elaborate on, am I right?" Lamont asked.

She kept her expression grim. "Right. It's an ongoing investigation."

Saunders tapped the table with one hand. "You're going to prove our Jamie innocent, though, right?"

He asked the question as if he were a concerned friend, but he was also the dean who'd brought his old friend to the college. She had no doubt the guy was in the hot seat with the president of the university and the Board of Regents. "Absolutely," she said. "He's my Jamie, too."

Saunders cleared his throat again. A nervous tic, Heat realized. He had something to say, but he wasn't sure how to say it. "You're taking some heat over this, aren't you?" she asked, saying it for him. "Need to make a change?"

The room fell silent. Jennifer Daily stopped her rustling. Rook, who'd been leaning back in his chair listening to the others talk about him and the situation, sat up at attention, and Raymond Lamont let out a quick and unintentional nervous laugh.

Saunders slowly looked at each of them, ending with Rook. "I've been asked to put you on leave."

Rook's normally relaxed face tensed. "Why?"

"Oh, Jamie, come on," Saunders said.

"Okay, okay, I know why, but . . . *why*? I did not kill that girl."

If the room had been silent before, now it was a graveyard. Daily and Lamont swiveled their heads from Rook to Saunders as the men conversed. "The fact that you even have to say that is the problem. There's a dead student, and . . . well, you know the rest. The university needs to separate itself from the . . . situation."

Lamont, for all his bombastic nature, was quiet when he spoke. "Kade, is this really necessary? We know Jamie didn't do this thing."

The provost lifted his hands in helplessness. "It's out of my hands."

"The Board of Regents has spoken," Rook said with a mocking tone. He shoved his chair back as he stood, looking at Heat. "Let's go, Nik."

Jennifer Daily heaved the strap of her overflowing briefcase over her shoulder and followed them out, letting the door shut on Lamont and Saunders, who still sat unmoving at the conference table. "Mr. Rook, a minute, please," she said once they reached the main hallway.

Her bag gapped open, the weight of the papers pressing down on the outer side. If the woman moved again, the soft side of the case would give and the papers would tumble out. Which is exactly what happened next. The professor took a step toward them and the side of the case collapsed, spilling the contents onto the floor.

"Damn!" Professor Daily dropped the strap to the crook of her arm. She sidestepped closer to the wall, put her hand against it, and started to lower herself down.

Rook leapt to her, taking her by the arm and lifting her back to standing. "We'll get it, Professor."

She nodded gratefully, leaning her age-worn body against the wall. "Thank you."

Nikki had already crouched down and was gathering the woman's work into a pile. Rook quickly helped her, took the stack, and carefully slid it into the case, taking care to zip it up.

"Can we help you to your office?" Rook asked once she was a little less discombobulated.

"Yes, please. That's perfect. I wanted to talk to you privately anyway."

He took her briefcase and carried it for her. They walked by her side. Nikki was surprised at the briskness of the woman's pace. Aside from her stiffness at trying to squat down to the floor for her papers, she was spry for her age and girth. She kept constant tabs on her case, as if it might suddenly vanish and she'd miss it.

Their progress was a bit slower on the stairs down to the lobby from the second floor where they'd been, but once they made their way out into the bright daylight, Daily once again increased her pace. Heat considered talking on the way but discarded the idea. If Professor Daily had something to talk about, Heat wanted to have complete focus. They entered the old brick building, then the stairwell. Daily's voice echoed as she finally spoke. "This old building doesn't have an elevator. I've requested to move, but it hasn't happened yet. Still a good ole boys' network."

*The bane of feminism,* Heat thought.

They stopped in front of room 211. Nikki held her breath as Professor Daily unlocked the door and flung it open. They stepped over the threshold and she sighed, relieved. The woman's office space wasn't as bad as she'd feared. There were stacks of paper, but only a few, and the professor seemed to have a specific shelf dedicated to those piles. The chairs were clear of papers, and her desk held only the typical office paraphernalia. Daily gestured to the chairs, and Heat and Rook sat.

Instinctively, Heat took her small pad of paper from her jacket pocket, uncapping her fine-tipped pen. The professor had information. Heat would bet her life on it.

"I'll cut right to the chase," Daily said after she'd perched on the side of her desk to face them. "I was Chloe's academic advisor. We met once or twice a month. Sometimes more, sometimes less. Lately less."

"Why less?" Rook asked.

"She was busy. A lot of kids plan their last semester so it's a light load, but not Chloe. She was a remarkable girl. Bright. Dedicated. Incredibly conscientious. She was in one of my advanced photojournalism courses, had an upper-division international journalism class, and two independent study courses. I was her advisor for those."

Heat made notes of everything Professor Daily was saying. "Do you know what she was working on?" she asked. Maybe the woman had information that could help them corroborate the secret society theory.

But the professor shook her head. "As I said, she was busy. I, of course, am always busy, too. When we met, it was usually just for me to ask her about her progress, to see if she had any questions or needed guidance, which she rarely did, and to review her photographs."

Heat zeroed in on one word. "You said rarely. She did need help at some point?"

At this Daily nodded. "I don't know if it will help, but that's why I wanted to speak with you. She came to me about a month ago. She was going through an insecure moment, something quite unusual for her. She sat right there," she said, indicating the chair Heat sat in, "and she cried. Students cry in here all the time. Far too often for my taste, in fact. We have a generation of young people who do not know how to cope with stress or failure because they've been coddled their whole lives. But that was the first and only time I'd seen that side of Chloe. She was tough."

"What had her so upset?" Rook asked.

"She wouldn't tell me much, only that she was in the middle of what could be a big story and she was afraid she was in too deep."

Heat opened her mouth to speak, but Daily interrupted her. "Before you ask if I tried to find out what she was talking about, I did. She wouldn't give me anything."

Maybe Chloe had been afraid of getting her professor involved in something she felt had become dangerous. She asked the next obvious question anyway. "Why'd did she come to you, if not to get your advice?"

"Believe me, I've given that a lot of thought. If I'd gotten her to share, could I have stopped her death?" She frowned, her chin disappearing into a series of folds. "What I've realized is that she didn't actually want help. She just needed to get her tears out, pull herself up by her bootstraps, so to speak, and forge on. When I think back on that meeting, I see that she was convincing herself to keep at it. I've lost sleep over this. Are we doing enough to intervene when we have a student who is genuinely on a cliff? It's been a topic of discussion in our department and at the university. With suicide rates of college students at an all-time high, it's obvious we're not doing enough—"

"Chloe didn't commit suicide," Heat said, redirecting the conversation back to their case.

"True. But she was heading into dangerous territory. It's one thing for students to break down because they've been taught they can put in little effort and still succeed, or that they can get redo after redo after redo without consequence. It's quite another for a student to feel as if she's taken her commitment to a project so far that she's in some sort of trouble she's unable to handle."

Rook shifted in his chair. "Without knowing what Chloe was investigating, we're circling around the landing strip."

Professor Daily maneuvered her ample body off the edge of the desk and went to one of the two tall filing cabinets along one of the side walls. She riffled through the middle drawer, withdrawing a folder. "This is Chloe's," she said, returning to her previous position on the desk.

Heat and Rook shared a glance, hopeful that this could help flesh out their secret society theory.

"I saw her last week," Professor Daily said. "These were her latest photos. I hadn't critiqued them yet."

"Photos of . . . ?" Heat asked.

"Buildings, mostly," she said. "They supported the article she was working on."

Daily handed the folder over. Rook moved his chair closer to Heat's so they could look together. Inside the file was a series of pictures. They went through them one by one, studying each for some clue as to location. "This was taken right here on campus," Rook said, pointing to the fourth photo. "That's the building being renovated, if I'm not mistaken."

Professor Daily took the picture back, then picked up a small object from her desk. Heat recognized it as a loupe, a powerful magnifier used to view photo proofs and slides. She held it to one eye and examined the pictures.

"I believe you are correct. See that?" She pointed to the front entrance. Barely visible on the left side of the picture, hidden behind a shrub, was the name of the building. Only parts of some of the letters were visible.

Rook peered through the loupe, then looked up triumphantly. "That is clearly a Z there between the leaves. There is only one hall on campus that begins with a Z."

"Zabro Hall," Professor Daily said.

"Zabro Hall," Rook agreed.

They looked through the other twenty-seven photos. There were more outside the same building, and a series inside. Several focused on a particular area of an interior hallway.

There was only one logical conclusion Heat could draw from Chloe's photographs: this building had something to do with what she was investigating. "Can we take these with us?" she asked the professor.

"Absolutely. It won't bring her back, but I hope you figure out what happened to her."

Outside, Heat and Rook looked at each other, each thinking the same thing. Professor Daily may have just given them the vital clue that would break open the case and help them solve it. Without needing to say a word, they turned on their heels and headed for Zabro Hall.

# TWENTY-ONE

Heat and Rook stood shoulder to shoulder outside the cordoned-off building they'd passed several times during the brief time Heat had been on campus at Cambria. It had seemed like any other building under construction before, but now it felt ominous. It could very well hold the answers they sought.

Rook had one arm folded across his chest. The other was crooked at the elbow. He stroked his chin as he stared at the building. "So we've come full circle."

Footsteps sounded behind them, followed by a familiar voice. "Ah, but this time you have help."

Rook turned his head and his eyes widened at the sight of Miguel Ochoa and Sean Raley. "Roach!"

Heat stared. "What are you boys doing here?"

Ochoa grinned. "We solved the case, had a day off, and decided we couldn't leave our man Rook stranded without us."

Rook put his palm flat on his chest. "You came up here for me? Admit it, guys, you love me."

"I admit that I loved those barbecue ribs you grilled that one time," Ochoa said.

"When was that?"

"Last Father's Day. Remember? All of us. No kids. So you thought—"

Rook chuckled, interrupting. "That's right. I thought it would be fun to have a non–Father's Day day. Knowing that it was a memorable experience for you, Miguel, well, that just warms my heart."

"You need to just take the love where you can get it," Ochoa said. "In your case, it's the baby back ribs."

Raley looked up at the sky, considering. "I don't know. I think I'm partial to the quiche Lorraine you made on Mother's Day."

Ochoa backhanded him on the shoulder. "Man, what is wrong with you?"

Raley took a step back. "What was that for?"

"I'll tell you what it was for," Ochoa said. The intensity of his opinion didn't vary based on subject. He was as indignant about quiche versus ribs as he was about meeting the parents of a woman he was casually dating. "Only you, Raley, would choose *eggs* over *barbecue*."

Ochoa had baited his partner, and Raley bit. "Only *me*? What's that supposed to mean?"

"That quiche has stripped you of a man card," Ochoa said, dead serious.

But Raley wasn't done. "If I lost a man card over liking Rook's quiche, how many man cards did Rook lose for *making* the quiche in the first place, huh?"

Rook stared slack-jawed at Raley. "Hey, why are you throwing me under the bus?"

"Sorry, Rook." Raley glared daggers at Ochoa. "Collateral damage. Sometimes my partner just pushes my buttons the wrong way."

Before anyone else could make another retort, Heat stepped in. "As fascinating as this debate is, could you fill me in on Joon Chin? You got a solve?"

Roach spoke in unison. "We did."

"You were right, Cap. 'Coffee' does not always mean coffee."

"In this case, it means cheating. Our vic was in it thick . . ."

"What does that mean?" Rook asked.

Ochoa chuckled. "Rales, get a load of that. The man with a brain like a sponge doesn't know the meaning of cheating."

Rook smirked. "I know what cheating is, funnyman."

Heat put a stop to their ribbing by turning to the most mature of the men. "Rales, tell me."

"Sure thing, Cap. Joon Chin was part of a group of college kids who wrote essays for their classmates. His work was in high demand. According to one of his fellow 'cheaters,' he was tired of splitting his earnings. He wanted to eliminate the middleman, so he went out on his own and formed 'Coffee Night.'"

"A euphemism for meeting with a client, I presume," Rook said.

Ochoa tapped a finger to his nose. "You've redeemed yourself, Holmes."

Rook dipped his head, looking far too satisfied.

"What else?" Heat asked.

Raley continued his narrative. "Coffee Night was quite lucrative. Chin expanded by hiring on some of his former fellow 'cheaters.' The founders of the original cheating ring were a little pissed about that."

Heat drew the logical conclusion. "You're saying Joon Chin was killed over cheating?"

"That he was," Raley confirmed. "The killers lifted him onto that sculpture to send a message. They didn't want any other defectors from the original cheating ring."

"Great work, guys," Heat said.

"Couldn't have gotten there without the coffee clue," Ochoa said, giving credit where credit was due.

Heat explained to Roach what they knew about the Chloe Masterson murder and what had led them to this moment.

Raley gave a low whistle, while Ochoa muttered, "Whoa. That's a trip."

"A long strange trip," Rook said, channeling Jerry Garcia.

Heat was growing impatient. She wanted a solve on this case, too. "Let's get moving, shall we? I'd really like to go home." She looked pointedly at Rook. "And by home, I mean Manhattan."

Rook pressed his palms together, steepling his index fingers and pointing toward the building. "Then let's do this," he said.

Heat, Ochoa, and Raley followed him up the walkway. The odds of getting in easily were slim, but they thought they'd try the front door first. As Heat had anticipated, though, it was locked. "Plan B," she said, leading them over a sagging strand of construction tape strung between sawhorses and around the building. They walked all the way around before finding a haphazardly boarded-up window to try to jimmy open.

Rook peered through the glass and immediately crooned a line from an old Beatles song: " '*She came in through the bathroom window.'* " He followed it up with a second line sung in the same melody: *"Does anybody have a crowbar?"*

"Oh yeah, I just happen to have one right here in my pocket," Ochoa said, and then he laughed. "Oh, wait, that's not a crowbar."

Heat rolled her eyes. She might be their captain, but to Miguel and Sean, she was also one of the guys. No need for them to censor what they said for her delicate ears. "Nice," she said.

Ochoa grinned. "I know, right?"

"I'm sure your, uh, *crowbar* is quite impressive; however, it won't open a window. Scour the grounds, boys. We need to get inside this building."

"Did anybody think to ask someone with the university to just let us in?" Raley asked.

"No can do," Heat said. "We know that Chloe's father is part of the Freemasons. Rook told me about how Yale's Skull and Bones is possibly a pipeline to the CIA org. What if Cam U's Tektōn society is a pipeline to the Freemasons? But *not* the Freemasons."

They all stared at her, but Rook spoke for them. "You lost me."

She looked at Rook specifically. "Remember the pad in Chloe's nightstand? The one with those random sketches?"

"Sure I do. Eyes and feathers and shapes."

"Here's what I'm thinking. She suddenly struck up a relationship with her father, who happens to be a Freemason. She found evidence of Cam U's Tektōn order. She was afraid about something, and wanted to share her findings with you, Rook, because you're a known conspiracy theorist. She wanted to know if any of your old notes could corroborate what she'd discovered, or thought she'd discovered."

"One problem," Rook said, playing devil's advocate. "The Freemasons are not a secret group, nor are they into clandestine activities that are less than aboveboard."

"Are you one hundred percent sure about that?" she asked. One thing she'd learned in the past few hours was that there were hidden levels of every organization. Even the handshake shared between Raymond Lamont and Kaden Saunders hinted at something deeper than an ordinary friendship. It was probably something going back to their college days together.

Rook had to answer honestly. "No, not irrefutably."

Ochoa cleared his throat. "So what you're saying is that this college has a secret organization that has some double secret pipeline to the Masons, which has some double secret level that is a pipeline to something else, did I get that right?"

"Sounds far-fetched, I know," said Heat. It did to her, too, listening to Ochoa summarize it so succinctly. "It's all we have to go on at the moment, though. Now let's figure out how we can get inside this building."

"Spread out," Raley said. "Let's scour the area. There's got to be something we can use to pry the wood off with."

Roach went in one direction, while Heat and Rook headed in the other. "Nothing in the trunk of the car?" she asked him.

"My car at home, yes. My rental car here? No."

They circled around the building, intercepting Roach at the front door. Heat saw they were empty-handed, but she asked nonetheless. "Anything?"

They both spread their arms. "Nada," Ochoa said.

They scattered again, eyes on the ground, in case they'd missed something. They hadn't. Ochoa and Raley joined her in front of the building again. Somehow she'd lost Rook along the way. She cupped her hand over her eyes, turning as she scanned the college grounds around the unused building. As she came full circle, facing the front entrance again, she stopped short. There, standing at the threshold, was her husband.

"Would you all like to come inside?" He swung the door open wider and gestured for them to enter.

"How'd you get in there?" Ochoa asked, eyes narrowed.

Rook's eyes danced. "When it became clear that we weren't going to find a tool lying around that can pry plywood from a window, I started trying all the windows again. You know, just in case we missed one."

Raley nodded approvingly. "And you found one that was unlocked?"

"Not exactly," Rook said. "I did, however, find one with a loose pane of glass. I barely touched it, and *kabam!* It fairly shattered at the gentle touch of my fingertips."

"Kabam?" Ochoa repeated.

Raley raised a brow. "It 'fairly shattered'?"

Heat kept quiet. She'd been on the receiving end of his gentle fingertips and knew firsthand just how shattering they could be.

She led the way, skirting past Rook. Roach followed, and behind them, Rook closed the door. "Okay, guys. Let's fan out."

"What exactly are we looking for?" Raley asked.

"A concealed space," Rook said, nodding knowingly.

"In fact, a lair. A place not easily found. Hidden from sight. A—"

Heat held her hand out to stop him. "We get it, Rook. It's a secret room."

"Well, fine, if you want to call it something as mundane as that."

"So it's a place where people get together and do hush-hush things?" Raley asked.

"Exactly," Rook said.

"Sounds exactly like a secret room to me," Ochoa said.

Heat clapped her hands. Instantly, they stopped their banter. "If you're done, let's find the secret, confidential, hush-hush lair, okay?"

"Aye, aye, Cap," Ochoa said.

Before they scattered, she held up her phone with the picture she'd taken of a page from Chloe's notebook. On it was what she now thought was a symbol of the Tektōn society: a triangle with the letter T inside of it. "Look for this, too," she said, and once again, they fanned out in search of a way in.

"Hey! Hey, guys, I found it!" Rook's voice bellowed through the ground floor of the vacant building.

Heat tried to pinpoint the direction of Rook's voice. She thought it had come from her left. She headed in that direction, calling to Rook as she walked. "Where are you?"

"The two hundred hallway. All the way at the end."

"One hundred hallway right here," Raley called. His footsteps grew louder as he came back toward her.

"I got three hundred," Ochoa called.

Heat could clearly hear where they were coming from. She started for one of the two remaining hallways. Just as she read 200 on a placard at the entrance to the corridor, Rook called to them again. "Are you coming, or am I on this adventure by myself? I will say, it's very dark down in the depths of hell."

Ochoa looked at Raley. "He doesn't have a clue about what he's saying, does he?"

"Not a one."

"We gotcha," Heat said, walking down the two hundred hallway, Roach by her side.

But they didn't actually have him. Or know where he was. The end of the two hundred hallway was empty. Rook was nowhere in sight. Display cases were mounted to the walls, all of them currently empty and covered with a thick layer of dust. Doors to offices or classrooms lined each side of the corridor. They tried each door they passed. Every one of them was locked.

"Where is he?" Raley turned around. "Dude, where are you?"

"He's a ghost," Ochoa said.

"No, not a ghost." Rook's voice drifted to them, but he was still hidden from sight. "Although now that you mention it, I kind of feel like a being from the shadowlands."

Heat spun around one more time, her irritation mounting. "Dammit, Rook. Where are you?"

Ochoa joined in. "Bro. Seriously. Show yourself."

The three of them stood in a circle, back to back to back. Heat wanted to count to three, as if she needed the leverage to coerce a rascally child to cooperate. But Rook was an adult—and far more mischievous than any kids she'd ever met. Which, granted, were not many. Her niece, but she was perfect and didn't require any extra supervision.

Just when Heat was about to put her foot down and shout out that he had better show himself, and right now, the display case at the end of the corridor suddenly opened outward. Out stepped Rook, arms spread wide. He stayed frozen in place like that, a goofy smile on his face. He was waiting for their reaction, Heat knew. She was thrilled that he might have found what they were looking for, but her aggravation trumped her curiosity.

It was like a game of chicken: Roach and Heat against Rook. Finally, Rook caved. He dropped his chin to his chest, heaving a sigh. "All right, all right. I get it. But look, it's a hidden door."

"I can see that." Heat came up to him, scanning the doorframe and the backside of the built-in shelving unit. There were no obvious clues to suggest that it doubled as a door. She really did have to give Rook credit for the discovery. "I give. How did you find it?"

He perked up again. "I thought you'd never ask."

Heat stepped back so Rook could close the secret door. It clicked into place. This time, she ran her hand up one side of the shelving, across the top, and down the other side. There were no levers. No obvious means of detecting that it was a door or how to open it.

"It's very well done, but I once wrote an article on the history of magic. I came across quite a bit of information on secret passageways. You might be surprised to learn that they were a fairly common occurrence in houses of old. They led to hideaways. Think Prohibition and speakeasies, illegal gambling dens, and the like. Of course I put two and two together. Magic and secret door. I realized that there didn't seem to be a basement floor—"

"Right, no stairwell or elevator leading down," Ochoa said.

Rook snapped his fingers and pointed at him. "Exactly. If there was a secret door, it would lead to a basement, and if there was a secret lever to open said door, it might come in the form of the triangle T symbol."

"Is there one?" Heat asked, impressed by his discovery, despite the dramatic flair. He came by his histrionics honestly. His mother had taught him well.

Ochoa was running his hand around the perimeter of the display case just as Heat had. "I give. How do you open this bad boy?" he asked once he came up empty.

"Allow me." Rook walked past the next door and crouched at an old-fashioned ventilation grate in the floor. He pried it off and plunged his hand into the darkness. Heat heard a click and, voilà, the locking mechanism released. Still holding the grate, he returned to them triumphantly. "The symbol," he said, showing them the faint image of the T in the triangle pressed into one corner of the metal.

"Impressive," Raley said.

"Yeah, nice work." This time Ochoa clapped Rook on the shoulder. "Your neediness comes in handy now and then."

"Try 'comes in handy all the time,'" Rook said.

Roach gave him no reaction.

Heat turned to the dark entrance in front of her. The smell of dank soot hit her first. It was thick and heavy, like the remains of a massive bonfire after a warm drizzle. The cool air coming up from the insulated basement hit her next. She peered into the darkness, stifling the shudder working its way up her spine. She felt as if she were in a bad horror flick where the heroine has the choice to proceed into obvious danger or retreat to safety. The heroine, of course, in a too-dumb-to-live move, goes right into the lion's den.

At the moment, she felt like that B-movie character, ready to descend into unknown depths where, like in *Raiders of the Lost Ark*, they might come across a room full of decades-old skeletons. Or worse, a pit of spiders.

Rook took hold of her arm so she couldn't go any farther. "Be careful. There is a flight of stairs, and they seem pretty steep."

She tamped down her runaway thoughts. Rook was the one with the active imagination, not her. She was the sane, sensible one. But right that second, their roles had reversed. She put her palm against the cool stone wall and took a deep breath, forcing her mind back to Chloe Masterson. She pulled up the images of the photographs they'd gotten from Professor Daily. Heat had snapped pictures of each one with her cell phone. Skimming through them now, she came to the one she wanted. It was a photo of a dark open doorway with a glimpse of stairs leading downward. "She was here. Chloe was exactly where we are right now, only she was alone."

"Maybe she wasn't alone," Rook said. "What if the killer was with her?"

There were two reasons Chloe might have been with someone. Heat voiced them aloud. "Either she thought she could trust the person, or she knew she was with a killer but thought she could protect herself. Either way, she walked down into the depths of hell and to her own death."

That was a sobering thought. The four of them stood in silence for a moment. Nikki had seen the lifeblood drain out of a person. One second they were alive, the next they were a shell, all semblance of the person they'd been completely gone. She'd seen it happen with her own mother, or at least she thought she did at the time. It was that personal experience that drove her to take a moment to honor each victim. Working through the scene of an actual murder and replaying it in her mind made it real. She could see Chloe in her mind's eye, standing in awe at the threshold of the secret passageway, her killer perhaps by her side, ushering her down. Cautioning her to be careful. Maybe even guiding her with a hand on her lower back.

"Let's have some light," she said, needing to move on to the next part of Chloe's actions.

At the same moment, as if it had been choreographed, Ochoa and Raley took out their cell phones and turned on their flashlights, aiming them down into the depths below. It smelled stale. Dungeon-like. Not a place Heat would choose to go alone. But Chloe had—maybe.

Roach took the lead, aiming their flashlights on the crumbling stone steps. Rook brought up the rear. They all walked carefully, testing each step before putting their full weight down.

"There must be another way in." Rook's voice echoed against the stone walls. "There is no way the members of Tektōn traverse this stairway to secret meetings together."

Heat had to agree. This didn't strike her as a regularly used meeting place. "But Chloe was here. I can feel it."

"Since when do you act on a feeling, Heat?"

In front of her, Roach mumbled their agreement. They were right. Heat looked at the clues and broke down the evidence into facts. Rook, on the other hand, acted on gut and instinct. He provided the story. They balanced each other out, but right now that balance was skewed.

She didn't have to answer Rook's question, because they had reached the bottom of the stairway. Ochoa and Raley shone their flashlights into the dark room and stopped in their tracks. Heat and Rook flanked them on either side.

The walls were rough stone, the ground packed dirt. There were no windows. No natural light filtered in. The single room was simply dank and dark.

Rook gave a low whistle. "This is a bona fide dungeon if I've ever seen one."

Ochoa arched a brow skeptically. "Have you actually seen one, bro?"

"I have, actually. I did a story once on torture devices in seventeenth-cent—"

Ochoa put his palm out. "Forget I asked."

Raley shook his head. "Why'd you go there, man?"

"Momentary lapse."

Rook's face fell, but Heat stepped in to put a stop to their squabbling. "Focus, guys. Let's take a look around."

They split up. Roach started around the perimeter of the room from the left. Heat and Rook both took out their own cell phones, turned on their flashlights, and took the right side. She kept hers directed at ground level, while he shone his on the wall and ceiling. They moved slowly, taking in every square inch. A few minutes later, Raley's voice sliced through the room. "I think we got something."

Heat and Rook were by his side in an instant, all of their lights shining on the wall. "It's a loose stone," Raley said. "And look. The symbol."

The stone wobbled under his hand as he pressed it, but he couldn't immediately dislodge it. Rook stepped up to it, running his fingers around the edges. "Fascinating. I bet this is how messages were left. A secret way to correspond."

It was a good theory. Raley touched the edges again until he found a groove. He gripped it with his fingers and, after a minute, he managed to pry the stone from its housing.

They four of them shone their light into the exposed crevice. There, shoved into the back of the space, was a slip of white paper.

Heat tugged on one of the nitrile gloves she always had with her, stuck her hand into the open space, and pulled out the paper. The three men gathered close around her as she unfolded it.

*Darkness falls*
*To the night we come*
*The bird sings*
*The forest beckons*
*And to the end of the game*
*We go*

"It's like a message in a bottle, but better," Rook said, unable to keep the excitement from his voice.

"It's like a movie," Ochoa said. "Secret messages behind a rock in a hidden dungeon? Who does this?"

Rook looked as happy as a pig in a mud pit. "It's a *poem* in the *wall*. It's like the *Dead Poets Society*. It's a clue, people. And we get to decipher it."

# TWENTY-TWO

R oach had left Cambria late the night before, and Heat and Rook had pushed the case aside for a raucous tumble between the sheets. They'd needed to forget for a little while, and that had done the trick.

The next morning, she stared at the murder board, back on the case. Lines crisscrossed down from Chloe's photo to the different things they'd learned. A photo of Chloe's long-lost biological father, Christian Foti, was on one side. Her roommate, Tammy, was on the other.

Heat and Rook had made a connection between the article Chloe had been researching and Cambria U's secret society, Tektōn. From there, they'd formed a tenuous connection to the Freemasons. Chloe's own photographs had led them to Zabro Hall on campus, and to the hidden room.

And to the message in the wall.

*Darkness falls*
*To the night we come*
*The bird sings*
*The forest beckons*

*And to the end of the game*
*We go*

Heat had taken pains to write it exactly as it had been put down on the paper, and had used a magnet to hold the original at the top right corner of the board. She'd told Ian about it, but was holding off turning it in as evidence. After staring at it until the letters blurred together into one mass, she wrote the words again, this time on a blank page of a notebook.

When she'd been a theater major in college, before the switch to criminal justice, she'd been exposed to plenty of literature along the way. She tried to pull hidden meaning from the lines of the poem, but was drawing a blank. "Darkness falls" could be interpreted in a few different ways: It was nighttime. The sun set. There were no stars in the sky. But these were all literal translations. What could the subtext be? *Was* there subtext?

*To the night we come?* Who was "we"? The night wasn't an actual place, so where were they going?

She moved on to the next line. Who was the bird? Could the bird be a person? She pondered this before realizing the meaning. "Chloe!" she said aloud. "The bird could be Chloe."

With his typically perfect timing, Rook walked in at just that moment. "The bird could be Chloe?"

It was a far cry from solving the murder, but if she was right, then they could at least connect the poem to the victim. It would validate that they were on the right path. "I'm trying to decipher the poem. To look for hidden meaning."

Rook beamed. "I'm so proud. My sweet little analytical

Nikki Heat, delving into the abstract world of words."

"Trying," she corrected. "And not doing a bang-up job at the moment."

"What have you got so far?"

"Just that Chloe could be the bird."

He raised his eyebrows. "That's it, huh?"

"I gave up on the first two lines."

He sat down next to her on the edge of the bed, reading aloud from the page on her lap. "'It was nighttime. The sun set. There were no stars in the sky.' All of that is fairly obvious, don't you think?"

She bristled, embarrassed at her amateur poetry analysis. "No, I don't, which is why I moved on to the bird."

He studied the poem on her paper for a moment before standing and moving to the murder board. He withdrew one of his special Blackwing 602 pencils from the inside pocket of his tweed blazer, using it to point to the poem she'd written there. "Here's what I think. Are you ready?"

She slid to the very edge of the bed, forearms on her knees. "I am more than ready."

His expression instantly shifted from professorial to flirtatious. "Why, Detective Heat, I didn't think you were—"

She didn't let him finish. "I'm not. Carry on, Professor."

He nodded, but gave her a stern look. "Very well, but we will come back to this discussion at a later date."

She had no doubt. "Great. Now, what's your take on the poem?"

He used the black eraser of the pencil to point to the first line. "'Darkness falls' is clearly a metaphor for the fact that the jig is up. If we assume, as you suggest, that the bird is, in fact, Chloe, then we can make a connection that it is because of the bird that darkness has fallen. 'To the night we come,' therefore, would symbolize the fact that whoever the bad guys are, they are backed up against a wall. They must take action."

As Rook jotted down his analysis, Nikki stared at her husband, rethinking her refusal of his sexual innuendos just moments before. "I have never been more turned on than I am right now."

Rook's shoulders inched back as his spine straightened. He preened like a peacock. "Well, then, let me continue."

She tossed the notepad aside, crossed her legs, and leaned forward. "Please do."

" 'The forest.' That symbolizes something, but at this point, I'm not quite sure what, so I'll come back to that." He slid the pencil behind his ear, trading it for an Expo marker and circling the word.

" 'And to the end of the game we go'?" she prompted.

"This can only mean one thing, my dear wife. This is the call for Chloe's death. They must eliminate the problem, and the problem is the bird. If Chloe is the bird, then she would be represented by something lovely. A bluebird, or a swallow, or a dove. These birds do not live in a dark and threatening environment. So the end of the game can only mean the end of Chloe. In the forest—the dark place where the murder took place—they will kill her."

"They *did* kill her," Nikki corrected.

Rook finished noting the interpretation of the poem on the whiteboard before capping the pen and sitting next to her again. "They did."

A moment of silence passed between them, and then they both sat up just a little straighter, looked at each other, and said, "They."

"They . . . as in the organization, not a person," Nikki said. "It wasn't just one person who killed her."

"Well, it might have been one person's act, but it was orchestrated by the group. Whoever is in charge wrote the poem. It's the battle cry."

"For Tektōn to act? Or . . ."

They looked intensely at one another. "Freemasons," they said in unison.

Nikki thought through the direction the poem had taken her, and then worked backward. She focused her attention on Christian Foti's picture. "Do you remember what Chloe's father said when Ian asked him about Chloe's childhood?"

"Sure," Rook said. "He saw her for a while. That he was a weekend dad. And that he eventually stopped coming around."

"Right. Because he moved back home and went to college." Nikki started to form a connection. "Home to Cambria. And to college at Cambria U."

"He could very well have been a member of Tektōn when he was in school here," Rook said.

Nikki got stuck again. "So let's assume he was. How does that factor into his daughter's death?"

They pondered this for a minute.

"Things didn't work out like I planned," Rook said quietly. And then louder. "Things didn't work out like I planned."

She'd heard that before. Recently. But where? And then it came to her. "That's what Foti said to us about his family."

Rook uncapped the marker and started writing.

TEKTŌN SCHOOL SOCIETY ➞ PIPELINE TO
SOMETHING ELSE
THROUGH THE MASONS?

DID CHLOE DISCOVER THE CONNECTION, AND IS THAT
WHY SHE REUNITED WITH HER FATHER? HOW DEEP IN IS
FOTI? WHAT DIDN'T WORK OUT THE WAY HE'D PLANNED?

Rook turned to face Heat. "What if he wasn't referring to how he ran out on his kids?" He tapped the pen against the photograph again. "What if he was actually *involved* in his daughter's death?"

Nikki knew better than to stop Rook from concocting a story. He saw things in a way that she didn't. "Go on."

He put the marker down, then shoved his hands in his pockets. "What if he didn't intend for her to die . . . or didn't know they were going to kill her?"

"She was the bird, because whatever she discovered needed to be kept secret. They had to stop her from singing, so to speak."

"She was acting on her own, investigating a story she didn't want the *Journal* to run," Rook said.

There was only one logical reason why that would be. "Just like when your old story was killed, someone on the *Journal* must be in Tektōn."

"Michael Warton," they said together.

She continued the line of thinking. "Michael kills the story, but she doesn't want to stop. Why?"

"Because through her father, she figured out it was more than just at the university level."

"So she kept digging," Heat continued, "but her reunion with her dad and her questions gave her away."

"Why keep digging?" Rook asked.

It was rhetorical, but Heat answered anyway. "She may have harbored resentment against her father because he'd left them."

"Good thought, good thought. And maybe," Rook said. "But in my experience, investigative reporters follow the story because they feel it. They know, or at least hope, it's going to reveal something and they'll be the ones to break it. They might get involved initially because of curiosity or some personal reason, but it's the potential of uncovering something big that drives them to continue. It's Watergate. It's Al Capone's vault."

"It's the exposé," Heat said, recalling what Jada had told them. Nikki got up from the bed and stood in front of the murder board again. *Something sinister,* she thought. "What would be threatening enough that they'd want Chloe silenced?"

She went back to what Foti had said. *Things didn't work out the way I'd planned.* Nikki pointed to the poem. "Let's get back to this. If Chloe is the bird, and the darkness is the fact that she discovered something that someone—possibly some faction of the Freemasons—wanted silenced, they were the ones to kill her. Whatever or wherever the forest is, they got to the end of the game with Chloe."

"If things didn't turn out how her father had planned," Rook said, "then he knows what happened."

# TWENTY-THREE

A quick search on the Internet provided Nikki and Rook with Christian Foti's address. If he wasn't there, they'd try the Masonic Lodge again.

Turns out they didn't have to go far. Foti lived in a boxy duplex across town from the university. They knocked three times before he finally answered the door, looking more haggard and forlorn than he had the last time they'd seen him. His skin had turned pasty, made paler by the dulled color of his hair and tired eyes. He looked like he'd aged ten years. Maybe more.

"Mr. Foti," Nikki said as she flashed her badge. "We have a few more questions. Can we come in?"

As Foti bent to take a closer look at the badge, he stumbled. Rook caught him by one arm while Nikki grabbed the other. She made the mistake of inhaling, recoiling at the smell of sour alcohol on his breath. Her best guess? Foti had been numbing his pain with Jack Daniels.

"Let's get you inside," Rook said, guiding him into the house.

Foti shook himself free and wobbled over to the brown corduroy couch, collapsing onto his back. He flung his arm over his eyes. The dark lines of a tattoo peeked out from beneath his sleeve. "I don wanna talk," he mumbled.

*Drunk as a skunk,* Rook mouthed.

Nikki sat on the coffee table opposite Foti. "We'll be out of your hair just as soon as you give us a little help."

He didn't move. If it hadn't been for the shallow rise and fall of his partially exposed stomach, she might have wondered if the man was alive. "Mr. Foti?" she said.

"She shoulda stopped," he finally said.

It was the opening Nikki needed. "But it was a good story."

"No, no, no. It was a *dangerous* story," he slurred. "Not a *good* one." His back curved as he propped his elbows on his quivery legs. "Why didn't she stop?" His voice rose with agitation. "I told her to. She just needed to stop."

Front and center in Nikki's mind was Foti saying that things hadn't turned out the way they'd planned. "Did you know what would happen if Chloe didn't stop?"

Foti's mouth moved as he spoke, his lips pulled back to bare his teeth, but he kept his eyes covered. "I told her to stop, but she didn't listen." He began moving his head back and forth as if he were trying to shake out a bad nightmare, and then added, "Of course, why would she?"

"Why wouldn't she?" Rook asked.

Foti scoffed, saliva pooling in one corner of his mouth. "I wasn't there for her when she was little, so why would she listen to me now?"

Nikki answered his question with one of her own. "Who wanted her to stop?"

He was too inebriated to follow along with them. "The story, it wasn't worth it."

"To a reporter, the story can be everything. Chloe must have felt it was a good one if she was willing to put herself at risk." Rook gently nudged Foti's arm until the man's eyes were visible. "Let us tell you what we know, okay? And then maybe you can fill in some of the blanks."

Foti heaved himself to a sitting position, sinking into the worn back pillows of the sofa. "The only thing you need to know is who killed my daughter."

"You mean we need to figure out who killed her," Nikki corrected.

But Christian Foti shook his head. "I mean you need to know who killed her. I'm going to tell you."

Rook and Nikki stared at him. "Are you saying you know who killed Chloe?" Rook asked.

His head wobbled as he nodded, but he managed to look at them straight on. "I killed her."

Nikki's spine stiffened. "Mr. Foti," she said slowly, "are you confessing to the murder of your daughter, Chloe Masterson?"

He pressed the flats of his hands against the sides of his head, as if he could squeeze out the pain he was experiencing. "It's my fault. I told her to stop, but she wouldn't. I *told* her she was going to get herself in too deep. 'You're going to get in too deep,' I told her, 'and then it'll be too late.'"

"Mr. Foti," Nikki said again, "did you kill Chloe Masterson?"

He hung his head, his skin turning red from the pressure of his hands against the sides of his face. "I led her right into the lion's den. It's my fault. I didn't kill her, but I might as well have."

He got up and stumbled to the bedroom, collapsing onto his stomach on the bed.

"Mr. Foti," Heat said from the doorway of the room. "Where was Chloe killed? Who killed her?"

*"Into the woods,"* Foti murmured before he passed out. He wasn't going to give them any more information at that moment.

Rook's face had grown flushed. He debated something silently, then grabbed Nikki's hand and dragged her back outside and to the car. Once he'd closed the door behind her and had slid into the driver's seat, she turned to him. "We need to call the local police."

"Fine, fine," he said, but she could see that he had something else on his mind. She'd seen the look a thousand times before. He was going to construct a narrative, and Nikki was all ears. This was Rook's gift. He could see things that she didn't. Not for lack of effort, but because they viewed life through different lenses.

"Did you notice Foti's tattoo?" he asked her.

"Inside left forearm."

"Very good, Detective Heat. Do you know what the tattoo is?"

"It was mostly hidden under his sleeve, so no." She angled her head at him. "Did you see it?"

"Enough of it," he said. "At first, I saw only the lower two lines, one thick, the other, just above it, thinner. But then his sleeve pulled up, revealing more. It's a triangle," he said triumphantly.

"Like the Tektōn symbol?"

"Yes . . . and no. The shading inside the triangle was

quite dark. While you were pressing him on his *confession*, I managed to get a closer look. I could only see part of it, but I'm sure that inside that triangle is an eye. Chloe had drawn eyes on that pad in her room." He paused for dramatic effect, as he was known to do. "An eye, Heat. A triangle. An eye."

She narrowed her eyes, visualizing it. An eye inside of a triangle. They looked at each other as realization dawned. "The Illuminati," she said.

He nodded. "Exactly. The Illuminati."

# TWENTY-FOUR

The police station was as deserted now as it had been the first time Nikki had visited. Cambria seemed to have a surprisingly low amount of crime happening. They also only seemed to have one other visible officer, the much-put-upon Officer Breckenstein. Nikki asked for Ian, but Breckenstein was stony-faced behind the bulletproof glass. Her chestnut hair was pulled into the same severe bun it had been a few days ago. Her uniform was pressed just as crisply. It felt like *Groundhog Day*.

"Detective Heat. What can I help you with?" she asked. Her voice was as stern as her demeanor, and she did not sound as if she wanted to lift even a single finger for Nikki.

"It's a personal matter," Heat said, annoyed. It was none of Breckenstein's business. She geared up, ready to give a retort that would put the young officer in her place, but Rook flashed one of his signature smiles. "We're helping Chief Cooley look into the murder of Chloe Masterson, Officer."

Heat grumbled under her breath, but she stood back and folded her arms over her chest. She knew her demeanor was tough and unyielding, but it was okay by her. She was done playing games with this rookie. Let Rook play a hand.

The young officer's face softened just a bit with Rook

smiling at her. "That was so sad."

"Yes indeed. Poor girl." He frowned, closing his eyes for a moment as he nodded his sympathy.

Officer Breckenstein slid open the glass divide, eliminating the barrier between her and Rook. Nikki stood back and let Rook work his charm. His winsome personality was a definite asset in his career. It didn't hurt in situations like this, either. The officer responded by leaning into the now open window. "That's what we want to talk to the chief about. Is he in?" Rook asked her.

Heat felt the rookie's hard facade start to crack, but then she caught sight of Nikki again and the air in the room suddenly felt heavy. *It shouldn't be this hard to give a message to the chief,* she thought. She could hold the officer's gaze all day, if necessary, but after another few seconds, the woman broke eye contact. Breckenstein tried to maintain her stern manner, but Heat could see that she was unnerved by the detective's mere presence. It had been a game of chicken that the younger woman had no chance of winning. Nikki was a veteran cop; she knew how to handle people. Identifying their weaknesses and playing to them was one of her strengths. Officer Breckenstein was still green and insecure in her role. Nikki suspected that the young officer didn't usually get any pushback from the citizens of Cambria. She'd been able to use that to her advantage.

Officer Breckenstein averted her gaze from both Heat and Rook and snatched up the wireless phone receiver, aggressively punching in a series of numbers. Her voice wavered slightly as she spoke, a sign of her agitation. Nikki almost felt sorry for her. Almost. She ended the short conversation with a brisk, "Yes, sir," then punched the OFF button on the phone.

Officer Breckenstein glared at Nikki. "He'll be right out," she said, her tone even more clipped than before.

"Great," Nikki said. "We'll just wait over here."

She and Rook stood by the door, awaiting Ian, but Officer Breckenstein kept her eyes on them. "If looks could kill," Rook muttered.

"Right? She's not the most astute police officer. Flies and honey, sweetheart, you attract more flies with honey."

Rook rubbed her shoulder. "Sadly, not everyone has the top-notch brain capacity that you do, Heat. You put most people to shame."

Her lips curved up into a smile. "Why, Jamie, you do know how to get me hot and bothered. Complimenting my intelligence. Brilliant."

He slipped his arm around her and pulled her close. "Brainy and beautiful. It's a winning combination, and you wear it well."

She felt her cheeks flush. She loved Rook more than she ever thought she could love anyone, and he knew just what to say to make her whole body tingle with need. She lightly kissed his lips, but they pulled apart when they heard the click of the door behind them.

Ian Cooley sauntered into the police lobby. "Sorry, am I interrupting?" The sarcasm dripped from his words.

"Not at all, Ian," Nikki replied. She gave Rook's hand a squeeze before letting it go. Right now she was Captain Heat, not the brainy and beautiful wife of Jameson Rook.

Cooley folded his arms and rocked back on his heels.

"Well then, to what do I owe the pleasure so soon after we parted ways?"

What was it with her and choosing men who had a flair for the dramatic?

Apparently he wasn't going to invite them back to his office, so Nikki got right to the point. "We'd like to take a look at Chloe Masterson's notebook. We have a theory, but need to refresh our memories."

"Since you looked at it yesterday?"

She didn't need to actually respond for him to know her answer was yes. "It's a theory, but one worth checking out."

"What kind of theory?"

Nikki scanned the empty room, letting her gaze linger on Officer Breckenstein. "I'd rather not go into it here," she said.

"Come on, then," he said, punching in a code on the security pad next to the door. The lock clicked, they all passed through to the back of the station, and they headed down the hallway to Ian's office.

It was much smaller than Nikki's, but then she was captain of the Twentieth Precinct, not of a small upstate New York college town. It had all the basic elements it needed: a desk and chair, two chairs opposite the desk, and a tall bookshelf. A long table sat flush against the wall behind his desk. It held a compact black printer and various stacks of paper and binders. A computer sat on the desk, and despite an organizational three-tiered tray set, the desk itself was littered with paper.

There was no doubt Cooley was a patriot. A large painting of the American flag hung on the wall above the long table behind his desk. On the left stood a flagpole with another American flag. On the right was a flagpole with the New York State flag. It hung loosely, showing only part of the state's coat of arms. The CEL of the word *Excelsior* was visible, as well as the green of the mountain, the yellow of the sun, and the center of the eagle atop a world globe. Nikki noticed other details, as well: an open case of Mountain Dew; a coatrack draped with a police-issue jacket and a windbreaker; a half-eaten sandwich and a jumbo-sized bag of Doritos, the opening like a gaping black hole. They'd interrupted Ian's lunch, but Nikki didn't care.

Ian gestured to the chairs. "Take a seat."

"Here's the theory," Nikki said after Ian had settled himself in his own chair. She proceeded to tell him about the university's secret society, the fraternal order of the Freemasons, and the possible connection to the Illuminati.

He narrowed his eyes skeptically. "The Illuminati? Are you serious?"

"Dead serious," Rook said, speaking for the first time.

"Because of a tattoo you caught a glimpse of on the victim's father's arm, do I have that right?"

"Ian, don't be an ass," Nikki said.

He leveled his gaze at her. "I didn't think I was. I do think, however, that this theory of yours sounds a little conspiratorial."

"Conspiracy theories are grounded in fact," Rook said. "Most people choose to dismiss them out of hand, but if they would take a closer look and consider the facts, they'd be more open-minded."

"And your mind is open, I take it?" Ian asked Rook.

Whenever he talked conspiracy, Rook got his sharply

angled grin. The sides of his mouth curved up and the center angled down so that his smile looked like a shallow V and his eyes lit up with anticipated excitement. "As a matter of fact, it is. Wide open to the possibilities that things are not always what they seem."

Ian rolled his eyes, obviously not convinced and looking as if he didn't care all that much, to boot. "What else do you have that supports this theory?"

Nikki took over the narrative, telling him about the secret room in Zabro Hall at the university, and about Chloe's notes on the matter. "She was on to something, Ian. She figured it out, and we need to see her notebook. Now that we know the track she was on, we want to look at things through the lens she did."

Ian propped his elbows on his desk, steepling his fingers. He gave a light, scornful laugh. "Secret societies. Really?"

Rook's laugh matched Ian's. "Indeed. Secret societies. They seem to be everywhere. Especially around here."

Nikki breathed a sigh of relief. She remembered something about Ian Cooley in that moment. That sigh. That laugh. It was resignation, of a sort. Right now that meant he was on board with them.

Ian stood. "Wait here," he said. He left the office, returning a few minutes later with Chloe's composition book. He handed it to Nikki without blinking an eye, which gave her pause. Being beholden to Ian for information that was normally at her fingertips at the Two-Oh made her uncomfortable, and she was suddenly skeptical of his ulterior motives. Her work had taught her that people usually put their self-interest first; police officers were no exception.

Rook could hardly contain his eagerness. He scooted his chair closer to hers, waiting for her to crack open the notebook.

"Officer Breckenstein and I spent the afternoon scouring that," Ian said. "We found a few trails to follow, but nothing that panned out. I'm entertaining the idea that the victim's death was not related to any story she was working on. We think there was a boyfriend. It's another avenue to pursue."

He might have avenues, but she and Rook had speedways. Heat knew how to play this game. "We spoke to her roommate, to the editor in chief at the newspaper, to her father. Not one of them has mentioned that she had a boyfriend."

He shrugged. "Could be a friend with benefits, I guess, but we know his name, anyway." He nodded to the comp book in her hand. "Places and times they hooked up. Doodlings. Now we're looking for him."

Heat tried not to begrudge Ian a win. If she'd had more time with the notebook, she'd have made the discovery.

"What *is* his name?" Rook asked.

Ian cleared his throat. "Todd Reynolds."

That name . . . Heat thought back to the photographs in the apartment Chloe and Tammy had shared. One of them featured Tammy's brother. Hadn't she said his name was Todd?

From the way he was biting his lip, stopping himself from bursting out with the information, Rook seemed to have had the same realization. "Half brother?" he whispered to her.

She nodded. It was the logical conclusion.

Ian looked from her to Rook and back. "That name rings a bell, I take it?"

Nikki addressed the question. "It does, actually. You've interviewed the victim's roommate, I assume."

"This may not be Manhattan, but give me some credit, Captain Heat. Officer Breckenstein did the honors." He was more serious now, leaning forward, tamping down his insecurities. "Why?"

"Because her roommate, Tammy Burton, has a brother," Nikki said.

Rook cleared his throat and went in for the kill. "And his name is Todd."

# TWENTY-FIVE

Captain Heat watched Tammy Burton as she led her to the interrogation room. The first time she'd met her, Tammy had had red-rimmed eyes. This time, her eyes were tinged red from anxiety. She had to be wondering why she was at the Cambria police station. She had a very bohemian vibe to her with her gauzy skirt and peasant blouse. Her auburn hair was pulled into a loose bun, strands carelessly cascading around her face.

Heat ushered Tammy to a chair at the table, closing the airlock door to the room behind them. Tammy looked nervously at the rectangular mirror on one wall of the small room. She'd obviously seen enough TV crime shows and movies to know it was a two-way and that someone was behind it, watching everything.

Heat excused herself. She wanted to let Tammy sweat it out for a minute. The more anxious she was, the easier it would be to rattle her and get to the truth.

She entered the small observation room to find Rook standing alone at the window. "Ian's gone?" she asked.

He didn't take his eyes off Tammy, but he answered, "Said he'd be back in a few. You're letting her stew. Good plan. It'll make it easier to break her, if, that is, there's something *to* break."

She and Rook had been partners for so long now that he knew her moves and motives. They stood side by side, observing Tammy Burton. Heat always focused on the eyes first, the hands second. Tammy twisted hers, then clasped them, bringing them to her nose. She dropped them to the table, and then raised them to tuck loose strands of her hair behind her ears.

"What do you have to be so nervous about?" Heat muttered.

"Looks to me like she has something to hide. But then, in my experience, most people do," Rook said.

She shot him a sideways glance, noting his taut jaw and intense stare. She frowned. He was usually a pillar of optimism. It was one of the things she loved best about him. Seeing murder after murder after murder meant she saw a vast array of darkness in humanity. Rook was the sliver of light that kept her grounded and helped remind her that there was a lot of goodness on the planet. But maybe so many years in her world had begun to snuff out that light. "You're beginning to sound cynical, Rook. That's not like you."

"Not cynical. Realistic." He turned to her. "Come on, Heat. You know what I'm talking about. That's what the job is, right? Someone is murdered, and it's up to us to sift through all the lies and deceit in order to get to the truth. Along the way, almost everyone has something to hide."

"Do you?" she asked him. "Have something to hide?"

"No. I'm an open book, Heat."

"No hidden creases in the binding that I don't know about?"

"You mean like having a former spouse that was heretofore unmentioned?"

"Touché," she said, knowing that if it weren't for the sly rise of one side of his mouth and the twinkle in his eyes, the comment would have had a different connotation.

"So what does Tammy Burton want to keep close to the vest? That's the question that needs answering. Because from her body language, I'd say there is definitely something she doesn't want us to know."

"That her brother had something to do with Chloe's death? That's my first guess." Heat was itching to get started. She left Rook to his musing, returning to the interrogation room. She took the chair opposite Tammy. "Sorry to keep you waiting."

The young woman moved her visibly trembling hands to her lap and out of view. She didn't quite manage to look Nikki in the eyes, and her voice quavered. "What am I doing here? I told you everything I know."

"Did you?" Heat had brought her notebook with her. She flipped it open and consulted it. "Because looking back on our chat, you didn't mention anything about the fact that Chloe was dating your brother."

The statement was a heavy cloud hovering between them. "They, um, they broke up, so I didn't think it was important."

Heat let that go for a minute. "Tell me about your brother. Or is he a half brother?"

Tammy blew out a breath, no doubt relieved that Heat had changed to a different line of questioning. "Same mom, different dads," she said.

"Right. So your half brother, Todd, was dating your best

friend, Chloe. And Chloe ends up murdered." Heat leaned in, keeping her gaze steady and watching every move— every twitch—that Tammy made. "Why wouldn't you think it was important to share that information? Unless . . . are you protecting him, Tammy? Is that it? Because that I might understand. He is your brother, after all. If I had to choose between my best friend and *my* brother, well . . . blood *is* thicker than water."

Tears pooled in Tammy's eyes. "Todd didn't have anything to do with Chloe's murder. You have to believe me," she pleaded.

Here Nikki shook her head, not giving an inch. "Why should I believe you, Tammy? You already withheld some pretty important information in a murder investigation."

"I'm telling the truth."

Nikki's phone buzzed with an incoming text. She glanced at it, nodded, and then pushed up from the table. "I guess we'll see."

"What do you mean? Where are you going?"

"You are free to go, Ms. Burton." Heat stood at the door, waiting and watching.

Tammy walked out on shaky legs, but she stopped short when she saw Chief Cooley leading a young man down the hallway. Heat acknowledged Ian with a slight nod that said *perfect timing.* With his own perfect timing—or perhaps just a sixth sense whenever Ian was around—the door to the observation room opened and Rook stepped into the hallway.

Tammy spun around to face Heat. "What the hell. What's going on? This is all some game to you, isn't it?"

Rook, hands deep in his pockets, shook his head in utter

seriousness. "Au contraire, Ms. Burton. This is far from a game. Murder is far too serious a business for dalliances."

Tammy puzzled through Rook's response while Ian led Todd Reynolds into the interrogation room Heat and Tammy had just vacated. "Wait!" Tammy rushed forward. "Toddy—"

She stopped abruptly when Ian kicked the door shut an inch from her nose. She spun around again. The trepidation and anxiety they'd witnessed earlier had been replaced with desperation. "You don't seriously think Todd killed Chloe, do you? I'm telling you, he didn't."

"I'm sure Chief Cooley will sort all that out, one way or another," Heat said. The words were encouraging; the tone was not. She wanted to keep Tammy unsteady. Until she knew what Tammy and her brother were hiding, Heat wasn't giving the girl an inch. She walked the girl down the corridor, showing her the way out. Tammy gave one more furtive backward glance at the door her brother was behind, and then she was gone.

Back in the observation room, Rook stood at the window, this time watching Ian and Todd Reynolds. Nikki could hear the textbook questions Ian lobbed at Todd, but the guy seemed to have taken a vow of silence. "He's not giving anything up, huh?" she said, coming up next to Rook just in time to hear Ian's frustrated voice shouting at Todd Reynolds. Todd's voice snapped through the intercom. Even through the glass, Nikki could see the beads of sweat on his forehead. "Do I need a lawyer?"

"That's up to you, Mr. Reynolds. Do you have something to hide?" Ian said, challenging him.

"Honestly, Heat," Rook said. "I'm not sure what you

saw in that guy." He lifted his chin to indicate Ian. "He does *not* have the finesse you do. He's an amateur, and you—you are an artist. You interrogate circles around the chief. You smoke him. Clobber. Destroy. Annihilate—"

"Got it," she said, cutting him off. Inside, she grinned at the compliments from her husband, but outside, she smirked. "Do you think you might be a touch biased, though?"

"I'm a journalist. I can't afford to be biased," he said in all seriousness.

She slid her hand onto his backside, giving a suggestive squeeze. "Really? No bias at all? You sure about that, Mr. Rook?"

"Mmmm." He grinned and waggled his brows. "Well, when you put it that way, Mrs. Rook . . ."

A loud bang rattled the window. Ian had stormed out of the interrogation room. Heat turned to see him standing in the doorway in front of them. "The guy's a brick wall."

Heat disagreed. Todd hadn't opened up to Ian, but maybe he would to her. "Mind if I take a crack at him?"

Ian flourished one arm wide. "If you think you can do better."

Heat shot a glance at Rook before skirting past Ian and going back into the interrogation room. Over the years, she had conducted interviews using a variety of methods. Her approach depended on several factors: the reason for the questions and the time frame they were working with was one. The interviewee's state of mind was another. Heat's level of knowledge going in. While lawyers made a point of asking questions they knew the answers to, cops were seeking information they didn't already have. They needed to lead the interviewee to reveal the very things they wanted so badly to hide.

Sometimes she went in like a bull in a china shop with the sole goal of intimidation. This was the approach Ian had taken with Todd. As Rook had commented, no finesse. It hadn't worked. Chloe's ex-boyfriend was clearly nervous, but he had a tough-guy air about him. Heat had observed Todd enough to know that he wasn't going to give in easily.

Todd was wound tight as a drum after Ian's verbal assault. As Heat entered the room, she could feel the heavy weight of tension in the air. Todd sat up straight, his spine stiffening, his shoulders square. He was not going to take any shit from anyone.

Heat took a completely different approach. She smiled, greeting him in an effort to put him at ease. She slid into the chair opposite him, careful not to cross her arms or ball her fists. Instead, she placed her hands flat on the table. A gesture of openness. "I apologize for my colleague," she said, knowing that an apology on his behalf would infuriate Ian, but also knowing that it was her best chance at breaking down the wall Todd had up around him. It was a classic good cop/bad cop, which was not a game Nikki particularly enjoyed playing.

"He's a real asshole."

Whether or not that was true, Heat wanted to validate his feelings. "Murder in Cambria is pretty rare. The department is using all of its resources to bring a killer to justice. Chief Cooley wants to get to the bottom of it, as you can imagine."

"Yeah? Well, I didn't kill Chloe." He looked up at the two-way mirror and shouted, "Do you hear me? I. Didn't. Kill. Her. I loved her."

"Love is complicated, isn't it, Todd?" Heat's calm voice drew his gaze back to her. "It doesn't always go like we plan, does it?"

Behind the glass, she thought of Ian stewing, imagining that she was talking about their failed marriage, and Rook preening because of the unexpected romance that had burned bright and hot for them.

For the first time since he'd been in the room, Todd hung his head. "She was too busy—too into whatever article she was writing—to be in a relationship. I wanted it more than she did."

"So she broke up with you?"

To her surprise, he shook his head. "No. I called it off. She was the smartest person I ever met, but she couldn't read the signs in a relationship. I couldn't take it anymore."

The challenge of an interview like this one was sifting through the truth, the half-truths, and the lies. Todd hadn't revisited the topic of calling a lawyer. And despite his tough-guy persona, he was cracking. His wall was coming down. If Heat had to lay odds, she'd bet that Todd was being honest with her. "How did she take it?"

He flicked away a single tear that had slipped down his cheek. "I don't think she gave it a second thought."

Unless he was an award-winning actor, Todd had real feelings for Chloe. She gently pushed him for more. "What do you mean?"

"She was an obsessive personality. She lived and breathed whatever story she was working on. She didn't give that same attention to the people in her life."

But she'd been the one to call her father, over and over,

and to foster that relationship. If what Todd was saying was true, that supported the idea that she hadn't been rekindling a relationship with her long-lost father, but had wanted something else from him—something related to her investigation.

Todd went on, unprompted. "I broke up with her. It didn't even faze her."

Heat brought her fingers together on the table. "Mr. Reynolds, we need your help."

He closed his eyes, his chest rising and falling with his shallow breaths. Nikki took a moment to really look at him. Where his half sister had a more rounded chin, Todd's was squared. They shared the cleft chin, although the dimple that bisected Todd's was far more prominent. Like Tammy's, his eyes were a clear brown. They were clearly siblings, with the strongest dominant traits manifested in both of them.

"I'll do anything. What do you need from me?" he said a moment later, looking back up at her.

"Did she talk to you about the story she was currently working on?"

"That's *all* she talked about. She was obsessed."

"Todd, listen." Heat gave him a sincere, imploring look. "We suspect that her pursuit of this story is what killed her. If there's anything you can tell us that might help, we can bring her killer to justice."

He didn't have to think about it before he started talking. "It started with some rituals we both witnessed happening on campus. But here's the thing. They weren't fraternity hazings."

Despite the fact that their conversation was being

recorded, Heat took notes as he talked, interjecting here and there as necessary. "How do you know?"

"Their heads were covered with black hoods. Very cloak-and-dagger, you know? But the other guys—the ones without hoods? They weren't students. They wore suits. One of them had a pretty big book under his arm. And they led the hooded guys to a van. It was weird."

"It sounds it," Heat said. "And Chloe was intrigued by it?"

"That's putting it mildly. I had to stop her from following them."

"Where was this?" Heat asked.

"I'd just met Chloe at the newspaper office. We were walking back to my car, approaching Zabro Hall. That's when we saw the first man coming out of the front entrance—"

Heat's heartbeat ratcheted up. It was the building with the secret passageway to the dungeon-like room. "One of the men in the suits?" she asked, her calm demeanor never changing.

"Right. We were far enough away that he couldn't see us, but the lights near the building meant we could see him."

"Go on," she said after making a few notes.

"The building was closed for construction. It still is, actually. So she thought it was unusual that he was there, especially in the evening. I didn't think much of it. I told her it was probably a professor, but, I don't know, she had some kind of sixth sense. I wanted to go to dinner. We started walking again, but that's when the others came out of the building."

"The men in the hoods?" Heat asked, her pen hovering over her notebook.

"Right. There were seven of them. They kind of

stumbled along. Each guy had his hand on the shoulder of the one in front of him. Another man in a suit walked beside them, and the last one brought up the rear. As soon as she saw that, she wouldn't budge."

"And her reporter instincts kicked in," Heat said. It was something she understood. She and Rook were similar in this way. If they saw something unusual, something that piqued their interest, they were both instantly intrigued. Her cop radar went off, while his reporter hat went on.

"Exactly. Why were they there? What were they doing? Where were they going? From the second she saw those guys in hoods, there was no going back for her. And it was the beginning of the end for us."

Todd couldn't tell her much more. Only that the van was large and windowless, white with no lettering or distinguishing marks. "And they were willing participants," he said.

"Why do you say that?" Heat asked.

"They were talking. And laughing."

"Could you hear what they were saying?"

Todd shook his head. "Nah. We were too far away. All I know is that wherever they were going, they were excited."

Heat was fairly certain that what Chloe and Todd had witnessed was the opening stages of initiation into the secret part of the Freemasons that was a pathway to the deeper level. If their conspiracy theory was to be believed, then that meant those college boys were heading into the world of the Illuminati.

# TWENTY-SIX

**H**eat called the Cambria precinct but hung up before she connected with Ian. She and Rook had a lead to pursue. She didn't want to slow down so Ian could catch up. If it came to it, she'd ask for forgiveness later.

The lobby of the hotel had plush oversized chairs gathered in clusters around an enclosed gas fireplace. It looked tempting, but instead she headed straight to the concierge desk.

The concierge, a woman dressed in a crisply pressed white blouse, navy blazer, and matching slacks greeted her with a pleasant "It's a beautiful day! How can I help you?"

Nikki noted the woman's name from the badge clipped to her lapel, then smiled amiably. Daisy Malone. She looked the part of a concierge. Bright and friendly. "I'm new to town and want to look around. Do you by any chance have a map of Cambria?"

"I do, in fact." Daisy turned to a pocket stand against the wall behind her, turning back around with a map in her hand and handing it to Nikki. "This is a map of Cambria proper, as well as some of the surrounding area. There are some lovely sites once you get outside of town. Lake Washington is lovely this time of year. Hamilton National Forest has some very popular trails. And of course there's the river. Too cold for rafting this time of year, but maybe for your next visit. We are lucky, though. The weather couldn't be more perfect."

Daisy was right. The weather hadn't topped seventy-three degrees during the day since Nikki had been there. The sun setting brought it down to the high thirties or low forties, but they weren't experiencing the frigid temperatures they might have been. Nikki took the map and thanked Daisy Malone for her help.

Back in Rook's suite, she opened it up and spread it out on the table, smoothing down the creases. She and Rook spent thirty minutes going over every inch of it, trying to pinpoint where the secret sect of the organization Chloe had uncovered might meet. Zabro Hall, they determined, was merely the site of the initiations, not a location for regular meetings. Nothing jumped out at them.

"What about the forest or woods?" Nikki suggested. "There must be secluded caverns or caves. That would be the perfect spot for clandestine meetings."

Rook hemmed and hawed. "I don't think we can take Foti literally. If Chloe was a bird, the forest was a metaphor for someplace else. We have to assume they have fairly regular meetings. A cavern in the forest in the dead of winter, with snow on the ground, would make it highly inconvenient. Same with mud season. Secret meetings mean unobtrusive. Coming home covered in mud would set off a few red flags."

"And in spring and summer, there would be too many people on the trails."

"Exactly."

They alternated staring at the map with staring at the

murder board. After few minutes of thought, she got up, uncapped one of the whiteboard markers, and drew a line through Hamilton National Forest. It had been something to consider, which is why she'd written it, but now it seemed unlikely that the forest was where Tektōn, the Freemasons, or some faction of the Illuminati would meet.

"There's only one place that makes sense," Rook said after another few minutes of contemplation.

"I know," Nikki said.

And then they spoke in unison: "The Masonic Lodge."

"I love it when that happens," Rook said, pulling her to him and planting a kiss on her lips.

"Me too," she said. It showed her how in tune with each other they were.

"I wonder . . ." Rook trailed off, stroking his chin as he pondered whatever thought had drifted into his head.

"What?"

"The entire Freemason membership can't possibly be involved in the Illuminati. Think about Chloe's notes. She drew staircases, remember?"

Nikki could picture the pages in Chloe's notebook. One pages had a staircase going diagonally down the page. Next to it, Chloe had jotted down some notes about what Nikki now knew was Tektōn. On the adjacent page, Chloe had drawn another set of stairs. These she'd shaded and added little lines along the edge like a ruler. Finally, on the following page, she'd drawn a third staircase. She'd doodled all around the pages, most heavily on this third one. Suns, moons, letter Vs, the flag, a pyramid, triangles, circles, and squares. Heat pulled up the pictures of the notebook on her phone, finding the images she wanted to examine. Chloe had drawn a series of geometric shapes with a circle in the center. It was like a clock, with a triangle at twelve o'clock, followed by a square, a pentagon, and a hexagon. At six o'clock was a triangle with curved lines, making it look like a Christmas tree. The next several were stars with different numbers of points. When she'd first taken the photos, Nikki hadn't thought much about the drawings, but now they took on new meaning.

"What if her drawings of the staircases were symbolic? A way for her to make her notes cryptic, yet still convey what she wanted to."

"I don't follow," Rook said.

Nikki held out her phone, scrolling through the pictures. "Look. The first set of stairs she drew had the school's crest, so they must represent Cambria U. Now look more closely." She drew her fingers apart on the screen, enlarging the image so he could see what she did.

"The Tektōn symbol," he said.

She went on, scrolling through the pictures on the phone. "Look at how she drew the stairs. The first set starts in the upper left corner and goes about halfway down the page at a diagonal. The next set still starts on the left side, but down about a quarter of the page. It follows the same diagonal, but ends well before the bottom of the page."

"I see where you're going," Rook said, looking at the next picture. "The third staircase starts even lower than the second, but ends in the lower right corner of the page."

Nikki took a minute to draw three sets of staircases on the murder board just as Chloe had in her notebook. "Look," she said, pointing at the different staircases as she spoke.

"They descend, starting with the university, passing through the Freemasons, and ending up with the most well-known secret society of them all: the Illuminati. Chloe discovered the pipeline. We know that not everyone in the first two tiers of the organizations can pass on to the next one. There must be scouts in each group. Someone who evaluates candidates and recommends them to move into the next tier."

"Not a higher level, like you might think," Rook said, "but a lower level, descending into the depths of secrecy."

"Into the lion's den," Nikki said, repeating what Christian Foti had said.

"The Order of Tektōn might not be willing to do something as heinous as killing a journalist digging into their order. The Freemasons wouldn't, either. But whatever tier falls below them—"

"Some part of the Illuminati—" Rook said.

"Might easily do so without compunction."

## TWENTY-SEVEN

"I'm starving," Rook said.

"What I wouldn't give for a kimchi taco," Heat said. Her stomach growled.

"Or Korilla BBQ," Rook said. "Any food truck would do."

"We'll have to do with a brick-and-mortar. But rest assured, Souvlaki GR, we will be seeing you soon."

"The lion's den," Rook mused as they drove toward Cambria's downtown in search of a suitable culinary experience. "There's got to be a meaning to that."

"It could just mean a room somewhere," Heat said. "Wherever they hold their meetings, like the ceremonial room for the Masons."

"Have you learned nothing about secret societies during this investigation?" Rook asked. "We are talking about the final tier in a progressively secretive organization, each level having more at stake than the previous. The room is more secret than secret."

She looked at him. "What does that even mean?"

Rook's smile sparkled. He let go of the steering wheel long enough to rub his hands together gleefully. "It means Tektōn's little hidden dungeon at the college pales in comparison to our Illuminati faction. This is it, Heat. I can feel it."

"Simmer down, tiger," Heat said.

"But the Illuminati! I never—not in a million years— dreamed I'd actually come anywhere near the most infamous secret society there is. Okay, well, maybe I did dream I might, but here we are on the cusp of . . . something."

"Yeah, but what? What do I need to know about the Illuminati?"

"A better question is what do you *not* need to know?"

She swallowed a growl. "Rook, so help me—"

He waved a hand at her. "Okay, okay. Let's start with Freemasonry. It began in Europe. First England, then Ireland, then the US. The order of chivalry dates back to the Crusades. Think an order of knights. It's symbolic."

"I get it. The Freemasons are all about their connection to the past."

"There's what's called a Grand Lodge. Here each state has its own. Pennsylvania, then New York and New Jersey, were the first in the country. The Provincial Gran—"

She held up her hand to stop him. "Do I need to know this?"

"Patience, my dear—"

"Rook, I don't want a dissertation. I want you cleared. I want to get back to the city. Both of which mean we need to figure out who the hell killed Chloe."

"I want those things, too, Nik. More than you know. Which is why I'm sharing my knowledge with you. In the organization, the Grand Master is elected and oversees the Masonic jurisdiction. But every jurisdiction is autonomous. They make their own rules. How they do their rituals, how many officers are present. The layout of the meeting room. It makes perfect sense that Tektōn is a pipeline to the underbelly of this particular Freemason order, which, in turn, leads to some faction of the Illuminati. They make their own rules."

"Everything we've figured out leads us back to the lodge, but we have a lot of unanswered questions."

"Shoot."

"What is the point? Why have this pipeline? To what end? The secret Freemasons feed the Illuminati, but why?"

"Power, of course. Imagine the Illuminati as the roots of a climbing garden vine. Each pipeline grows the tendrils, and those tendrils invade society. Government. Religion. Education. You name it, they are there."

If Rook's explanation was true, the Illuminati was worse than Big Brother watching. "Is there some universal goal?"

"World power."

She scoffed. "Oh, is that all?"

"Mock if you will, but it is true. They are after an authoritarian society. In 1776, while the United States was declaring independence, the Bavarian Illuminati was born. What has developed today is quite different."

Rook pulled into a parking lot and turned to face her. "Historically, it was a secret society in the Enlightenment era. They had the very lofty goal of fighting against superstitions, abuse of power, abuse of religious authority, and those opposed to intellectual enlightenment. In other words, they fought the good fight. They, along with the Freemasons, I might add, were outlawed in the late 1700s. But critics, primarily religious and conservative groups, believed the Bavarian Illuminati continued to operate underground and that the French Revolution, among other things, rested squarely on their shoulders. The society was vilified."

"Well, sure. I mean, if they caused the French Revolution . . ."

"Louis the sixteenth and Robespierre played a part, too," Rook admitted. "Oh my God."

This could be one of Rook's brilliant moments. "What is it?"

"Louis the sixteenth. Robespierre. What if one of them was Illuminati!"

"What if one of them . . . ?" Oh brother. She snapped her fingers in front of his face. "Focus."

He blinked, breaking the spell. "Right. Sorry. The point is, the Illuminati is worldwide. The belief is that they have one goal: world domination."

"World domination," she repeated, as if she hadn't heard him correctly.

"It sounds far-fetched, I know. But that's what they're about. Gaining political power. Influencing and infiltrating governments and corporations. Masterminding events that cause chaos and advance their agenda."

"Like?"

Rook scratched his cheek. "Where to start? The Kennedy assassinations. The attempt on Reagan. The mortgage crisis in 2008. The Syrian war. 9/11. The power of the NRA lobby. The list goes on and on."

"And you believe the Illuminati is behind it all?"

"Heat, it's not whether *I* believe it or not. I haven't researched it enough to say one way or another. It's what others deem to be true."

"You know an awful lot for not having researched it."

"I said I haven't researched it *enough*. I did preliminary background on it in college. You saw my notes."

"That was years ago."

He tapped his temple, a gesture she'd come to recognize as a symbol of his never-ending brainpower. If she hadn't loved him so much, she'd have thought he was the most arrogant man on the planet. Which was exactly what she'd thought when she'd first met him. But his charm eventually won her over.

"Mind. Sponge. Boundless capacity for knowledge."

She turned in her seat, bending one leg under her, to face him. "Then put your Victoria St. Claire hat on, squeeze that sponge, and spin me a tale, writer boy. What's the big Illuminati conquering-the-world plan that killed Chloe?"

He shook his head. "You're looking at it wrong. This isn't a 'give me the facts, and just the facts' kind of solve."

"Rook, there have to be facts—"

"The facts will lead us to the who. But the why is more . . . loosey-goosey."

"The DA can't convict on *loosey-goosey*."

Rook ignored that annoying detail. "Chloe didn't interrupt a specific plan. She discovered the pathway, which would have revealed the very existence of this particular faction of the Illuminati. That's a big reveal for a secret society that operates on the down"—he pointed his index finger south—"*doooown* low."

"So you're saying the organization killed her."

He shrugged. "Yes and no. Obviously a *person* actually committed the crime. But that someone was acting on behalf of the *organization*."

"I can't arrest an *organization*, Rook. Which means I need the *person*."

"Remember what we talked about," he scolded, and then reminded her, "Patience. Now bear with me."

She exhaled. Patience was sometimes hard to come by, especially when she was on the verge of a solve, but like a word on the tip of her tongue, it was just out of reach. "Shoot."

He held out his hands, balling them into fists. "Two organizations," he said, lifting one fist, then the other. "They're separate, yet connected. If one feeds into the other, it will happen within an accepted organizational structure."

"I get it. Like the salesperson who reports to the manager who reports to the VP who reports to the president," she said.

"Precisely. In our case, we have three groups: Tektōn, the Freemasons, and the Illuminati. A new recruit in Tektōn isn't going to have any knowledge of the group's connection to the Freemasons. Likewise, a Tyler isn't going to be the conduit to the Illuminati. There is a hierarchy."

"So only someone in the upper level of Tektōn would have anything to do with the Freemasons," she said slowly, "and only an officer in the Freemasons would have anything to do with the Illuminati."

"Which means there is a chain of command," he said.

The solution was forming. "Which also means only a few people have the power to call the shots." She thought of the mystery man who'd paid Joseph Hill to steal the notebook. She hadn't recognized the voice on the other end of the phone in the police station, but it could have been disguised. She thought of the poem—the call for Chloe's death.

They looked at each other, and then spoke at the same time. "Holz."

**Murder came before food, but there was always time for coffee.** They swung by a local café. "New York food trucks win, but this coffee is pretty damn good," Heat said, sipping her usual nonfat sugar-free vanilla latte.

Rook raised his cup in a toast to Cambria coffee as they mapped their way from downtown Cambria, where they'd been headed, to the Masonic Lodge. Heat texted Ian to meet them there. At the lodge, they were greeted by a young man who couldn't have been more than twenty-five. Nikki sized him up. He was a Tyler. Low man on the Masonic totem pole.

"Can I help you?" the man asked.

Rook held out his hand. The young man hesitated, but then took the proffered hand. It started like any handshake, but Rook shifted by pressing the top of his thumb hard against the first knuckle joint of the kid's first finger. Again, the boy hesitated, but then he threw his shoulders back and returned the grip.

"Jameson," Rook said.

"Garrett." Rook lowered his chin and raised his eyes, and the boy filled in the missing information. "Charles. Garrett Charles."

"You're a new member?" Rook asked.

Garrett Charles's face fell. "Is it that obvious? Was my handshake wrong? I thought I got it right. Too much pressure? Not enough?"

"Garrett—" Rook said, trying to cut him off, but the kid was on a rant.

"I've been practicing. I really thought I had it." He looked up at Rook, eyes imploring. "Can we try it again before Mr. Holz gets back? I wanted to impress him."

"Garrett," Rook said again, and this time the kid met his gaze. "Let's do it again, and I won't tell."

They went through the handshake a second, then a third time. After the fourth go, Rook gave his approval. "Perfect."

Garrett beamed. "Thanks, Mr. Jameson."

Rook didn't correct him on the name. It was better that way. But then his face fell. "So Holz is not here?"

Garrett sensed Rook's disappointment and quickly checked his watch. "He'll be back soon. Like forty-five minutes, probably?"

From the lilt of his voice, Heat knew they held the cards. They just had to play them right. She lifted her hand as if she'd just remembered something. "Of course. He's at the—"

"Right," Rook interrupted, realization lighting up his face.

Garrett leapt right into the web they'd spun. "Do you want to wait?"

"Absolutely. We'll be in the ceremonial room," Rook said, already striding across the hall.

Garrett looked from Rook to Heat. "Is . . . is that allowed?"

Rook stopped, slowly turning around. "Son, how long have you been a member?" He went on before Garrett could answer. "Longer than me?"

Heat was impressed. Rook had phrased the questions ambiguously and, just as he'd intended, young Garrett mistakenly assumed that Rook was actually a Freemason. "Oh no, Mr. Jameson, I never meant to—"

Rook waved his hands, stopping him in his tracks.

"Don't worry. It's no problem." He held open the door to the ceremonial room and Heat passed through. "Let us know when he's back," he said without a backward glance.

"Nicely done," she said once the door closed behind them.

He tipped an imaginary hat. "Thank you, Captain Heat. A high compliment, indeed."

They strode side by side up the center aisle of the room toward the Worshipful Master's chair. It sat on a double platform on the eastern side of what Nikki thought of as the altar. The chair sat atop a ten-inch platform that sat atop another larger one. When the Worshipful Master climbed up the two steps to his throne, he had to look like a king readying himself to face his subjects.

"I keep coming back to the lion's den," she said, slowly turning and looking at the room with fresh eyes. If there were a secret room, there would be a secret entrance, which would require a secret lever of some sort to open said door. She said as much to Rook.

"Now you're thinking like a conspiracy theorist," he said with a grin.

"Oh no. I'm thinking through the problem logically." She looked at the medieval tools adorning the walls, and then studied the floor. She remembered what Rook had said about the black-and-white checkerboard pattern representing the dark and light in each of us—or perhaps the light symbolized the Freemasons, while the dark signified the secret faction that was connected to the Illuminati.

"Everything has meaning," Rook muttered.

"Everything has meaning," she repeated, looking at the tools of the craft again. Holz had described the square of morality, the compass, and the plumb rule. She walked over to the wall and stretched her arm up. The tools were out of reach. Too high on the wall for any to serve as a trigger for a secret passageway.

Her gaze traveled around the room again, landing on the two stones, each on its own pedestal. She took out the notebook she always had with her, flipping back to the pages of notes she'd taken when they'd first visited the lodge. The stones represented man. The transformation of man from apprentice to his improved version. That could mean the moving from Freemason to Illuminati. "Sacred stones," she said aloud. Rook joined her. "Holz didn't want you touching them."

They looked at each other, then at the stones. With a smile and a nod, they each reached a tentative hand out, Rook toward the rutted stone, Heat toward the smooth one. Their hands hovered above the stones for a beat before they lowered them down. Heat pushed hard, but nothing happed. The stones didn't budge.

She sighed. "Should have known it wouldn't be that easy."

"You're not throwing in the towel already, are you, Heat?"

"Not yet."

"Good," he said as he circled the pedestals, sinking to his haunches and stroking his chin at one point. He studied them from every angle, finally turning to her. "I guess we're reading too much symbolism into it," he said, putting one arm out and resting his hand on the raised edge of the inch-tall platform on which the rutted stone sat.

Heat heard a faint click at the same time Rook jumped back. "It moved," he said. Heat scanned the room, hoping something would open, but everything was still. As he went back to examining the rocks, Heat faced the paneled wall behind the throne. She ran her palms across the wall, the pads of her fingers playing across the cool wood as if it were the keys of a piano. She felt along the beveled edges of each section. Nothing.

She was on to the next section when Rook let out a whoop and a "Yes!" Heat whipped around just as the gold velvety throne lurched. She froze as it moved again. Finally, the square platform it sat on started rotating. "What did you . . . how did you . . . what the . . . ?"

"The smooth stone," Rook said. His face showed a mixture of bewilderment and excitement. "I felt around the base of it. There was a little gap. I worked my finger in and hit a button. And voilà!" He pointed to the moving platform. "There's a gap between the two steps."

He bent down to get a closer look at the mechanism, but Heat had already walked around to the other side of the throne. "Rook," she said, staring at the dark space below. They'd been right; there was a secret room, and they'd just found it. "Come here."

He must have sensed something in her voice, because he was by her side in an instant. "We were right," he said as the moving throne revealed an opening beneath the chair. Once again, Heat and Rook faced a dark stairway down into the depths of the unknown.

# TWENTY-EIGHT

**H**eat led the way down, shining the flashlight from her phone in front of her to light up the steps.

"Concrete," Rook said. "How pedestrian."

"You got your crumbling dungeon stairs at Cam U."

"When you're talking secret societies, you can never have too many crumbling dungeon staircases."

She took the last step, spotted a light switch, and flipped it up, drawing in a breath. She didn't know what she'd expected, but it wasn't this. She'd thought the symbolism in the ceremonial room above had been thick, but this far exceeded it. The tools of the craft were present, as was the same black-and-white checkerboard floor. A large square table sat in the center of the room. The throne, more ornate than the one above them, faced the table on one side. There were chairs, but instead of being in orderly rows, they were in three groups, each facing the center of the room.

Rook bypassed her and moved past the groups of chairs to the table. "Fascinating."

"It's a table."

"In a room with a throne." He pointed. "And the symbol of the Illuminati."

She followed his gaze to the center of the table. There,

in the middle, was an eye with a delicate swoop coming from the inner corner, which was inside a triangle, which was inside of a circle. Around the perimeter were the words NEW WORLD ORDER.

"It's like a huge sweeping crash, Heat. Three rivers converging. This is it."

"The three rivers being Tektōn, the Freemasons, and the Illuminati."

"Of course."

She leaned against the table. "A new world order. There has to be someone connected to Tektōn that ushers the apprentice members through the channels. The Worshipful Master of the Freemasons is just a man, after all. So whoever is the true head honcho, over even the Freemason master, he's also just a man. But he's a puppet master."

"Makes sense," Rook said. "So we're looking for someone who wields power at the university, who knew Chloe, and who has a connection to the Freemasons."

A memory skirted along the edges of Nikki's brain. "Christian Foti's tattoo," she said.

"The Illuminati."

"Could he be the man in charge? Responsible for his own daughter's death?"

"No," Rook said. "Holz was in charge, not Foti."

"Does he have a connection to the university?"

Before they could consider the question, they heard a noise. Footsteps. Garrett Charles stopped halfway down the stairs. "You shouldn't be down here."

Heat stood, quickly surveying her surroundings. There was a door at the back of the large room. Other than the stairway, it was the only way out. Garrett seemed harmless enough, but Heat never took chances. "What happens down here, Garrett?" she asked.

He looked over his shoulder, back up the stairwell, then back at her. "I didn't know it was here."

"The Worshipful Master must spend time down here. Have you seen Mr. Holz—"

"Mr. Holz isn't the Worshipful Master," Garrett said, his brows pinched.

Heat and Rook shared a glance. "We assumed," Heat said.

"Christian Foti isn't—" Rook said.

"The Worshipful Master? No."

"He has the tattoo," Heat said, touching the inside of her wrist.

"All the leaders have one."

"Always on the inner wrist?"

Garrett descended the rest of the steps. "As far as I know. It's part of the brotherhood."

"Not the Freemason order, though."

He stopped, thinking about this. "Not all the Masons have one."

Just the leaders. Heat thought back to when she and Rook had first met Chloe. She'd been so determined to meet Rook. There had to be a connection to the university, she thought. Someone had to feed the beast. Her thoughts crashed as she realized that she'd caught a glimpse of a tattoo that could be the same as Foti's. She'd seen just the edge of it more than once over the years. She shot a glance at Rook before she asked the question she didn't want to hear the answer to. "The Worshipful Master, Garrett. Who is it?"

Garrett's face had lost all its color. "This is about Chloe, isn't it?"

"Did you know her?" Heat asked.

"Sure. She came around to see her dad."

"What about from school? Have her in any classes?"

"Yeah, of course."

The most obvious question came next. "Garrett, do you know who killed Chloe?"

Heat thought there had been an infinitesimal beat before he answered, but she couldn't be sure. "I wish I did," he said.

So did she. Heat directed the conversation another way. "How did you become a Freemason?"

Once again, he looked over his shoulder and up the stairway. "We shouldn't be down here."

She didn't acknowledge his concern, instead staying on point. "Were you recruited?"

"If Mr. Holz finds—"

"Garrett," she said, "were you recruited into the Freemasons?"

Slowly, he nodded. "That's the only way to join. Sponsorship, they call it."

Rook had walked across the room and stood by the door in the back of the lodge, but now he turned back to them. "Who is your sponsor?"

"Michael Warton. He's the editor in chief of the *Cambria Journal*."

"We've had the pleasure," Heat said.

Rook came back next to her. "Michael wanted Chloe's story," he said to her, his voice quiet. "He knew she was on to something. If he alerted someone higher up—"

"But not Holz," Heat interjected. "He's not connected to the university and he's not the Worshipful Master."

"Which is why it would be someone *like* Holz, if not Holz himself. Warton may be on a path to the next level, but he's still a newbie."

"He was tapped almost two years ago," Garrett said. "He was one of the youngest recruits, he said. Usually you have to be a senior."

*Power,* Heat thought. This faction of the Masons leading into the Illuminati was all about power and control. Why would the order bring Michael Warton into the fold early? There was only one reason she could think of. "Was he already editor in chief when he was recruited, or did that happen later?"

"This is his fourth semester as chief, so I guess he was appointed to the position not too long after he became a recruit," Garrett said. He tried to usher them toward the stairway. "We should go up."

Rook was walking around the room again. He examined the adornments on the walls, taking his time as he absorbed the details of each one. "Who's Michael's academic advisor?" he asked.

Heat followed his train of thought. Chloe had had Jennifer Daily. They'd formed enough of a connection that Chloe had come to her. Whoever Michael had formed a connection with could be the missing link they needed. Becoming a Freemason was different from being selected as one of the elite Masons.

"I don't know if he's Michael's advisor, but I know he's really tight with Professor Lamont."

Rook drew in a sharp breath. "Raymond Lamont might be Michael Warton's academic advisor?"

Garrett shrugged. "Like I said, I don't know for sure. I just know that they spend a lot of time together."

"The tattoo," Heat said, remembering the glimpse of ink she'd often seen on Lamont's inner wrist. It was the same arm, and the same location, as Christian Foti's. "Does Michael Warton have a tattoo?" she asked Garrett.

"Yeah," he said, after thinking about it for a second. "Inner wrist."

*Bingo.* "A triangle?"

"Maybe," he said, but he sounded uncertain. "I don't work with him too much, so . . ."

"What do you know about him?"

Garrett ticked off on his fingers as he named a few things. "Big ego. Was pre-med before switching to journalism. Never seen him date. His life is the paper. That's about it."

"The handshake," Rook muttered. "Of course. How could I be so stupid?"

"The handshake?" Heat asked, not sure where he was going.

He turned to her. "Remember Holz and Foti?" When he held out his arm to her, she clasped her hand in his. Then he placed his other hand on her forearm, wrapping his fingers around and almost meeting his thumb on the other side. "Now you," he directed, and she did the same, encircling his forearm with her free hand.

"Remember who else did that?" he asked her.

She did remember, because it had been only a day. "Raymond Lamont and Kaden Saunders."

"It's a higher-level handshake," Rook said.

"Lamont has a tattoo on his inner wrist. He tries to keep it covered, but—"

"It's probably the same as Foti's."

"The Illuminati," they said in unison.

Behind them, Garrett started muttering under his breath. "This is about Chloe?" he asked shakily, but he didn't wait for an answer. He turned and stumbled up the stairs and out of sight.

Heat debated going after him, but she left him to his shock. Their time was limited. She checked her watch. They likely had only another fifteen minutes before Holz returned.

Rook seemed not to hear Garrett go; he was busy muttering to himself. "Lamont and Saunders?"

Nikki felt for him. If they were right, which she believed they were, some of his oldest friends were involved in a clandestine organization they valued more than a human life.

"Rook," she said, drawing him out of his shock.

He blinked twice. Then a third time. "Lamont and Saunders," he said again, but this time his voice was filled with rage. "Those sons of bitches. They're responsible for this. You know that, don't you, Heat? Whether or not they killed her, they are responsible for her death. Remember at the Nellie Bly awards? Lamont said that even Saunders had met with Chloe. Why would he do that? He's the provost. He's bloody admin. Why would he meet with her? Because he needed to feel her out. To see what she knew and what she didn't."

Heat heard out his rant, then redirected him. "I know this is hard, Rook, but we have to stay focused on the facts."

He scrubbed his face with one hand, exhaled, then went

back to pacing. It was a distraction, she knew, but he would process through the information with her at the same time.

"You start," he said.

She launched into the narrative. "Chloe had dug up dirt on the pipeline between Tektōn, the Freemasons, and the Illuminati. Michael Warton figured out what she was up to and tried to get her to give up the story. She refused—then came the fight in his office. That was the argument you saw."

Rook picked up the story. "Don't forget our first meeting. Lamont said Saunders had met with her. Michael has the tattoo, we think?"

So he had been paying attention. "Possibly. Or probably."

"He's in the pipeline, then, and must have alerted his elders. Once Chloe refused to give her story to Michael, and Lamont and Saunders got involved, I imagine Chloe's fate was sealed."

"Basically they ordered a hit," Heat said.

Rook turned and paced in the opposite direction. "The girl was stabbed, stripped, and laid out on my bed to bleed out."

A tableau befitting a clandestine organization seeking a new world order, Heat thought.

One question that had lingered in her mind was how the killer had gotten into Rook's campus house. They'd pieced together their ideas, but talking out the time line and telling Chloe's story now, knowing where the university connection was, gave the narrative strength. "Let's assume that the call Chloe got during her yoga class with Jada was, she thought, from you. She goes off to unburden herself with the one person she knew would understand—"

"Because she'd read my archived and killed stories—"

"But instead she encountered her killer. But how did that killer get into your house?" Heat asked. According to the police report, there had been no evidence of a break-in and no prints. Hence the suspicion that Rook had been involved.

Rook scoffed. "If they're part of this Illuminati faction, it would be a piece of cake for Lamont or Saunders to get a set of keys." His eyes turned feral. "Son of a bitch," he growled and then, suddenly, like a boxer, his arm shot out in a series of quick bursts, hitting the wall. His knuckles beaded with blood. "They were setting me up to take the fall. But why?"

The answer to that question was crystal clear to Nikki. "Two birds with one stone," she said. "Chloe picked up what you'd started. With you back here, the two of you were suddenly a double threat."

Rook looked as if steam might start billowing from his ears at any moment. "Frame me for Chloe's murder, get rid of us both. Son of a bitch!"

"Rook!" He had every right to be as mad as hell, but she'd never seen him like this. From the stunned look in his eyes, she guessed that he'd never seen himself like this, either.

He flung his arm up, spinning around. "I'm okay, I'm okay."

She didn't believe that, but she went on with the story, keeping an eye on him as she spoke. "Surely Foti didn't kill his own daughter. The elders used him to get intel on Chloe and what she knew about them and the organization."

If they thought about the players in this tableau as a pyramid, Saunders, who hadn't even been on their radar, was at the top, followed by Lamont, then Holz and Foti.

There had to be others in the organization, or those being groomed for it, but Chloe's investigations were centered on this group. Heat had told Rook that she couldn't arrest an organization, but she still didn't have a person to target. The kill was ordered, but who executed it?

Rook had begun pacing again, stopping at the wall he'd smashed with his fist. The paneling had splintered, revealing a hollow behind it. "A false wall," he said.

Instead of trying to repair the damage he'd done, he dug his fingers into the spaces and yanked. With a sickening cracking sound, a chunk of the thin wood came free. "Look," he said.

Heat came up beside him and stared into the narrow space behind the wall he'd just officially destroyed. "So?"

"It's a double wall. Like the false bottom of a suitcase. A hiding place."

"It's not very practical to create a hiding space you can't get to," Heat said, pointing out what she thought was quite obvious.

"There has to be a trigger." He began feeling the walls, paying special attention to the beveled edges of the different sections.

Heat went back to her thought process, letting Rook have his conspiracy theory about hidden spaces and secret hiding places. Ian had had no reason to look for alibis for any of the suspects they'd just identified, with the exception of Christian Foti. Where had Saunders and Lamont and Holz been?

"Eureka!" Rook's exuberant voice echoed in her ears and she went running. "What did I tell you?"

Rook had found a hollow piece of molding, removed

it, and there had been the lever he'd been so sure he'd find. The panel had popped right off the wall, revealing a gaping space. Scrolls of what looked like blueprints and maps stood on end. Rook grabbed one, slid off the rubber band holding it in place, and unrolled it.

"Blueprints for a bank," Heat said, skimming over the page.

Rook unrolled the next one. "This one's for the New York Supreme Court."

One after another, the scrolled papers revealed the layouts of banks and government buildings, churches and malls, schools and businesses. Heat suddenly understood what this faction of the Illuminati was all about. "Tools for the new world order," she said

Rook had moved on to the next panel. He found the hollow molding and easily popped out the next panel. Empty.

The next three were also empty. "Rook. We need to—"

"Holy shit," Rook said. The quiet tone of his voice was more alarming than his pounding on the wall.

She stopped abruptly as he removed the next panel. At first glance, she thought the space was empty, but then her gaze settled on something at the bottom. Rook bent to retrieve it. He turned slowly. "Holy shit," she said.

He was holding a laptop computer.

# TWENTY-NINE

**W**ithout a password, they couldn't get into the laptop, but the very presence of it brought Heat and Rook back to the question of who committed the actual murder. Heat went back to the hierarchy and their working theory. Saunders at the top. Lamont and Holz in the middle. Foti at the bottom.

This all made sense, but there had to have been a whistleblower. Someone who'd discovered what Chloe was up to and who'd reported it to the higher ups. Most likely someone in Chloe's peer group. Someone being groomed for the order.

Heat laid her palm flat against the laptop. They didn't need to know what was actually on the computer, she realized. "Presumably everything she wrote and researched is right here. This is what led to her death. Rook, there's only one person who knew what Chloe was working on."

They looked at each other. Rook had come to the same conclusion she had. Completely in sync, they headed back to Cam U and the place where it had all started. The Merritt School of Journalism was a beehive of activity when they walked through the lobby and headed straight for the editor in chief's office in the newsroom.

They could see him sitting behind his desk from between the slats of the window. Heat knocked on the door, but she didn't wait for Michael Warton to open it. She walked in, Rook on her heels. Warton shot to his feet. "What the hell are you doing?"

Heat didn't respond to the question. Instead, she set the laptop on his desk and watched his expression go from furious to horrified. "I see you recognize this," she said.

He reached for the laptop, but Heat snatched it back. "Nice tattoo," she said. She'd caught only a glimpse, but her allusion to it was enough for him to yank down his shirtsleeves. "We have a theory we want to run by you."

Michael looked over their shoulders as if someone might appear to save him from having to answer to Heat and Rook. There was no cavalry. "I don't have to talk to you," he said, but the words had no bite.

"You're right. You don't. But here's the thing, Michael—can I call you Michael?" She didn't wait for a reply. "We know you killed Chloe."

He started to bluster, but she stopped him by holding the palm of her hand out. "Shh, shh, shh," she said to quiet him down. "No need to object." She tapped her finger on the computer. "It's all right here."

"You got in—"

"Michael," Heat interrupted, "why don't you let me do the talking? Have a seat and let me tell you what I know."

He sat, but fidgeted, first leaning back, then putting his arms on the desk, then crossing and uncrossing his legs. He didn't know what to do with himself. If he hadn't been a murderer, Heat might have sympathized with him.

"Tektōn." She let the word hang there between them. His eyes darted from her to Rook. Twice he opened his mouth to speak, twice closing it up again.

"The Freemasons," she said, planting the next seed.

The color had drained from his face. "I—"

"Shh, shh, shh. I said not to talk. Now is your time to listen."

His eyes opened wider and he nodded.

She spoke the next word slowly, enunciating each syllable. "Illuminati."

Michael sucked in a breath, choking on the air he pulled in. He coughed, doubling over until he stopped. Heat and Rook watched his every move. Desperate people did desperate things. Heat wouldn't have put it past him to pull a gun from his desk drawer. He didn't, though. He pulled himself together and Heat went on. "Chloe discovered Tektōn, didn't she?"

Michael stared at her, mute.

"Now you can talk, Michael. Now you need to answer my questions. I'll repeat it for you. Chloe discovered Tektōn, didn't she?"

Michael nodded.

"And you tried to dissuade her from writing about it?"

Again, he nodded.

"And why is that, Michael? Why didn't you want Chloe to write the article about Cam U's secret society?"

"It . . . it wasn't a good story. She thought . . . she thought it was some exposé, but it wasn't there."

He was trying to sound like an editor in chief, but he couldn't quite pull it off.

"But see, here's the thing, Michael. There's a witness that saw a ritual taking place right here on campus. He was with Chloe when the new recruits were led out to the Freemasons' white van, heads covered for dramatic effect, I imagine. What I think, Michael, is that you were once a new recruit, but one of the elders saw something in you. They wanted to groom you, so you were taken under their wing. Raymond Lamont was your . . . is your . . . academic advisor. Is it his wing you were under?"

Michael nodded. His fingers curled into a fist, then uncurled. Over and over and over. The guy was cracking.

"So, when you told your mentor, Lamont, that Chloe was on to Tektōn, he told you to kill the story."

Again, Michael just nodded.

"But Chloe wasn't letting it go, was she?"

This time he shook his head. "I tried to convince her. I really did, but she was stubborn."

"That's a common trait among investigative reporters," Rook said, speaking for the first time. His tone was not pleasant.

"Here's where I get a little lost, Michael. You're low man on the totem pole. I get that. You have the tattoo. You are destined for great things with the new world order, clearly. But why kill a college journalist who was writing about a college secret society? Did they threaten you? Was it a test? A rite of passage?" Heat put her hands on the desk and leaned closer to him. "The elders wanted her dead, didn't they? They wanted her stopped so she wouldn't reveal the group's plans to rob banks or blow up town halls, or whatever dastardly deeds they concocted. They needed Chloe to stop."

Michael moved his hands to the tops of his thighs, rubbing them up and down. "She wouldn't."

"But the elders . . . who? Lamont? Saunders? Even Holz? They certainly wouldn't get their hands dirty. My guess is Holz took a chance trying to recover Chloe's notebook, but he wasn't going to bloody his hands by silencing the bird."

Michael's eyes widened, and Heat nodded. "That's right. We found the poem. Or the kill order, I should say. Handy way to communicate with each other, leaving notes— poems—kill orders in that secret room in Zabro Hall. The poem was a big help, actually. Instrumental, I'd say."

Michael opened his mouth to speak, but Heat kept on, a thought suddenly coming to her. "It was you in the lecture hall, wasn't it? Assuage your own guilt by trying to lay more blame at Rook's feet."

His silence and the complete lack of color in his face were all the answer she needed. "And then there's Christian Foti," she continued. "They tricked him, didn't they? Let him get close to her to find out how much of a threat she was, then took her from him. He didn't realize they were using him, did he, poor man? Not until it was too late."

"I—"

"Let me cut to the chase. You were the hit man, Michael," Heat said. "No point in trying to deny it. You are especially qualified, aren't you?"

"W-what do you mean?" he stammered.

"Chloe was killed by someone low on the totem pole but, more importantly, by someone who knows something about human anatomy—the femoral artery, specifically. You were premed, Michael. You fit the bill. But help me understand. Why did you do it? Why didn't you say no?"

Michael didn't answer. He just hung his head and cried.

# THIRTY

Nikki and Rook walked hand in hand down West 47th Street, she in a little red cocktail dress that drove him wild, and he in a dapper black tux that made her feel feral. They'd spent the evening at the opening night of Margaret Rook's new play. "Your mother is a force to be reckoned with," Nikki said. She meant it. Mama Rook had been mesmerizing from the moment she'd stepped onstage to the last line she'd uttered.

"She says that about you," Rook said.

They walked together, talking about the performance, but at a break in the conversation, Nikki changed directions. "I heard from Ian," she said. Not exactly the sexy come-on she wanted to say, but something he'd be interested in nonetheless.

"Let me guess," he replied with a smirk. "Your ex-husband, chief of Cambria Police, the cool Mr. Cooley, has wrapped up the Chloe Masterson case?"

"With a bow. Lamont and Saunders are the holdouts, but Foti and Michael Warton gave them up. The DA will prosecute to the fullest. Foti is an accessory after the fact. Holz, as well as our young recruit, Garrett, were in the dark."

In the glow of the streetlights, Rook's face looked eerily solemn. She wound her hand around his arm, their stride in sync. "I'm sorry, Jamie. We got the bad guys, but I am sorry they were your people."

He stopped and cupped her face between his hands. "I am, too, but let's be clear, Nik. *You* are my people."

"Two college students, Rook." She shook her head sadly. "Losing anyone is hard, but somehow losing the young is more gut-wrenching."

He squeezed her hand. He knew her personal loss, so he knew how deeply she felt everything when it came to victims and their families.

"I don't condone what Joon Chin was doing, but he was an entrepreneur. And Chloe . . ."

He trailed off. "Chloe was a bright light snuffed out too early."

They both were. And nothing she or Rook said could change the reality that Joon and Chloe were gone.

"I heard back from April Albright," Rook said after a half block. "We were right. Chloe pitched her story and April wanted it. Chloe hadn't sent any of it, though."

"Mmm." Heat held Rook's arm tighter as they walked on.

"I also heard from Sparky. The three-part history of New York is on hold."

"Let me guess," Nikki said. "She wants you to write the story Chloe died for?"

"Nail on the head, Heat. Nail on the head."

Rook leaned toward Heat and they walked in silence. The cool night air seeped into Nikki's skin, her brain, her lungs. She exhaled, letting her tightly wound nerves float away. After a few minutes, they both seemed to put all that had happened in Cambria to rest. Rook looked up at the skyscrapers that created the NYC landscape, and he grinned. He adopted a Shakespearean manner as he spoke. "But soft, what light through yonder window breaks? It is the east, and Manhattan is the sun. Take not the sweet sounds and smells of my city. They're like no other and shall not be forsaken."

Nikki laughed. Margaret Rook would be proud. The dramatic flair had passed keenly from mother to son. "To which sounds and smells are you referring?"

"You name it. Sirens. Music. Horns. Laughter. Steam. Chinese food. It. Is. All. New. York. City." Rook pulled her close to him. "Remind me never to leave my beloved city again."

"Never?" She pulled away from him, walked ahead a few steps, then turned to face him. Walking backward in her dress and heels wasn't easy, but she managed to do it gracefully.

"Wine tasting in California?"

He shook his head. "They import it to us here."

"Dude ranch in New Mexico?"

He scrunched one eye in temptation, but shook his head. "Nope."

She arched one brow, giving him a seductive smile. "Reykjavík."

A statement, not a question.

He melted before her eyes. Or maybe it was her melting before him. He loosened the black bow tie around his neck. He really *was* ruggedly handsome, and God, he wore a tuxedo well.

She crooked her finger, beckoning him to her . . . tempting him . . . but staying just out of reach.

Rook followed her like Odysseus, who, tempted beyond reason, was seduced by Circe. "Are you toying with me, Captain?"

Nikki wagged her finger at him. "Jamie, oh, Jamie. You know me better than that, don't you? I don't play games."

"Au contraire, my fair lady. There are games you play quite well."

She smiled, knowing just where he was going with this. "Do I?" she asked coyly as she hailed a cab to take them home.

He nodded sagely. "Games in the dark, Nikki Heat. With those, I must say, you are quite adept."